Motive

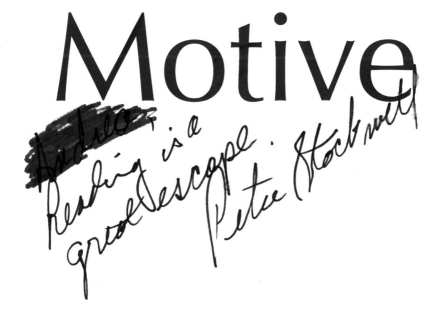

Peter Stockwell

I dedicate this debut novel to my magnificent and ever patient wife, Sandy, who listened to my ideas and offered sagacious advice to help improve many rather primitive early drafts.

CHAPTER 1

R oger sat on the floor holding Mary's warm, but lifeless hand. The acrid smell of gun smoke lingered, the ear deafening reverberation long abated. As he sorted events into a plausible scenario, he could taste the cordite in his mouth. Blood droplets spattered the end of the bed sheets, rumpled from sleep, a wall and some of the furniture exhibiting the same evidence. A 9 millimeter caliber revolver lay beside his wife's other hand. *Why now? I didn't mean to have this happen.* He stood, surveyed the scene again, then picked up the phone and called her parents. The conversation lasted only a few moments.

Hanging up, he returned to his wife and held her in his arms. Blood from her wound stained his shirt and tie. His hands became covered. After a seeming eternity, he sat her next to the dresser, stood, and took the blanket from atop the cedar chest by the window. Unfolding it, he placed it near where she had fallen. He then placed her on it letting any remaining fluids soak into it. He held the revolver in his hand, checked the remaining cartridges, and then replaced it next to her hand. Tears welled up in his eyes.

"I love you. I love you so much," Roger whispered. "I'm sorry I failed you. We should've been happier."

He stood and said, "I wanted more for us, but I guess it wasn't to be." He checked his bedroom one more time. His dresser escaped any spray, but the end of the bed displayed the blood spatter from the head wound. Three pale blue walls had no marks except for one bullet hole. All was as it should be. The blood ruined his new shirt and tie. It mattered little. The completed deed changed his life forever.

No more suffering for you, Mary. He returned to the phone and picked up the receiver for his second call. His future depended on believability. Did the scene create it? Time would tell and he was running out of it. What forgotten detail would corrupt his plan? The complications of a future without her raced through his mind. He sat on the bed where sheets were clean and dialed the universally known three digit number.

CHAPTER 2

S heriff Detective Marcus Jefferson and his wife Joan returned home from church with their three children. His wife of fifteen years had planned an afternoon family movie and dinner, a rare day together when his cell phone buzzed. He looked at the caller and said, "I've got to take this." The children left the kitchen sensing what next would happen.

Clicking off the cell, he faced her Irish green eyes, unable to speak. "What's up, now?" she said, arms pinned to her slim waist. Joan understood police work, but this day had been promised. Her brunette curls splayed as she shook her head. "I suppose this means no movie or dinner."

"There's been a shooting. Tom asked me to come to the scene," Marc stared at the floor, frozen in place. He reached out for her but she pulled back.

"Why can't he field this one, alone? We haven't had a day together for months. The kids are looking forward to being with you." She glared at Marc. "It seems to me you prefer your police buddies over us." In his heart he knew she might be right.

"I'm sorry. Look this may not take long, but as head detective I wanted to be notified of major events. You and the kids go to the movie and I'll join you there or for dinner."

"Alright, you've been notified something big has happened. It doesn't mean you have to be there. Call him back and tell him to do his job. You can be caught up later. You're not the only detective in Wendlesburg."

"I know, but he requested I come and if I don't go, you know Sheriff Fellington will be on my back." He turned to leave.

Joan responded, "Someday, you're going to come home and no one will be here."

Without turning around he headed out to uncover what happened.

At the scene a deputy was securing its integrity. Marc asked for a cursory report. "A man reported his wife shot herself. His name's Roger Waite."

"Where is he?"

"In the kitchen."

Marc signed the security log and entered the house. The foyer was small with oak flooring which led into a kitchen. A sunken living room stood off to the left with a dining area visible at back. Marc turned into the living room. He studied the area for a moment, a sofa, two wing chairs, a coffee table, and side tables with lamps. Flowers on the coffee table provided a sweet aroma. Shelving held books, pictures and knickknacks. He turned back to the foyer.

Another deputy directed him to a bedroom at the back of the house. "Oh, hi," said Tom Knudson, the detective who had inter-rupted his day. "I'm glad you're here." Marc stood in the door-way and smelled the residue of burnt gun powder.

"Yeah, what'd you need from me?" A young woman's body lay next to a dresser, a 9 mm caliber Smith and Wesson revolver close by. Blood spatter marked several areas around the victim. Some of them seemed out of place. Blood trickled down her head across her neck.

"You said to notify you of anything that seemed big as far as this town is concerned." A crime lab person busily extracted something from a wall opposite the bloody area. "But that's not the only reason I called you."

"Go on."

"A couple of years ago, we received a call from this house about an OD. I arrived along with Danny Brandenburg. It was just before I became a detective. We discovered a woman who probably tried to commit suicide. Nothing came of it. So coming here again, I figured another suicide. Since her husband isn't the warmest guy I've ever met, I began thinking maybe he had something to do with her dying."

"Have you questioned the husband?" Marc asked. She looked peaceful enough, her blond locks stained crimson, but her position contrasted the blood spatter. The CSI busily collected evidence which would be studied and reported by the end of the week.

"He keeps saying the same thing," Tom said. "She shot herself."

"Do you believe him?" Marc asked.

"I don't know, but remembering this guy, I assume there's more to this than meets the eye. That's why I called you. I figured two set of eyes were better than one." Marc sighed.

"Well, let's go ask him again." Marc and Tom left to find the husband. "Maybe he'll have more to say by now."

In the kitchen, Roger Waite sat at a table with head in hands. The room was clean, as if no meal had ever been prepared. In contrast, he was covered in blood on hands, face, and black hair. A white shirt and a tie with a tan and green pattern were now stained. His six foot frame crumpled as he sat.

"Good afternoon. I'm Detective Marcus Jefferson." Marc's voice was calm. "Could you please tell me what happened?"

Waite raised his head and looked at Marc. His hazel eyes were bloodshot, the sockets swollen. "She shot herself. I came home from church and she shot herself right in front of me." He put his head back into his hands and began to whimper. *Tears? Caused by genuine sadness or onion juice? This guy's got to be hiding something.*

Marc moved away from the table and asked a deputy to get Waite a change of clothing, collect what he was wearing, and take him to the stationhouse. The deputy left to retrieve a set of county jumps and a tarp from a squad car.

"Mr. Waite, we're here to close this incident as quickly as possible," Marc said. "Now you said she shot herself. Do you own the gun in the bedroom?"

"No, well, I mean, I didn't know about it until she showed it to me when I got home from church."

"So, what you're saying is that your wife obtained the gun and then used it to shoot herself." Roger nodded. "Mr. Waite, when did you get home from church?"

"I don't know; around 12, I guess."

"How was your wife acting when you arrived?"

"She was acting strangely, like she had a secret but didn't want to show me. Then she opened a drawer and took out the gun."

"What happened next? Did you think she might use it?

"No, she handed it to me and said she wanted to die but just couldn't do it."

"Do it? You mean shoot herself?"

"I guess. I took the gun from her and asked her where she got it. She said she bought it at Mike's Guns and asked me to return it. I stupidly put the gun on the dresser and turned around. I yelled at her about being thoughtless. She got mad, picked up the gun and pulled the trigger."

"Was she aiming at you?" Marc asked.

"I don't know. The bullet ended up in the wall. When I turned to see where it went, she shot herself in the head." The deputy returned with a county jumpsuit.

"Mr. Waite, I'm going to have this deputy take you to our office. Please take off your clothes and put these on."

Roger did not resist but stood up looking dejected. "I hope you find what you want in there," he said. "You probably think it's my fault. I can only tell you what I know." The deputy folded the clothing into the tarp after Roger stripped.

"We'll talk later." Marc did not want to Mirandize Waite, plenty of time for that. He had to find out what the forensics showed. A preliminary report could be ready by evening, although much more evidence was needed to secure what really happened.

Before they left, Marc turned to see the chief CSI investigator, Perry Andrews, enter the kitchen. He hesitated to speak privately with the investigator until Waite and the officer were gone.

"Tom, ask around the neighborhood about these people. Maybe something will shake loose about who they are. I'll look around here and see what pops." Tom nodded and left. "Alright, Perry, what happened?"

"I'm not sure yet. She has a gunshot wound to the right side of her head. The gun was near her hand and the wound appears consistent with a self-inflicted injury. We have some prints that we'll match with the victim and the husband. The blood spatter and gunshot residue are close range. She was lying on the floor next to the bed. A blanket was on the floor. I'm not sure why, or even when it was placed. There are bloody fingerprints on the edge as if someone handled it after the shooting. As you saw, the husband was covered in blood. He states he was in the room at the time of the shooting. The phone has blood on it, probably the wife's. There are prints on it. We took his prints and will get hers at the lab. Two bullets were fired, but only one entered the victim and is still in her. The other was in the wall opposite. We have it and it matches the caliber of the gun, a 9 millimeter. Of course we'll match them in the lab. We took plenty of pictures. She was lying in a weird position like she had been sitting on the floor. Arriving at the scene, the officer said he found the husband sitting on the floor holding the victim's hand. I asked the husband if he had moved anything and he stated he had held the gun after his wife showed it to him. He said he put it on the dresser and she picked it up and shot herself."

"Do you think he's telling the truth?"

"The evidence doesn't lie. We'll process it and see what's what. As for whether he is lying or not, I cannot say. It appears to me there's an awful lot of blood spatter for the type of wound the victim has. But the head can bleed profusely." Jefferson trusted Andrews who knew better than to suggest something which later could be refuted. "I'll write this up and have the prelims on your desk in the morning."

"When did she die?"

"M.E. Wilson says she died between 10 and 12. He'll know more after the autopsy." He turned, picked up the tarp, and left the house for the lab.

Marc went into the bedroom to see it up close. The coroners were removing the body. The blanket was still on the floor covered with blood. He could see an outline of the head and shoulders where the blood had not stained. He noticed the hole in the wall where one of the bullets entered. The phone had been removed as evidence. Blood was on the dresser, end of the bed, and the wall beside the dresser. Little blood was on the floor. Marc wrote a note in his pad about the floor. The bedding had blood on it. He watched one of the CSI bag and remove it for examination. He imagined the wife shooting herself. He imagined the husband shooting her. This shooting was far more complicated than his last one. He wrote copious notes and kept his mind clear of forming preconceived notions. But was it a suicide or a murder? *The blanket doesn't fit and he moved her. Why? What else did he move or change?*

The last of the evidence was bagged and tagged; the forensic people completed their work. Robbed of a quiet afternoon, Marc felt tired, wanting very much to go home. He called Joan on his cell. She did not respond, probably at the movie with the kids. *Guess I'll be in trouble for missing it.* He left her a message and hung up; relieved he did not have to speak to an angry wife. He left the house. If he believed so strongly Uncle Jerry couldn't do it, why would he think this woman would commit suicide?

Entering his car, he planned to drive through the neighborhood, a seemingly quiet middle class place. He wrote another note to check on any domestic problems with the couple. Remembering pictures on the dresser and in the living room, he got out of the car, returning to the house to find them. One family picture on the dresser showed Roger and his wife sitting with two children on their laps. He picked it up and studied it. "Where are the children?" He thought aloud. No one had mentioned them. He went down the hall, finding three other bedrooms. One was certainly a girl's and another, a boy's. No evidence of foul play existed. His suspicious mind rambled through possible scenarios. *What if the father had eliminated them elsewhere? Or the mother had sent them away with relatives fearing her husband? What if the father knew the danger of leaving them with the mother and secreted them at another location? Were they safe and cared for?* He thought about his own kids abandoned for this investigation. He missed them. He craved forgiveness but wouldn't seek it.

He returned to the living area to find other family portraits. He noticed an older couple in a picture on one of the side tables. On another side table a picture had several people in it, probably an extended family. He took the picture out of the frame to see if anything had been written on the back. Nothing!

He crossed the room, removed one of the books from a shelf, which looked like a photo album, and thumbed through the pages. Each contained a note about the picture. 'Mom and Dad at Christmas.' 'Sis and her husband'. He continued to turn pages and found a name under another picture of the older couple. The name was the same as the tragic family. He took out his cell and punched in one of the preset numbers to the office.

"Sally, I need you to find an address for me. Last name, Waite. First name, Walker." He waited for her to find the address and a phone number. "Thanks, Sal. You're a lifesaver." He disconnected and put away his cell. He thought about calling but changed his mind. Better he drives to the address and meet the parents.

The afternoon slowly waned and Marc desired to get home. The movie was history and dinner would be lost as well. He needed to get to the office and talk with Waite. This case seemed twisted. *Why were the children not at home? Why did she shoot herself, if that's the case? He went to church without her? Who owned the gun? Was it registered?* This was a small city, but he did not know everyone. Small towns have a propensity for everyone to know everyone. No one could do anything without someone knowing. He knew most of Wendlesburg, but this neighborhood somehow did not register.

He left the house again. Police patrols would guard the scene for the night. Tom would canvass the neighborhood asking questions of neighbors; he would read his reports later. Right now he had to find the children.

He entered his car a second time and drove away; not through the area as planned but the way he came in, arriving at the other Waite house in less than 10 minutes. It was in an upper middle class area of town, the yard neatly manicured. The bushes and lawn were far neater and greener than he had achieved with his grass. He suspected a professional yard care company.

Marc parked his car and sat for a few minutes. The information he had to deliver would be devastating if this was the right family. He dreaded this role. He consoled mothers, parents, children, and extended families and felt fortunate his family had not experienced such heartache.

Leaving the car, he looked up at the front door, pausing. No reason to delay, however. The family would be no less happy receiving the news later than sooner. He stepped slowly up the walkway and ascended the three steps to the front door. Ringing the doorbell on the left side he thought of words to say.

The door opened. "Good afternoon. I'm Detective Marc Jefferson of the sheriff's office." Dressed in his casual church clothes he did not look like an officer of the law. He showed his badge to the woman behind the screen door. "Are you Nancy Waite, Roger Waite's' mother?"

"Yes, what's this about?" she responded.

"May I come in?"

"Has something happened to Roger?" Her face showed surprise rather than concern. "I just spoke with him at church this morning."

"Are his children with you?" Marc asked.

"Yes." She opened the door, the look on her face now demonstrated concern. "What's happened? Please tell me." Marc entered the house. "Honey, the police are here."

Marc stood in the foyer as the elder Waite stepped in. "What's this about, officer?" Two children were with him. Before getting an answer from Marc, he turned to his wife, handing her the toddler boy, and said, "Take the children into the family room." Returning to Marc, he restated his question. "What's happened?"

"We received a call from your son earlier this afternoon. I've been to your son's house and noticed he had children. I'm glad to discover they are here and safe."

"They're here. What's this about? Where's my son?"

"He's at our office. When did you last speak with Roger?"

"At church."

"Why are the children with you?"

"He received a call from home and asked us to take the kids with us. We agreed and brought them here."

"Are you aware of any animosity between your son and daughter-in-law?"

"What?"

"Well, I don't know them. Has the marriage been good?"

"Why?"

"Just wondering if they had any … disagreements."

"Like what?" Waite wrinkled his brow.

"Oh, you know, about raising the children, where to vacation, how much money is being spent."

"Not that I ever saw." Waite grimaced. "What's this all about? I want to know right now."

"What have you observed about Mary's mental state?"

"What?" Waite shifted his feet as if anxious. "She's been a bit edgy lately."

"What do you mean?"

"I don't know. Recently, she's been kind of depressed."

"Is she capable of harming herself?"

"What kind of a question is that? Has something happened to her?"

"I'm sorry to report. Your daughter-in-law died this morning."

"That can't be. I just saw Roger at church." Walker Waite's voice faltered. "There's got to be some mistake."

"I just came from your son's house. There's no mistake." Marc decided enough had been gained. "I'm sorry for your loss."

"And Roger knows?"

"Yes, he called 911 to report it."

"This is awful. How's Roger?"

"He's at our office. He's not hurt."

Waite widened his eyes. "And you think my son did this to her? Is he under arrest?"

"No, he claims to have witnessed the shooting. We need to ask him some questions." Clearly, Roger was at church in the morning and was called home. After that is pure speculation. Thank God for forensic science.

"Does he need an attorney?" Walker shuffled his feet nervously.

"He isn't charged with anything." Marc remained evasive. "Well, thank you for your time. I am glad the children are safe. You may come to the sheriff's office and see your son." Marc did not want to stay any longer and raise suspicions. He opened the door and left for the office.

CHAPTER 3

Back at the office Marc, asked the desk sergeant, "Where's Roger Waite?"

"Bob Watson brought him in and secured him in room 1." Marc nodded understanding.

He found Watson at a desk, "How did Waite act while being transported?"

"He appeared calm, but I think he wanted to go somewhere else. He kept on about his children losing their mother and how he would have to raise them alone. I don't think he was as calm as he was trying to be."

"Thanks Bob. Where is he?"

"I put him in 2. He asked for something to drink. I sent in coffee."

"Alright, I'll get to him right away. He knows more than he's telling." Marc grabbed a legal pad and pen. His notepad contained a cursory list of questions.

Marc peered through the mirrored glass watching Roger, who stood by the mirrored window looking at the glass blankly.

Eyes are very telling, and Marc studied him for a moment before entering the room. Realizing the intrusion, Roger turned. "Why am I here?"

"Please sit down. I would like to ask you some questions."

"I didn't do anything wrong."

"Let's close this as soon as possible. I just need to know what happened."

"Do I need an attorney?"

Marc cringed. *I hate when they ask for attorneys.* "You're not charged with anything. We need information about the event that happened today." *Waite's involved more than he indicated earlier.*

"I need to call my parents." Roger pled.

"I've just come from their house. They've been informed of your wife's death."

"All I want is to get my children and go home. Can I go home? I'm a victim here. My wife shot herself. I know this looks bad for me, but I'm innocent."

"Okay, let's begin with this morning." Marc sat down. He positioned his legal pad and pen. He continued. "How did the day begin?"

"Well, I woke up about 6:30. My family slept for a while longer. I got the newspaper from the porch and sat down in the kitchen to read it." It sounded like a typical beginning to a Sunday. Marc had done much the same thing in his home. "I read for about half an hour and then heard my daughter getting up. She's a good kid. She came into the kitchen and I fixed her some cereal for breakfast. She sat down and I went to check on her brother. He was still asleep so I left him. My wife had gotten up but had gone back to bed. I looked in on her, and then went back to the kitchen and fixed myself an English muffin and juice." He stopped talking and looked down. Looking up again, he continued. "I talked with my daughter for a while, ate my muffin and drank my juice. With the time getting near 7:30 I finished eating and asked my daughter to get dressed for church. I went to my son's room to wake him." *This guy talks a lot,* thought Marc. "I took him into the bathroom and then to the kitchen for some breakfast."

"Do you often take care of your children?"

"I'm the one who gets up with them in the morning. I get them ready for the day and take care of them until my wife gets up and then I leave for work. My wife is not… uh… was not a morning person. She often would be in bed and I would have to wake her before leaving."

Okay, Joan usually takes care of my kids. Why isn't Mary taking care of hers? Marc thought. *What if Mary couldn't take care of them?*

"Has your wife ever had any problems in the past?" he asked.

Roger responded, "What do you mean?"

"I'm wondering if your wife needed any medical or psychological help." He watched Roger's reaction. *Were you stuck in a bad marriage, Roger?*

"My wife was a complicated person. Yea, she had some problems. She wasn't very happy, lately. I asked her to get help, but she was not the type to admit she needed it." Roger dropped his eyes. Marc made a note on his pad.

"What do you know about her life growing up?"

"She had it rough through her teen years."

"What do you mean by rough?" Marc shifted body.

Roger glanced away. *Is he thinking up a good story for me?*

"I guess, you could say, she was unhappy."

"Unhappy about what?" Roger hesitated. Marc pressed him to answer. "How was she unhappy?"

"She was artistic as a child. Her mother showed me some of her work and I thought it was great. But her Dad said she was wasting her time. He never supported her ideas, always putting her down."

"You say her dad never supported what she wanted. What does that mean?"

"He demeaned her sometimes when we were at their house. He said things which hurt. She tried to be strong, but I know his behavior upset her. She would hide in our bedroom at home and not come out for days."

"Had Mary ever tried to kill herself before today?"

Roger lowered his head, stared at the table, and then looked Marc in the eyes. "I have nothing more to say."

"How did you react to any other attempts of your wife trying to kill herself? Were you upset, mad, disappointed?"

Roger stiffened. "I was concerned," he yelled. "It scared me."

Marc leaned closer, "It scared you because she was depressed and this wasn't the only attempt, isn't that right?"

"She was depressed but I didn't think it was serious."

"When did you decide it was serious?" Marc stood and leaned even closer to Roger. "Was it serious enough for you this morning?" He walked away, then turned and said, "Were you scared enough to make it look like suicide? Did you set a scene for us to find? Who pulled the trigger, Mr. Waite? Did you kill your wife?"

Roger reddened. "My wife killed herself. I watched it happen and couldn't stop her." Marc sat down again.

"Where do her parents live?"

"They live in Seattle."

"If you'll give me their address and phone, I'll inform them of what has happened. They can come here. Maybe they can help us resolve this." Marc thought: *let's uncover what you're not telling, Roger.*

"I already called them." Roger looked at Marc.

"When?"

"I called them after Mary shot herself. I checked on her to see if she was dead and then I called them. They're coming here as soon as possible."

"You called your in-laws? Was this before you called 911?"

"I guess so."

"Why?" exclaimed Marc. *What did you tell them?*

"I wanted help. I didn't know what to do. I couldn't call my parents since our children were there. I asked them to call Mary's sister and brother. I know it seems strange but I was hurting."

Or maybe you were establishing a timeline to support your assertion she shot herself. Marc wrote a note to check the time of the 911 call against the time of the call to Mary's parents. Marc let out a sigh of disgust. *Interesting, Roger, you did not get immediate help for your wife.*

"Are you expecting your in-laws to come here?" Marc was sure something was foul. He now suspected everything and everyone.

"I asked them to go to my parents' house. I figured I'd be hauled off to this place for a while. When can I leave?"

"As soon as I understand what really happened." A knock on the door interrupted the conversation. The door opened and an officer came into the room.

"Marc, may I see you outside, please." The officer said.

Marc excused himself "Roger's father is here with an attorney and wants to see his son." The interrogation was finished.

Walker Waite approached with another person Marc recognized as a criminal defense attorney. The attorney spoke first. "I want to see Roger Waite immediately and you are to cease any questioning without me in attendance." Jeff Woodbury, a small, overweight, balding gnome-like person, had defended people in and around Wendlesburg and Seattle winning controversial cases. Marc admired his ability but did not like criminals out on the streets when they deserved jail. The father and attorney entered the interrogation room, followed by Marc.

"Roger, are you ok?" asked Walker.

"Mr. Waite, could I speak with you?" Marc said, speaking to Roger's father.

"Detective, I am advising my clients to speak with me first. We will return tomorrow, if need be, and you can speak with them then."

"Mr. Woodbury, we're going to keep Roger over night while we complete our investigation." Woodbury turned to Walker.

"I'll stay with Roger for a while," he said. "You go home and take care of the family." Walker nodded and left the police station soon after. Nothing more could be done this evening. Marc wondered what awaited him at home. He had not attempted another call and figured the lost time with Joan and the kids was another mark against him. How many more could he accumulate without Joan's patience being exhausted and his one sanctuary crashing around him?

Marc picked up his notebook from the table and left the interrogation room. A manila envelope was on his desk. Picking it up and turning it over he observed the chief examiner's name and knew this was the preliminary report. Should he read it now, or go home to an irritated wife?

CHAPTER 4

O pening the report, Marc sat down to read. Creighton Wilson's medical examiner's report gave all of the standard information about the victim. Female, age 28, light blond hair - shoulder length, height – 5 foot six, weight – 129, eyes – hazel, gunshot to right temple. Stippling indicates close range but no skin contact. *Unusual.* Marc read on. The information matched much of what Perry had told him earlier at the house. But something just wasn't right. He continued reading. The blanket contained blood matching the victim's. The blood of the finger prints also matched. He thought, "Whose finger prints are they?" The victim had a slight garlic odor. Will check for DMSO use. *DMSO? What's that?*

Marc pondered. *So, Mary Waite, did you place a blanket on the floor after shooting yourself?*

Samples from the bed, walls, floor, and phone all matched the victim's blood. The pictures showed the victim sitting on the floor leaning against a dresser. She slumped slightly forward with her right hand on the floor. A 9 millimeter revolver was next to her hand. Some fingerprints on the gun matched the victim's. Other prints did not. The print on the trigger was smeared and not readable. The prints on the blanket matched the unknown prints on the gun. *Are they your prints, Roger?* The picture showed little more than what he had been told. But her position did not look right. Did Waite stage this? Did he shoot her or just let her die? He put the materials back into the envelope.

Nothing in Marc's training had prepared him for this case. He wanted to go home and hold his wife and children; tell them how much he loved them. He didn't comprehend why someone would entertain such a thought as killing themselves. He had seen it before with Uncle Jerry's hypothetical suicide and questioned it then. Death is so final, and tribulations, so changeable and fleeting. He wondered in his youth about death but never wanted to experience it. Some of his friends thought death was only a passage to something greater and expressed interest in finding out about it. None of them actually tried to kill themselves.

As he sat, an officer approached and gave him two folders "These are from the neighborhood canvass."

"Thanks Ted." Three neighbors had been home and questioned. He opened the first file and began reading.

The first neighbor lived next door on the corner. He stated Roger and Mary were a nice young couple, friendly most of the time. Mr. Waite was always friendly, but his wife could be difficult. She insisted a fence be erected between the properties. He noticed an occasional fight between them, nothing suspicious. He thought the family went to church regularly.

The second and third reports from families across the street stated much the same. These three reports did not raise much suspicion. *Check out the difficult wife angle and delve into the 'fighting'.*

He contemplated the gun, the model number, who bought it and when? *Whose finger prints are on it?* That could wait until morning. He rose and left the station to go home for the evening and see his family.

On the way home he drove to the Roger and Mary's neighborhood, wanting to see it before darkness obliterated his vision. The sun was lowering in the early evening of this fateful Sunday.

Nothing had gone as planned. He hoped Joan and the kids had enjoyed the movie without him. He realized he had not eaten and his stomach reminded him in a most embarrassing way. He was grateful to be alone.

The neighborhood appeared to be a well-kept and normal enough place where parents could raise children in safety. The yards were well cared for and houses seemed fairly new. A school was within walking distance for the children of elementary age. Two churches were within a mile. Trees lined some of the streets and a park was not far off. Marc figured if anything unusual had ever occurred, someone here might know. No stone would be left unturned.

Marc thought about his own home and neighborhood and decided his was not much different than this one. He departed the area and drove home. Parking his car in the garage, he sat for a moment, contemplating the day's events. Why would a seemingly normal family shatter so shockingly? He dismissed it from his mind, got out of the car, and entered his personal haven to apologize and hopefully, relax.

CHAPTER 5

Joan entered the kitchen, noticing Marc's return, and met him as he came inside. "Something terrible must have happened."

"I am so sorry about today."

She hugged and kissed him gently, her anger checked for the moment.

Marc returned the kiss and sat at the kitchen table. "Yeah, something terrible did happen." Marc removed his jacket and loosened his tie. His mouth released a sigh but curled a small smile again, "I'm tired. I just want a shower and to go to bed. I really am sorry about missing the movie. Where are the kids?"

They're in the family room playing on the computer." Joan followed Marc as he left the kitchen. "Have you eaten anything, today?"

"No, but I'll come back in and fix something." Marc replied.

"You go see the children and I'll heat up your dinner which I left in the refrigerator." Joan turned back into the kitchen. Marc continued through the door into the family room.

He sat down on the couch and his children surrounded him and showered him with hugs. He missed being with them today. "I hope you enjoyed the movie."

"Yes." They chorused.

"We missed you." Marc Junior said, "What happened?"

"I love you three very much, but I can't talk about it right now. Tell me about the movie." They related as much as they remembered while Marc feigned interest. He had wanted to see it, but exhaustion dulled his sense of compassion. A silence awakened his faculties. All three stared at their father's perplexed expression.

Sarah then spoke. "Did you hear anything we just said to you about the movie?"

Marc could only grin and admit he missed much of the conversation. Marc Junior then interjected. "I guess the shooting was really bad, huh." Marc reached out for the three of them and hugged each of them.

He kissed them and said, "Get ready for bed and I'll come up and say goodnight." They left to do so. Marc stood up and returned to the kitchen finding dinner and a glass of wine already on the table. Joan had prepared the kids favorite of mac and cheese with garlic toast. The salad came from a package. He knew he deserved no better.

"You take excellent care of me," he said. "How about a shower together?" He made an effort to kiss her again, but she turned her head and he only pecked her cheek.

"What about the kids?" she retorted.

"I've sent them to bed. Well, I asked them to get ready." He sat and ate his dinner.

"I didn't take the kids out for dinner after the movie." Joan explained, "I just didn't feel like it. Look, I know you have a job to do, but sometimes I think you put it before me and the kids." Joan sat with him, not asking for any details about the event which tore Marc from her. An icy silence followed.

She rose from the table, "I'll go check on the children. Just put the dishes in the sink. I'll clean up later." She left.

Finished, Marc took the dishes, rinsed them off and put them in the dishwasher. He did not mind helping around the house, knowing how much work it took to care for the place. With Joan employed helping was the right thing to do. He smiled thinking about her. The children had chores and were paid an allowance, earning extra money by assuming more chores than the assigned ones. Marc and Joan wanted their children to be responsible, caring adults.

Marc thought. *What happened to the Waite's family? Why would Mary Waite commit the ultimate sin of killing herself? What had her childhood been like? Why would Roger want her dead? What motives drove these people?*

Dispelling the questions from his brain, he left the kitchen to see his children. The family room was still well lit, so he turned off lights on his way to the bedrooms.

Marc and Joan Jefferson did not tolerate misbehavior. Both had been raised in happy families with strong work ethics and were determined to instill the same in their children. So far all had been successful. Each child was learning, was socially adept, and their friends were from good families. Marc truly felt he was a fortunate man.

The boys climbed into their respective beds. Marc gave each a kiss on the cheek. "Give me another chance to listen to your rendition of the movie. I promise to listen, really." They smiled and said they would.

He went to his daughter's room and sat on her bed. She sat up speaking to her father about the afternoon. "Dad, it's okay that you missed the movie. Mom was ticked but she'll get over it."

"Sometimes my job has so many hindrances to being a family I understand your mother's attitude."

"Dad, did this involve a family?"

Marc hugged and kissed her and then said goodnight to her. He left, finding Joan in their bedroom. The evening had slowly waned and Marc felt his tiredness. He lay down on the bed with his clothes on and closed his eyes for a moment. Joan sat down beside him, holding his hand. He opened his eyes and smiled.

"Are you ok?" she asked.

"Yeah, but this shooting isn't what it seems. I am sorry about leaving, but it was the right thing to do because of what happened.

I do love you and the kids. This job is a family killer, even more so than today's death of a mother and wife." Marc did not want to get up and go through the motions of day's end. When Joan stood and he swung his legs around and rose from the bed. Both undressed, went into the bathroom to complete nightly tasks, and then climbed into bed. "It'll be a busy day tomorrow, so I guess I should get some sleep." A shower could wait. He hoped Joan would, as well.

CHAPTER 6

Marc heard a buzzing in the air as he drove down the highway at breakneck speed. *Why is my car buzzing*? The highway was empty of other cars although it was rush hour. "I must get to her before he kills her," Marc shouted. Suddenly he was in a room, blood everywhere. The room shuddered.

Marc slowly gained consciousness "Honey, wake up," Joan gently shook him. "What were you dreaming about?" She had already turned off the buzzing alarm clock.

Marc sat up. "I was driving, trying to get to a crime scene. I don't need nightmares about my job." He rubbed his eyes and rose. The clock showed a little past six AM. Marc went to the bathroom. Joan left to rouse the children and begin breakfast. As he laid out his clothes, he thought about yesterday's disturbing circumstances and listed them mentally creating today's tasks. He returned to the bathroom for a shower, emptied his brain and relaxed. The warm water soothed him.

After dressing Marc departed the bedroom and smelled bacon. Breakfast usually consisted of cereal and fruit, but he guessed Joan wanted the week to begin with a fine flair. His family was unlike yesterday's victims.

As Marc ate the eggs, bacon and toast, conversations with the children ranged from school activities to weekly sports. James changed the subject. "You missed a good movie yesterday."

No one usually talked about police work, but Marc junior asked, "What happened yesterday, Dad?"

Joan scowled, "Marcus Junior, you know better. I don't want to hear about it."

Marc interrupted, "I've got a lot of investigating before I know what really happened. You finish eating and get ready for school. I'll fill you in when I have all the facts." They ate silently. Then the children prepared lunches and left the kitchen.

Joan scowled at Marc, "Don't promise them that." She finished cleaning the kitchen, as Marc scarpered for the office.

* * *

Arriving well before 9, he parked in his usual spot and entered the building. At his desk, he sat, picked up the phone, and called the morgue. "How soon will a report be available?" He listened and smiled. "Have you discovered whose finger prints are on the gun?" Wilson was the best and Marc trusted his work. "Thanks, I'll send someone over for it when it's ready."

Picking up one of the files, Marc opened it and read. He did the same with the other files. He gleaned as much information as he could. The Waite's knew more than what these files contained.

A deputy approached with another file. "Here's the information you requested about Mrs. Waite. The report states she called 911 two years ago. Something about a drug overdose. She needed help with her children. The husband was not home and she couldn't take care of the kids."

Maybe she did off herself. Or maybe this points to a disintegrating marriage and motive for Roger Waite. "Thanks," Marc opened the file and read.

The call came in at 8:03 AM. Mary Waite stated she needed help with two small children because she couldn't function. A car was dispatched to the address on the CenCom screen. Responding officer was Deputy Danny Brandenburg. He wrote: I knocked on the door. When no one answered, I entered through an unlocked front door and discovered Mrs. Waite in a bedroom. She was incoherent, appearing drugged. I looked into the other bedrooms and found two children, a girl about three and an infant, under a year. They appeared healthy. Deputy Tom Knudson arrived. I returned to the mother. She was on the bed unconscious but not in any danger of dying. I called for medical help.

Knutson assisted the children and asked the girl about the mother. The girl said, "Mommy couldn't feed us." He picked up the girl and put her on the floor. He picked up the baby. They went to the kitchen and found cereal on the counter. The deputy put the baby in a high chair and the girl sat at the breakfast table. He fixed a bowl of cereal for the girl. Baby food was found in the pantry and he fed the baby.

Soon after, the aid car arrived and the medics worked on the mother who had awakened again. She was more coherent this time. I questioned the mother. She stated she woke up and wanted to feed her children. She got out some cereal but knew she could not finish. She told her daughter to get in the crib. She put the baby in the crib as well. She stated she then called 911 for help. I asked about her husband and ascertained he worked with his father in a local real estate office. His business card was located by the kitchen phone.

Knutson helped the girl find some clothes for the day. He changed and dressed the baby boy.

I contacted Waite Real Estate, identified myself and asked for Roger. Discovering he was out of the office, I left a message for husband to contact his house or return as soon as possible.

The medics prepared to transport Mrs. Waite to the hospital. She was more awake now. I returned to Mrs. Waite and asked her what had happened. She claimed to have taken a sleeping pill the night before. One of the medics stated he had found an empty prescription bottle. The date of the prescription was such that the bottle should have contained many pills. I suspected an attempted suicide. I asked, "Mrs. Waite, how many pills did you ingest last night?"

"I think I took a couple before I went to bed. I couldn't sleep, so I took another around midnight." she stammered.

"Were you attempting to end your life?" I inquired.

"No, I have children to take care of. I love them."

The ambulance arrived and Mrs. Waite was transported. The medics packed their gear and left soon afterward. We stayed with the children until Mr. Waite was located and asked to return home. We left when he arrived. He was informed that his wife had been transported to the hospital. Duration of the call was one hour thirty two minutes.

Marc closed the file. *This wasn't the one you referred to yesterday, was it, Roger?* Maybe yesterday's was a suicide attempt gone badly. Maybe the husband came home, just as he stated, but he made sure that it was completed. Roger needed to explain the earlier attempts. He rose from the chair, left the office and drove to the elder Waite's house.

Marc contemplated how to broach the earlier events. Anyone who attempted two suicides may have more in their history. Digging into the family past would not be benign. He wanted a solid case for manslaughter or murder, because suicide couldn't be an option. He strongly believed his Uncle Jerry hadn't killed himself, and the death should have been investigated as a murder. The prosecutor's office would expect nothing less, and solid evidence meant digging deep. Without hard evidence, could enough circumstantial evidence add up to a conviction?

Marc figured Roger left the station when released and went to his parents, since his house still had police tape around it. Besides, what sane person would stay in a house where your loved one had died violently? Marc thought of his children and how they would react if something happened to Joan or himself. Waite's children were not old enough to understand something had happened to mom and she would not be returning home. How, as they grew older, would they handle finding out that dad killed her? He again thought of his own children.

Marc departed his car and strolled up the walk to the front door. Ringing the bell, he hoped for little trouble, but anticipated it. After a few seconds the door opened. Walker asked, "What do you want?" His demeanor seemed defensive, but one could hardly blame him.

"Is Roger here?" Marc inquired.

"Are you going to arrest him?'

"I hadn't planned on it. However, I am at a loss about a few things and need Roger to answer some questions." Marc felt his muscles tense.

"He's gone to see his in-laws. They're here from Seattle." He evaded.

"Thanks. Where are they staying?"

"I'll let Roger know you want to talk with him. Mary's parents can call if you have a card I can give them." Waite had not opened the screen door. Marc decided they could wait. He wanted to find out about the marriage and Walker might provide some insight.

"Do you have some time to talk with me?" Marc wanted inside the house again for an idea of how Roger grew up.

"I do have to get to the office before eleven as I have an appointment, but come in." Walker opened the door and stepped aside so Marc could enter. "How can I help you?"

"I want to know about Roger and Mary's life together. I'm curious about his relationship with her." They sat in the living room which reflected the success Walker had in the real estate business. Marc made a mental note to investigate his business just in case something lent itself to an unhappy marriage between son and daughter-n-law. "How did Roger and Mary meet?"

"They met in college and started dating."

"Did you know her parents before they started dating?" Marc thought he already knew the answer to this but confirming it would help.

"We met them soon after. We were at a school event, parents' weekend, if I remember correctly. Her parents seemed nice enough." Waite squirmed a little. "Mary was a nice girl and we were happy for Roger."

"However, you had some reservations."

"She had a history that concerned us."

"What were your concerns?"

"She'd been hospitalized as a teenager for depression. We felt maybe Roger would be better off with another woman. However, he was not concerned and we didn't say anything. With the current situation, maybe we should have."

"What caused her depression?" Marc's curiosity piqued.

"All I know is that she had been learning music or art and had received a grant or something that allowed her to go to New York to study. She injured herself which ended the study. She came home and soon after tried to kill herself."

"What do you know about your son and daughter-in-law's relationship recently? Have they been having any troubles?"

"They've been fine. Why? I told you before my son would not do anything harmful to his family." Waite became defensive. "I think we're through here. I'll let my son know you'd like to see him. I'll also speak with his in-laws." Walker stood up and moved toward the foyer. Marc followed, recognizing the deliberate action of a concerned father.

As they approached the front door, Marc turned toward Walker. "Oh, one more thing, do you know when and where they purchased the gun?"

"What? No, I didn't even know they had one." Walker opened the door. "Now if you would please leave. I have nothing more to say."

Marc left, thanking Walker for his time and handed him a contact card. In his car he converted his mental note to paper. Returning to the office he called the records department. Was there a record for the purchase of the gun used in Mrs. Waite's death?

CHAPTER 7

Marc picked up the phone and called the Prosecutor's Office to include them in what transpired the previous day. The receptionist answered. "This is Marc Jefferson at the sheriff's office. May I please speak with Duncan?" His mind wandered through scenarios while waiting to be connected.

Duncan Patterson, a very capable attorney, had been with the county for several years as an assistant DA and developed a reputation as thorough and tough. He did not lose many cases. People thought of him as one who could convict without evidence. He was one of a reliable staff of young guns, who knew the law and were eager to please. Many cases were easy to prosecute, but occasionally ones would come along challenging these minds. If anyone could take the evidence of this current case and find a reason to convict, it would be Duncan Patterson.

"Good morning, Duncan. I have a case involving a local real estate person and his wife. The wife allegedly shot herself yesterday morning at the family home." Marc laid out the details of the event as current as he had them. "I don't think the husband is innocent. I think he's the one who did the shooting."

Marc waited for Patterson's response, "Yes, I'll bring over what I have right away." He punched another button on the phone.

"Have you had a chance to locate that gun purchase?" he asked. "I'll need it as soon as you have it." Disappointed, he gathered the files on his desk and left for the DA's the office.

Patterson's office was nearby, as was the courthouse. Marc had not been assigned to a branch office for the last two years, happy to be part of the main operations. Every so often he would lunch with his father-in-law, Kendall Jackson, a county commissioner. The commissioners' offices were located in the courthouse. His father-in-law had been urging him to try for the sheriff's job in the next election. Marc was not sure he wanted that headache.

However, a case such as this one could help him win if he did try for the top spot. He had been with the department for seventeen years, was well known in the community, and well-liked by his fellow officers. His father-in-law's backing would be substantial. Only one other person, Joan, knew he was investigating the sheriff's job. The current sheriff was retiring in the next three years after winning the position the last four election cycles, sixteen years as head sheriff. His shoes would be hard to fill.

Marc entered the reception area and was directed to the conference room down the hall. He sat down and placed the files on the table. Duncan entered with one of the young guns he had not met, a woman of medium build and dark hair. She was remarkable.

"Marc, I would like you to meet our newest staff member, Monica Atherton. She recently graduated from University of Washington law school and was just admitted to the bar. She's been with us for a month. I thought it would be good for her to get her feet wet with this case."

"Very nice to meet you," Marc shook hands, "I'm Marc Jefferson." She responded amiably. Marc thought her young but probably talented. Her dark hair lay seductively on her shoulders, her eyes a penetrating blue. The dark blue pants outfit

34

accentuated her body. Her fragrance hinted of musk, peaches, and lesser a scent he couldn't identify. "Very pretty and motivated to succeed," he thought.

"What do you have for us?" Duncan asked.

"We received a 911 call at 12:15 PM about a shooting. Officers arrived to find a man in his bedroom with his dead wife on the floor. Blood was spattered about and a gun was near her hand. The husband, Roger Waite, claimed his wife shot herself in front of him."

"Do you believe he's telling the truth?" Duncan picked up the preliminary coroner's report.

"I don't know yet. I'm suspicious of the events as related to me by Mr. Waite. The room seemed staged. Tom Knutson told me about being at the house a couple of years ago because of an OD. He thinks the husband is suspicious. There seems to have been some trouble in the family and the wife has this one previous incident that may have been a suicide attempt. I've not yet been able to complete my investigation of the husband as he now has a lawyer, Jeff Woodbury, who his father retained for him." Marc watched Duncan's eyes widen at the name of Woodbury.

"A competent adversary. Do you need any warrants?"

"So far all the blood and DNA evidence points to the wife. The husband was not injured, and we have his fingerprints. The gun registration has not yet been located, but we have the weapon and will trace it quickly, I'm sure." Monica sat reading the officer reports as well as listening and observing.

"Sir, I can call Judge Chalmers office for any warrants?" Monica Atherton interjected.

"Hang on a minute," answered Duncan. "Now, why do you think the husband may have done something he shouldn't have?"

"The pictures seem inconsistent with a self-inflicted gunshot. GSR," Marc turned to Monica, " gunshot residue, was taken from both the husband and the wife, so either one of them could have been holding the gun when fired. There's stippling around the wound, so the barrel was not in contact with the skin, which is more common with a suicide. He may have had time to stage the event to make it look like a suicide. He called his in-laws before calling 911, which seems strange to me. We are getting phone records to verify this. I spoke with Walker Waite, Roger's father, and he related Mary Waite may have been a bit unstable. A report in this file," Marc picked up a folder, "explains the 911 call a couple of years ago from Mary Waite for an apparent drug overdose. That's the one Detective Knudson investigated. Her father-in-law also stated to me she had some kind of problem with depression as a teenager." Marc waited for the information to sink in.

"We've just begun, so there's much to find out. Mary may have had the required psych review after the overdose. I don't know, yet. I think it will be important to know who bought the gun. I'm also interested to see if a history of domestic misconduct exists. And the blanket edge is nylon and has fingerprints on it that are not Mary Waite's."

Patterson sat down in a chair near the whiteboard at the front of the room. The opposite wall had oak shelves filled with law books. Marc knew the office also had a library with many more volumes. The prosecutor's office consisted of DA Bronson Manderly, Duncan Patterson, the assistant prosecutor, and five junior prosecutors, like Monica Atherton, and various aides and secretaries. He had been part of several prosecutions over the years and had worked with Patterson successfully putting criminals behind bars. This could be another in a string of successful prosecutions for the county, if a case existed.

Duncan thumbed through the files and read quietly while Marc sat nearby. Monica smiled at Marc as she moved about the room. His eyes followed her.

His cell phone interrupted his musing. He retrieved it from his pocket and listened. "The gun registration's been found. Mary Waite purchased the it from Mike's Gun Shop, a local place, waited the requisite number of days for a background check, and picked it up ten days ago." Marc wrote the address of the store. "I'll stop by after leaving here."

Patterson said, "I want to know Mary Waite's state of mind at the time of the purchase. Someone should remember. I find it interesting she made a purchase and used it so soon." Marc stood to leave. "Maybe, she had a plan in her mind. Find out if the husband knew anything about this purchase." He pounded his fist on the desk. "Are you confident Roger Waite committed the shooting and we can get enough evidence to prosecute him?"

Marc answered with a slight doubt in his voice. "Maybe. Family history, psychiatric evidence, and neighborhood interactions still need to be gathered. Much of the evidence might be circumstantial."

"True, but with enough, a prosecution can go forward."

Marc responded. "More on the state of mind of the wife sure can help. She may be the key to understanding the husband's state of mind at the moment of the shooting."

"Get me enough to get a jury to understand what happened. Hard fact is easier for people to discern. Sorting out the confusing psychology can obfuscate any truth."

"I'll gather hard fact about the family and keep it neat for a jury."

"Find out about the wife, then. I'll give you as much support as you need. Oh, and be sure to push the husband as much as possible. If he cracks and admits his complicity, it sure would make my life easier." Patterson trusted Marc. "If there was a crime of any kind, find the evidence."

Duncan stepped to the phone in the room and asked for a secretary to come in. When she arrived he handed her all of the files for copying. She left. They made small talk about Monica's law education and life in general waiting for the return of the files. After a short period of time the secretary reentered and handed the new set of papers to Patterson and the original files to Marc, who thanked her. He said goodbye to Duncan and Monica whose smile unnerved him. She was attractive and seductive, but nothing she exuded held any allure for him. He left to find out about a gun purchase, and dig up other pertinent evidence.

CHAPTER 8

At his office Marc went directly to records. *If she planned a suicide, this woman must have had some serious mental issues. So he finds the gun and assumes she wants to try again. He loses it and decides to end her misery himself. But when did he know about the purchase?*

Marc left the records office with the report and went to his desk to read. Mary Waite had purchased the revolver from Mike's for $179.00. She paid with cash and left with her receipt. Marc surmised. *No record to follow here. Maybe she wanted to kill her husband. He discovers the plot and turns the tables on her.* She returned after 5 days, the waiting period for a gun purchase in Washington State. She received her weapon, a box of ammunition and left.

Not much here indicated intent to do bodily harm. "I wonder if the husband knew?" he thought out loud. "Tony," he called to another officer, "pick up Roger Waite and bring him to the office so I can speak with him. I am going to check with the coroner about Mrs. Waite's autopsy."

"Sure thing," Officer Wilkins replied. Marc gave him a card with the Real Estate office number on it, and left for the coroner.

As he entered, the smell of chemicals invaded his nostrils. He had seen plenty of autopsies, but the smell always nauseated him. He associated it with the crimes committed. Of course, many of the bodies were not victims of crime, but Marc linked the smell anyway. The receptionist directed him to autopsy room C. She obviously had become immune to the odor or maybe it was all in his head.

As he passed by rooms A and B, he observed work being done on other bodies. What were the circumstances for those unfortunate souls? Entering room C, the odor of chemicals was definitely not his imagination. "How's it going, Doc?" Marc and Tom Wilson had known each other a long time. They had begun working for the county about the same time. Tom was a little taller than Marc and had more weight on him. His hands were steady and his eyes caught everything odd about any-body brought in by him or for him. As the chief medical examiner, he managed the facility, but also liked to keep his hand in the work that needed doing. It seemed that nothing ever got by him.

"Thanks for coming by. You always seem to know when to show up." Tom laughed a little. "I have some interesting information for you. I have sent tissue samples to be examined for drugs. She had not eaten anything for the last 12 hours. She did not expel any waste product at the time of the shooting, so I guess she completed that business prior. Her health was good. She had had sexual relations sometime in the last 24 hours. We found evidence in the bed clothes as well as in her vaginal tract. No spermicidal was present. She had some bruising on her right arm that was a couple of days old and had yellowed. The imprint looked like a hand and fingers. We have sent the image to be compared to any known perpetrators. You might want to have the husband printed if he has not already been." Tom paused to look at the body again. He had been in the process of closing when Marc entered the room. "The gunshot to the head is the cause of her demise. No question there."

"Could the husband have held the gun to her head and pulled the trigger?"

"Possibly, but I can't be definitive about it. The wound indicates the barrel was not in contact with the head. Someone could have been holding it which seems more likely, but I can't say for sure."

"Thanks, Tom. Send the report to my office when it's finished. Also, send a copy to Patterson. I spoke with him today and he is interested in pursuing a case, if one exists."

"Oh, there was a slight garlic odor which indicates the use of DMSO, but I couldn't find any instillation evidence."

Marc made his goodbyes and left the room. Many thoughts intrigued his mind. *Bruising on the arm! Had they fought before the incident? Sex the night before. Maybe a goodbye to Roger? And she did not go to church that day. Must check on her attendance. Was it regular or spotty? Did the family usually attend together? What the hell is DMSO?*

Marc walked across the street to his office. He met Knutson in the parking lot. "If you have some time, Tom, I would appreciate you going back to the neighbors and asking more about the Waite's relationship. We may have missed something, yesterday. Take Crowell and Edison with you"

"You bet. I don't think that family was as happy as was made out to be. I'll probe about any loud noises or fights. Maybe someone heard the gun shots, but they did not call it in." The detective left.

In the office Marc rummaged through the files. He had Perry's preliminary CSI report, the neighborhood investigative questions and answers report, the first 911 call, the gun purchase report, and his own written report. He decided to follow up on the 911 call to uncover any psych work done as a result of the apparent drug overdose. If this matter was not a suicide attempt, he would have questions for Roger Waite.

Marc picked up the phone and dialed the prosecutor's office. "Duncan, I think we should obtain a warrant for medical records regarding Mary Waite and her apparent suicide attempt two years ago. I also need a DNA sample from Waite to compare with a sexual encounter the night before unless he cops to it." He listened and nodded. "I'll get right on them." He hung up. A thought occurred to him which might have a bearing on the case.

He called the coroner's office. He hummed while being connected. "Tom, Marc Jefferson, here. Did the GSR register on both of Mary Waite's hands?" He listened as the coroner responded. "Thanks." He hung up and opened the file with the crime scene pictures. He examined the wall with the bullet hole in it. *Why is a bullet in the wall? What if the wife had fired a first shot into the wall, but not the second? Or maybe the second shot went into the wall. The husband could be altering the scene for his benefit. Obviously, Mary would not be the one making the second shot hit the wall.*

The gun and the box of ammunition were safely put away in the evidence locker. He called the evidence room and asked that the ammunition be checked. He wanted to know how many bullets were missing. While he waited, Marc imagined again the wife putting the gun to her head and pulling the trigger. She must have been right handed. He then imagined the husband holding the gun to her head and pulling the trigger. He would have to be left handed to be facing her. Or he was right handed and shot her from behind. The pictures of her sitting on the floor leaning with her back against the wall indicated she may have already been sitting. Or the husband sat her up from lying on the floor.

The phone rang, startling Marc. He picked up the receiver, "Jefferson, here." A hearing had been set for later in the week to hear arguments for compelling the release of medical records. Something must be in those records damning to Mary Waite. If Roger was tired of his marriage and did not want a divorce, which could be expensive, motive could be established for a manslaughter or murder charge. Motive was the key to establishing a solid case. A jury could be compelled to believe a man would take drastic measures to secure a future without complications. Fortune may have shone on Roger Waite when he came home to his wife and discovered a gun and suicide.

Marc contacted his favorite judge, explained his need for a DNA warrant, and with that need filled, realized it was well past noon and he wanted lunch. Today, Joan had prepared a meal for him. He put the pictures back in the folder and stacked the folders neatly on his desk. He went to the break room, retrieved his lunch, sat down alone, and ate.

CHAPTER 9

A clerk from the judge's office arrived as Marc finished eating his lunch. He had the warrant with him, gave it to Marc, and left. Marc called the coroner's office to have someone present to take the sample. He did not want to screw this up, although not much was expected from the DNA sample.

Preparing for the interview, Marc reviewed the files again. He wrote a list of questions about Mary, the gun, her medical history, their relationship, and their families. He hoped Woodbury would not be present, but believed he would accompany Waite to keep family secrets, secret.

Deputy Tony Wilkins returned with Roger and Walker Waite. Attorney, Jeff Woodbury, scurried in shortly after. Marc escorted them into an interrogation room and asked if they wanted anything to drink. Woodbury declined anything for all of them.

"Thanks for coming in." Marc directed them to chairs around the table. Marc sat across from them and placed a recording devise on the table. "Is it o.k. to record this? I don't want us to have any information misinterpreted."

"If you think you must, but please send me a copy of it." Woodbury said. "After all, no need for misinterpretations." *Sarcasm, interesting.* Marc thought.

"I'll do that. Mr. Waite, we are here to find out as much about the incident yesterday as we can. You are the only witness, so we need to hear how everything happened." Marc turned on the recorder and announced the date and time of the interview and who was present.

Roger nodded.

"You related to me yesterday, your wife called you while you were at church."

"She asked that I have Mom and Dad take the kids home with them. She didn't want the kids to come home with me."

"Did she indicate any reason?"

"No, but I knew something must have been bothering her. She insisted, so I asked my parents to take the kids."

"When did she call?" Marc asked.

"About 11:30 or so. I went home as soon as the kids were taken care of. Our church is not too far away. I got home about ten minutes later." Woodbury leaned over to say something to Roger. Marc guessed it had something to do with talking so much.

"You arrived home around 11:45. What happened over the next hour?" Marc thought. *Keep talking, Roger.*

"Yeah, I guess that's about right." Roger said nothing more. Marc wrote a note about the lack of an answer to the second question.

"I would like to know if you suspected Mary of wanting to commit suicide."

"No, I didn't. She had been moody, lately, but that was nothing new." Woodbury touched him.

"Did you know about the gun before yesterday?"

"No."

"How did you find out about it?"

"She took it out of the top drawer of her dresser and showed it to me. I asked her where she got it." Roger relaxed a bit.

"What did she say?"

Roger leaned over and spoke with Woodbury. He then turned back and said, "She told me that she bought it for protection about two weeks ago. I asked her who she needed protection from. She was evasive. I asked her how she paid for it. She said she used cash. I asked her when she had gone to the bank. She said she went before going to the gun store. I noticed the withdrawal earlier last week."

"Did she need protection from you?"

"You don't need to answer that," Woodbury intoned. "Ask him questions about yesterday, please."

This is going to be difficult. "Roger, explain to me how she came to shoot herself."

"She said she had taken out the gun and had decided to shoot herself. She told me she laid out the blanket on the floor, loaded the gun and fired one shot which went into the wall. It scared her so she put away the gun and called me." *The blanket had bloody fingerprints. Are they your prints Roger? Was she testing the gun by firing it?*

"But when did she get it out and shoot herself?"

"She told me she had a gun and that it was in the drawer. I opened the drawer and got it out. That's when I put it on the dresser and asked about it. She told me about buying the gun and deciding to end her life."

No plan? Something's screwy here.

Roger continued, "She kept that from me, by the way. I knew she was unhappy, but I never suspected she was suicidal. I talked with her about getting help. I said I would go with her. We talked for about half an hour. I turned and looked at the wall where the bullet had entered. She picked up the gun, put it to her head, and pulled the trigger before I could stop her. I checked for a pulse but couldn't find one."

"Did she put the gun directly on her head?"

"I don't know. I guess." Roger groused.

"Did you move the body into a sitting position?"

"I decided I had to call for help. I had been holding her for a few minutes. I was in shock, I guess. I just laid her against the wall, got up and called you guys."

"Mr. Waite, did you love your wife?"

"Keep to the shooting Mr. Jefferson." Woodbury wasn't about to let the emotional feelings enter the questioning. Roger's father clenched his teeth and hissed.

"I'm curious, Mr. Waite, about some bruising on your wife's arm. It is a hand print and is a couple of days old. Did you have a fight with her?"

Roger looked at Woodbury again who shook his head. Roger remained silent. Marc looked at Woodbury and asked, "Aren't you curious about any fighting within the family?"

"If it had any bearing on the suicide, I would have Roger answer."

"Alright." He turned to Roger, "Why did you call your in-laws?"

"I thought they should know what happened. I didn't think anything was wrong with letting them know what happened. I didn't want to call my parents because they had the children."

"Who did you call first?" Roger looked at Woodbury, who nodded acceptance of the question.

"As I already told you, I called my in-laws first. They told me to hang up and call 911."

Marc engaged the elder Waite. "Mr. Waite, have you noticed any problems with your daughter-in-law's emotional state lately?"

"No, I thought everything was fine."

"I think we can call it a day for now," Woodbury wanted to leave to protect his client from self-incrimination. Marc stood up and thanked each of them for coming in. As they left he turned off the recorder and followed them out the door.

"By the way, did you and your wife engage in sexual intercourse the night before?" Roger blushed.

Woodbury intervened. "Why does that matter?"

Marc said. "Just wondering, who was saying good-bye to whom?"

The coroner's representative was sitting in the hall waiting for the interview to end. Marc called to Roger. "Mr. Waite, I have

a request of you. This person is here to take a DNA sample."
Woodbury approached Marc.

"Why do you want a DNA sample?"

"You know, to figure out if anyone was saying good-bye."

"You're really a funny person, aren't you?"

"I have a warrant." He handed the warrant to Woodbury who read it carefully.

Handing it to Roger, he exclaimed icily. "You felt a need to have a warrant?" *Anger!* Marc noted. "We would have consented to a DNA sample since my client has nothing to hide."

Marc felt Woodbury staged the anger but now would be defensive about any questions. The representative took the sample from Roger and left for the coroner's office.

"Are you charging Roger with a crime?"

"No but there are some anomalies in the answers your client gave. So I want to know if he staged the suicide to cover a murder."

Roger, his father, and Woodbury left the sheriff's office. Marc returned to his desk and laid down the folders. He removed the tape from the machine, took it to another room and asked the person to transcribe the information to a document and to create a copy of the tape and the document. The afternoon passed and Marc thought of home. He put the files away and left for home hoping an early reentry would quell any brewing storm there.

CHAPTER 10

Arriving home, Marc sat for his moment in the car, as he often did, to clear his head of the day's activities and thoughts. Long ago he had made a vow to himself and Joan to separate work from family. So far this philosophy succeeded in keeping the family cohesive if not always happy. The children were secure, Joan pleasant, most of the time. Marc needed to learn to release the day and live the home life.

Still, no matter how much one wants to separate work from home, events creep in. Concerning this current case, Marc wanted his family life disconnected from this dysfunctional family. He exited the car and entered his haven.

Stability is such a fleeting emotion. How many of us could collapse under the weight of lesser issues. Mary Waite did not approach the type of person that Joan was. She died because of a perceived weakness. Did she create an environment that induced an unconscionable behavior from the man who vowed to love and cherish her for better or for worse? It certainly went beyond worse. Are we exonerated for not wanting to live in 'worst?'

"How are you this evening?" Joan asked as he entered the kitchen. "I heard you come into the garage." Marc smiled, thought of reaching out for her but decided to wait.

"I'm fine. It's been a busy day. But let's not discuss it."

Sometimes, one's life does not turn out just exactly as planned. Roger Waite had discovered this yesterday. Marc comprehended life's unintended consequences. He observed the nastier side of living regularly because of the people who crossed his path. These people fell into situations his family knew not. He did not want them to ever know the nastier side of living. What happened to people, mostly self-inflicted, trapped them in untenable consequences.

Joan recognized Marc's thoughts. She hugged him as though letting him know it was alright to talk about his day at home. "I love you," she said.

He reacted peacefully to her admission, sensing the strain in her voice. They went upstairs where he removed the symbols of his profession. The revolver was safely placed in its lock box, his shield accompanying it.

He sat on the bed and asked about the children. "They're at friends. I asked them to be home by 5:30 so we could eat together." She worked all day and still prepared a nice dinner which he smelled cooking as he entered the kitchen. "If you need to talk about this case, I'm a willing listener. It seems to bother you. I'm sorry I got angry yesterday. I know you felt a need to be part of it. I just wanted time with you."

He smiled. "Thanks. You're right that I may want too much involvement in the serious events that cross through the office. And I'll take you up on listening about this case."

She sat beside him on the bed. "I would never have dreamed two people could have so much turmoil in their lives. I don't even know what the turmoil might be, but one is dead and the other is suspect. And the extended families may be covering up for each other, the old 'circle the wagons' syndrome."

Marc stood up and changed into more relaxed clothing. As he and Joan went downstairs, Marc Junior and James entered the house arguing about something. Competition existed between them despite their difference in age, but they always worked through what bothered them. Occasionally, Marc helped them by providing the proper incentive. The boys dropped the argument as soon as they saw their parents.

"Good evening gentlemen, anything I might help you with regarding these angered voices?" Marc did not want to deal with their disagreement. This comment usually stopped any further quarrelling for the moment.

"No thanks," they stated in a harmonious duet. James gave Marc Junior a look of disgust.

Joan interjected, "Get cleaned up for dinner. Have you seen your sister?"

Marc Junior replied, "She's over at Rachel's."

"Well, I hope she comes home soon. Dinner is almost ready." Just then the door opened and Sarah entered with a smile on her face.

She bounded upstairs before anyone could react. The boys disappeared up the stairs after her and Marc and Joan finished preparing the table in the kitchen for dinner.

When they returned, all enjoyed the meal with talk about the day. The boys seemed to have worked out their disagreement. Sarah spoke of a new friend she had met at Rachel's. He was a visiting cousin and he was the cutest, nicest boy she had ever met. An older boy of seventeen, so worldly and all knowing, she was sure she was in love.

"Yuck," her younger brother responded. Her older brother just voiced his concern for her to be careful. He knew all about older 'men,' he being one himself. The dinner progressed without any other conversation involving the parents. Marc and Joan smiled as they ate and mostly listened to their children. No need to interpose sagacious adult wisdom for the moment, plenty of time later. They chatted a bit with each other.

Dinner completed, the children cleaned the kitchen. They lived in the house and as such had responsibilities as to its care. They grew up with this philosophy and did not complain. Each received an allowance for personal expenses. Marc Junior wanted to drive soon and was looking for a job to cover an automobile.

Mom and Dad were willing to help him with a used car so they would be free of transporting him around. He would help transport his sister and brother.

Marc and Joan strolled into the den, closed the door and began to talk. The kids knew to leave them alone when the door was closed. Joan asked, "What happened to that family?" She knew Marc needed to release the tension. She had seen enough family interaction at the elder care center to understand how Marc was feeling.

"I don't know who did what. She's dead from a gunshot to the head. He's the only witness. I discovered she had a history of mental instability maybe causing at least one other attempted suicide. Her youth was rocky. I'm beginning to think this guy took advantage of a situation to extricate himself from an unhappy marriage, but the time of death doesn't seem to match his statements." Joan just listened. "I need to get psych reports they will not want released. I would like to hear the truth from the husband, but I'm sure he's not telling it. Their attorney will block any attempt at interviewing anyone else who might implicate the husband. Boy, this one is a doozie." He looked at Joan and smiled.

She returned his smile knowing that he had unburdened his soul and would now relax. She reached out her hands to his and they held each other for a few moments in silence.

"I am so glad I'm married to you," he finally commented. "Our life is easy compared with so many others. They don't know how good it can be." They looked at each other and then kissed a passionate, arousing kiss. Marc explored Joan with eager desire. Joan touched Marc in places that she knew awoke his libido. The passion lasted for much of the evening. Satisfied with each other, they dressed and went upstairs to sleep. The children had retired earlier to their rooms to study or entertain themselves. Life truly was good and in such contrast to Roger and Mary Waite. He recognized Joan had to be first in his life. But how could he ignore an apparent murder just to keep her happy?

CHAPTER 11

Marc woke from a restful sleep, and felt calm, much like one experiences just before a storm. His mind may not have dreamt. However, it felt in hyper mode, now. The medical records' hearing wasn't for two more days, but a long day lay ahead.

He looked at the clock. It was still early and Joan slept soundly beside him. He quietly slipped from the bed and went to the bathroom. He looked in the mirror and grimaced. *What have you gotten into?* He grabbed his robe, left the room, and went downstairs.

The newspaper on the porch declared the Sunday event in the headlines. "Nothing like a good old shooting to enliven the news," Marc sarcastically said aloud. He figured his name would not be present, not having spoken with any reporters in the two days since the incident. He felt sure that would be changing today. Yesterday's paper mentioned little about the event, since nothing had been released to the media. Now they knew more than he thought they should, much of it speculation on their part. He wondered with whom reporters had spoken. He knew of no one in the sheriff's office who had been approached.

"Must talk with the boss about this," he reflected. He understood reporters' need to gather information and suspected they'd be at the office when he arrived, but too much could taint the jury pool. Although he didn't know the Waite family, he figured they had some connections within the community. He didn't know anything about Mary Waite's family in Seattle.

After reading news articles, editorials, and the sports pages, Marc sauntered into the kitchen to get breakfast. Joan entered soon after. "You're up early. Did you have another dream?"

He turned from his breakfast to face her. "Fortunately, no. The paper has a banner headline about the shooting, though. I imagine reporters are gathering at the office as we speak." He shrugged his shoulders as if to say "Oh, well!"

Marc turned back to his preparations. Joan hugged him from behind. "You'll do well with them. What's for breakfast?"

"My famous pancakes and bacon. But I should get to the office so I'll leave the rest to you while I dress and awaken the kids."

"Not fair, Bub! You need to finish what you start."

"Alright, you get the kids, and lay out my best sports coat and pants, please."

Joan smiled and left the kitchen. Marc continued with breakfast. He knew his investigation would uncover much about this vitiated family which invaded his life. He finished cooking the bacon and worked on creating a stack of hot pancakes. Joan and the children showed up just as he finished the first batch. Marc Junior set the table while Sarah got out plates. Joan poured juice for everyone. They sat and enjoyed a family breakfast which would be the last for a while.

Marc retired to the bedroom to dress, while Joan and the kids cleaned the kitchen and loaded the dishwasher. He took a quick shower and put on the clothing laid out for him. He did admire his wife greatly. She came into the room as he dressed. "I wish you hadn't taken this one," she said. "It may cause us more harm than good."

"Why? It's no different than other cases I've worked."

A chill invaded. "I worry about us and what we'll be when it's over."

Great, I need this like I need another dead body. "Let it go, Joan." He picked up his revolver and shield. He turned to kiss her, but she moved away. He scowled and left the room.

* * *

As predicted, reporters congregated in front of the office. He parked in the back lot away from the crowd. Entering the office, Sheriff Glenmore Fellington intercepted him. "Sit down, Marc. We need to address the crowd gathering outside. Bring me up to speed regarding the Waite case. We'll have a media session as soon as we can put something together."

Marc nodded. He didn't want the limelight, but this case had spotlights all over it. He excused himself to get the files, and when he returned he related what had been done and uncovered the previous evening. Marc was thorough. The Chief and he devised a plan and called a spokesperson to address the media as to a time for a report. The spokesperson departed to deliver the message. It was about 9:00 AM and they planned a summit to be convened in an hour.

"What are the chances of a murder conviction?" Sheriff Fellington was ready to retire in the next few years. He had been easily reelected to the top spot three years ago but was not going to stand for office again and wanted to retire on a high note. This type of case was a good resume piece. Regardless of what he might do after thirty years of law enforcement, he still wanted employment.

Marc shifted his feet. "A conviction could be difficult if we can't get something solid on Roger Waite. Although he was present and had opportunity and maybe even motive, a jury could be sympathetic to a man whose wife is off her rocker. The hearing on Thursday may be a smoking gun or an empty chamber. This woman may indeed have had mental problems, and she may have wanted to commit suicide. However, I believe Waite helped it along and that's what we have to prove. He'll get off if we go to court without sufficient evidence of complicity."

"Alright, I trust you and your judgment. Get what we need. But you only have until the end of the week. If you can't pin it on him, it's going in the record as a suicide."

Fellington handed Marc the files. He returned to his desk glancing back at the Sheriff whom he admired. He did not envy his having to face the madding crowd and answer questions with words mostly consisting of 'We are still investigating and have no comment on that at this time.' Marc would stand with the sheriff when the time came to address the mob of reporters. He could see out a nearby window to the front of the building. He thought the crowd had grown a little. TV reporters had erected the microwave towers on the top of the trucks. A live broadcast was a real possibility. He returned to his work of preparing a report to accompany the sheriff's remarks as Fellington requested. His writing ability was adequate but not worth publishing. He would give enough to the frenzy to feed their lust but not enough to jeopardize a possible case.

He worked the computer and keyboard efficiently and knocked out his own statement within half an hour. Attempting to anticipate questions he would be asked, he wrote accordingly. He was satisfied with his editorial and stood up to show the sheriff. Fellington had his own speech which included turning over the media session to questions. This definitely involved Marc who would be answering much of what would be asked.

At 10:00 AM, as promised, Sheriff Fellington and Marc stood in front of the throng and began their soiree. Fellington related the events of that fateful Sunday, explaining the circumstances that existed at the time and the information that had been gathered so far. He did not reveal pertinent details that could taint the case. After what seemed like an eternity but in reality a mere 5 minutes, he asked for questions. The reporters noisily obliged him.

"Do you feel this is truly a case of suicide?"

"As far as we can tell, right now, yes."

"What kind of gun was used?"

"As I stated before, it was a small caliber weapon."

"Is there any evidence the husband may have shot his wife?"

"We are still investigating and will not comment on that matter."

"So he possibly could have shot her?"

"No comment." That would fuel the fire, he thought.

"Officer Jefferson." Here it comes thought Marc. "You are the lead investigator, are you not?"

Marc stepped to the mike. "Yes."

"What can you tell us about the shooting that has not already been addressed?"

"Well, as Sheriff Fellington has stated, this is an ongoing investigation. We have evidence to gather and process. Until we get done we'll not be sure of exactly what happened."

"Have you spoken with the prosecutor, yet?"

"I spoke with him yesterday."

"Will he be pursuing a criminal charge against the husband?"

"I am not at liberty to speak for the prosecutor's office."

"Yesterday, a warrant was issued for DNA. *How did they find that out?* Has that evidence been useful?"

"The DNA evidence is being processed. We have nothing to say about it at this time."

The questions continued for another fifteen minutes. Many of them were repeats with a different tack. Reporters knew how to ask questions to gather information before one knew that it was gathered. Marc was careful releasing nothing that shouldn't be released. Finally, Sheriff Fellington ended the torture and they reentered the sheriff's office. Questions continued flying at them, but they were ignored.

As Marc looked out of the window, the TV reporters were giving their reports to their broadcast stations. The print reporters were calling in their reports to magazines or newspapers. The radio broadcasters were busy as well. Marc sat down and picked up the phone. He dialed the prosecutor's office and asked for Patterson. When the assistant DA answered, Marc explained the media blitz and asked about their office. There had been some inquiries but no interviews. "What do you need for the medical hearing on Thursday?" Patterson asked for the 911 tapes of the Sunday call and requested the previous drug overdose report to be followed up by asking neighbors and family members about it. Marc promised to do so. He hung up the phone.

He picked up the transcript of Sunday's 911 call and began reading:

"911, what's your emergency?"

"My wife just shot herself. Send help. Please."

"Sir, explain to me what you mean."

"She shot herself in the head with a revolver. There's blood everywhere."

A pause in communication occurred.

"Sir, I'm dispatching services to your location. Please stay on the line with me. Is your wife breathing?"

"I don't know. I don't think so. I think she's dead. Oh God, this is awful."

Sir, please touch nothing before assistance arrives. Are you able to leave the area so as to let in the medics?"

"Yes, I can."

"Sir, are you injured in any way? Did you have a fight of any kind with your wife? Did she attempt to shoot you?"

"What? No, we didn't have a fight. She just pulled out this gun and put it to her head and pulled the trigger."

"Did she say anything before shooting the weapon?"

"I think I hear them." A pause followed. "Oh, why did she do this? She said she wanted to die, but she didn't have to do this."

"Sir, what is your name..." Marc stopped reading.

Nothing seemed so unusual about the call. But Marc discerned no real concern in the words of the Roger Waite. His experience with desperate 911 calls told him the panic element was missing. *I should listen to the recording.*

He created another list of people which included Mary's family. A file had been delivered while he was outside revealing a sister and brother who lived in Seattle. Marc decided a short auto ride would be in order. He picked up his recorder and pad and left the office. Not contacting them first, their reactions to be real, not contrived. He also wanted them available. No need to play hide and seek with them, if they ran. He didn't want additional attorneys blocking his investigation.

Benjamin Johnson worked at a software company in downtown Seattle. He was not married. Arriving at the company address, Marc parked his car in a nearby lot and entered the establishment. A receptionist directed him to a cubical in another part of the room. The cubical was large and had a window view of Puget Sound. The company, located on the fifth floor of the building, placed it above the buildings between it and the Sound. The slight rise of the hillside helped to create a spectacular view of Bainbridge Island, the ferries, and the Olympic Mountains.

Marc walked up to the cubical, displayed his badge and introduced himself. Ben stood and asked, "What can I do for you?" Marc discovered a different sort of person than expected. He was about the same height as Marc, although several years younger. He wore casual clothes with a slight flare for swanky. Marc wondered about his life but dismissed the idea of confronting his style, for now.

"Is there somewhere we can talk?"

"This is about Mary, isn't it? I spoke with my family attorney and he said I should not speak with anyone from your office without her being here."

"I am only going to take a little bit of your time. And I have only a few questions to ask." Marc called his bluff. "I'll be glad to wait while you contact her." Ben tapped a pencil on his desk.

"Okay. Come with me." The two of them retreated to a conference room nearby and shut the door. "What do you want?" Ben rephrased the earlier question.

"What can you tell me about your sister's life while she grew up?"

"I don't know, she had a normal life, like the rest of us, I guess"

"Are you older or younger than she?"

"Older."

"By how much?"

"Three years."

Were there any times in her life that you could describe as medically challenging?"

"What do you mean?"

"Did she at any time have to see medical personnel about her emotions?"

"Do you want to know whether she saw a psychiatrist? She saw one when she was about 14, I think. She had a disappointment in her life that caused a severe depression for a while. She worked through it and that was that. She went on with life."

"Did she have any medical traumas or accidents at that time?" Marc avoided saying suicide.

"I don't know much about what happened. My parents told me that she fell and hurt her arms. She stayed in the hospital a couple of days and came home. She had bandages on her lower arms."

"Were you and your sister close?"

"Not really. She and I hung out with a different crowd. I was in high school at the time you're speaking of and she had her artsy group. I was more interested in technology. But I loved my sister and she shouldn't have killed herself. By the way, I don't think she did it. That's what you want to know, isn't it?"

Marc contemplated asking more questions but decided to wait. Was Ben evading the truth about Mary? He thanked him for his time and left the building.

The sister was a student at a local private university, Seattle Pacific, located on the north end of Queen Anne Hill and several years younger than her brother and sister according to the information he had gathered. He went to the office of the registrar to have her contacted. He waited while the receptionist called security to send a guard who would escort Marc to her class. Marc thought it strange that neither of them had left their own lives to be with their family. Maybe life did have to go on after all. A memorial service or whatever would be later anyway.

The security guard arrived and led Marc across a quad area to another building. The guard had the name and classroom in his hand and escorted Marc to the building and floor in which Victoria Johnson's class was located. The guard went into the room and brought her out. She was a younger version of her older sister. Her dark blond hair was cut to shoulder length. Her body was superbly shaped. The jeans and loose fitting shirt did little to accentuate anything, but she exuded a sensuality that asked for attention. Her deep blue eyes penetrated a man's soul. The guard stepped back to let the two people talk privately.

"My name is Marc Jefferson. I am with the Wendlesburg sheriffs' department. I am here about your sister, Mary. I would like to ask you some questions about her."

Victoria showed some emotion. "I guess. What do you want to know?"

"What was your relationship with Mary?"

"She was my best friend. I miss her very much."

How old were you when she attempted her first suicide?"

"Boy, you really cut to the chase. I was very young when she was a teenager. I'm sure I can't be of much help."

"When she was around 14, what happened to her that led to her being so depressed she attempted killing herself?"

She furrowed her brow as if surprised. "Wow, I haven't thought of that in years. She had this talent for drawing and painting pictures. She was always drawing things for me."

"What happened?"

"As I remember it, she went to New York with Mom and Dad to show some of her work to an art gallery and there was an accident. She got hurt and didn't paint after that. I think she was depressed because she couldn't anymore."

"How did your parents react to this?"

"Dad was never very supportive of her art work. He wanted her to get through school and go to college and get a job that would pay her real money. He thought art was not a lucrative enough vocation."

"What about your mother?"

"She wanted what was best for Mary, so she helped my sister with her artwork until Mary just stopped creating any more pictures. She drew lots for me. I still have them all."

"Were your sister and brother close?"

"Not like me and Mary. I don't know about their lives before me, of course. My sister was nine years older than me and Ben is 12 years older."

"Are you and Ben close?"

"No. He hardly talks to me. Here we live in the same city and the only time we do anything together is when we're at Mom and Dad's."

"Why is that?"

"We have different lives and friends and twelve years is a lot of years."

"When did you last see your sister?"

"We saw each other Friday. I don't have any classes that day so we tried to get together as often as possible. She seemed so unhappy. I didn't realize that she was planning to kill herself. If I had known, I would have tried to talk her out if it. She listened to me. She said I was the smartest member of the family."

"Did you know she had purchased a gun a couple of weeks before?"

"Yes, she wanted to have some protection from home invaders. At least, that's what she told me. I asked her if she was going to learn how to use it and she said she had signed up for a class. I bet she really didn't."

Marc had found a treasure trove of information. Victoria Johnson had not been informed about not speaking to the police or she didn't care. One more question and he would leave her, somewhat unwillingly.

A sensation penetrated his demeanor of professionalism. Victoria fascinated him in a way long ago lost in marriage and family. Her crystal blue eyes glistened. Her breathing raised and lowered her frame accentuating what he fantasized. Her waist curved delightfully to her hips which enticed a man to stare a second longer than appropriate. He followed her legs to her flip-flops. Her exposed toenails were a bright pink which completed the ceremonial magnetism of first encounters between man and woman.

"Miss Johnson, do you think that your sister tried to kill herself when she was 14?"

"We didn't talk about it in the family, but Mary and I did privately. After she came home from the hospital, she told me that she didn't want to live anymore. I listened. After all, what can a 5 year old say. I stayed close to her as much as possible so that she wouldn't try to hurt herself."

"Thank you for your help. I know this is a difficult time for you. I am surprised that you are still attending school."

"I have nothing better to do. If I'm not busy, I'll think about Mary. As I said, I'm going to miss my sister." She turned and Marc studied her as she entered the classroom. A seductive smile coursed her face when she turned and spied Marc's lingering attention. He thanked the security guard and left.

He was touched by her careful attention to the older sister. He couldn't help notice that, although the two sisters looked alike, this girl truly was more beautiful. A sinister thought entered Marc's head, but he let it go. What other information would be extracted from Victoria which could impugn Roger's innocence?

CHAPTER 12

Marc called Patterson as he left Seattle to be sure he was in. The day passed quickly, but Marc was not finished yet. As he arrived at the prosecutor's office and parked his car, he called the sheriff's office asking the day watch officer to contact Waite to set up another meeting.

The media crowd had moved from the sheriff's office to the prosecutor's office and began to assail Marc as he exited his car. He avoided answering the plethora of questions thrown his way, using the stock answer, "No Comment."

Patterson stared out a window as he entered. "Quite the feeding frenzy outside. We spoke with them about two hours ago and still they haven't left." He faced Marc. "What did you find out from Mary's sister and brother?"

Marc spoke as they moved to a conference room down the hall. "The little sister is loquacious while the older brother is protective of family secrets. He did relate that Mary was hospitalized when she was fourteen but didn't give much detail or he didn't know much. Mary spent a couple of days there and came home bandaged on her lower arms. Probably cut her wrists. The younger sister seemed to think Mary contemplated suicide as a teenager. She did state that Mary had been hurt in an accident in New York when the parents took her there to display some art work. Mary liked to draw and paint but did not do so after returning home from their trip. She also said the father wasn't very supportive of her art. I'll track them down and talk with them about it."

"This is good." Patterson smiled a wise thinking smile and turned to the library in the room. "Maybe there's a case here we can use as precedence. We push the idea that we support the suicide angle rather than suspecting Roger of anything. That way we may get the records for all of her medical history. I'll get my staff right on it."

"Are you interested in pursuing a criminal prosecution of Waite for murder?"

"If the evidence points at his complicity, this office will convict him." Patterson looked intent as he spoke.

"Well, I think he had something to do with the death," replied Marc.

"Okay, then go after him."

Marc left the conference room promising a written report about his visits. He would see the siblings again, of this he was sure, especially Victoria. The parents were next. The day waned toward evening, but Marc still had a puzzle to solve. He expected reports from officers he'd sent out to interview neighbors. And he hoped Waite would be available.

Entering the office, he strode to his desk, and found three folders on it from the deputies who had interviewed neighbors, and a note that Waite was available after 5 PM. A phone number was with the note. He picked up the receiver and dialed. The time was now 5:10. After several rings a person said hello.

"Mr. Waite, please," he asked in his most professional voice. Marc listened and responded, "Mr. Waite, can we please meet again as soon as possible?" Marc listened again. "That would be fine with me. I'll see you when you get here." Roger did not mention anything about a lawyer which Marc hoped would be the case. He wanted to have a clean shot at discovery with Roger. The information he gleaned from the Johnson siblings needed corroboration, a clear understanding of the relationship Roger had with Mary. Was she a bitch and needed elimination? Was Roger capable of her elimination? Or had she become so disillusioned with living that no amount of motherly instinct for the safety and welfare of two small children had the power to save her.

Marc picked up the first folder and read the report. The officer visited with the next door neighbor asking for clarity regarding the relationship of Roger and Mary Waite. He asked about the fighting mentioned initially. The neighbor explained hearing disagreements that escalated into shouting matches. Mary did not act very friendly to anyone. He heard her complaining about people staring at her. The neighbor said he stayed away from her, but he liked the husband and felt sorry he was married to that crazy woman. The officer asked if he knew of any other problems with the police. The man related the police had been at the house about two years before and he thought she had attempted to kill herself. He noted Roger acted unhappy after that. The neighbor decided to build a fence in order to keep the wife away from his family. He had nothing good to say about Mary Waite.

The next folder from the neighbor across the street had little additional evidence. One important comment by the wife of the family stated she had tried to befriend Mary and had only marginal success. However, when the lady introduced Mary to other friends of hers, Mary became very protective of her friendship with the neighbor. Mary attempted to isolate the neighbor and discredited her friends as beneath her. The neighbor finally broke from the friendship and stated she kept away from Mary. Mary then began berating her to other neighbors. She sought a court order to keep Mary away from her and attempted to stop the negative gossip.

The third neighbor on the other side of the Waite's had little contact with them as they had just moved in. Nevertheless, the previous owners had warned them about Mary. Intriguing, this woman alienated her neighbors. Maybe Roger grew tired of her antics, irked enough to kill.

Marc closed the folders and placed them with the others. The case was beginning to mount circumstantially, but lacked hard evidence. Marc looked up to see the duty officer escort Roger and his attorney, Jeff Woodbury, into the area. Marc stood, shook hands with the men, and ushered them to an interrogation room. He had grabbed his pad and recorder as they departed for the room.

Woodbury intoned, "You seem more interested in my client than necessary for a suicide. You're getting close to harassment." Marc nodded.

"Thanks for coming in. I know we can finish this business soon and get on with living. Mr. Waite, how are you doing?" Marc wanted to appear caring and not put Roger on the defensive.

"I'm okay. We're planning the memorial service for Mary. Her parents are staying at my parent's house if you want to talk with them. Do you still want to have medical records about Mary?"

The question surprised Marc. He thought a hearing would be the only way to get the records. Maybe Roger was playing a game of sorts. "Yes, I think some of the history we have discovered helps support the suicide cause. We can then get an idea of your wife's state of mind and complete this case."

Jeff Woodbury interceded, "Against my advice, Mr. Waite wants to release the medical records regarding her accidental drug overdose two years ago. He will stipulate that Mary had a problem with her mental state."

"Thank you, Mr. Waite. I do have some questions about that incident and another possible attempted suicide when she was a teenager. Can you tell me what you know about these events?"

"Mr. Jefferson, the difficulties in her teen years has nothing to do with Sunday," Woodbury responded as he turned to his client. "You don't have to say anything." Roger nodded but began speaking.

"I don't know much about that. I heard some things, but really, I don't know that much. Speak with her parents. They can fill you in on what happened. All I know is that she was crushed about a trip to New York. An accident happened and she was injured." Roger seemed genuine. "As for the drug over dose two years ago, she took too many sleeping pills and almost killed herself."

"Do you think it was accidental?"

Woodbury interrupted, "Don't answer that." Roger ignored him.

"What do you mean? Of course it was accidental." Roger squirmed. "She was not sleeping well. The baby kept her up late at times. She just needed to get some quality rest."

"That seems a bit drastic. What did you do that night?"

"I took care of Samuel and Rebecca, our children. Mary wanted to get some sleep, so she went to bed early. I went to bed about 11. Nothing seemed wrong."

"How did Mary get the pills?"

"She had a prescription from her doctor."

"Was she taking the pills as prescribed?"

"What? Of course she was. Some nights she went to bed after me. Sometimes I stayed up, but mostly we went to bed together. I didn't monitor her consumption, if that's what you want to know."

"So she could have been saving the pills for an attempt at killing herself on that night two years ago?"

"Don't answer that," Woodbury leaned toward Roger.

Marc continued, "What happened the next day?"

"I woke up, made myself some breakfast and read the newspaper. I then dressed and left for work."

"Did you often leave for work before Mary woke?"

"Yes, she and the children usually stayed asleep. I like to get my paperwork completed at the office before the hustle and bustle begins."

"What time did you leave for work that day?" Marc was curious as to why Roger would leave his children with a wife who had taken drugs the previous night. This guy's routine drove his life.

"I left about 6:45. I arrived at the office a little after 7." Roger shifted in his chair.

"I am curious as to why you would leave the house and not first check your wife's condition. After all, she had taken a sleep aid that night." The little probe by Marc seemed right. Woodbury whispered to Roger.

"I didn't think anything was wrong. I wouldn't leave my children in jeopardy. I just had things to do at work and Mary usually slept later than me. So did the kids."

"After the sheriff got a hold of you, how did you react to the news that your wife had taken an overdose?" Woodbury spoke with Roger again.

"I was upset. I realized then she may have accidently taken too many pills and I shouldn't have left until I checked on her. I made a mistake." Jeff Woodbury touched Roger's arm as if to say, 'Shut up'.

"Usually after a drug overdose a competency hearing is requested. Did this happen in Mary's case?"

Woodbury hastened to answer, "You should have that in your records. Roger, let's get out of here. It is late." Roger nodded and the two of them stood.

Marc stood as well, "Thank you for coming in. I'm really sorry to have to ask you these questions at such a terrible time in your life." Keep him calm, thought Marc. "Oh, one more question. Did Mary act any different that night?"

"What do you mean?" Roger looked perplexed.

"I was wondering about her demeanor."

"No more questions," Jeff had his client by the arm and was guiding him out the door with vigor, Marc let the question slide. It would be asked later, anyway.

After Waite and Woodbury left, Marc returned to his desk to type a report for Patterson. Completing the report, Marc noticed that the day was over and night had crept in. It was nearly eight o'clock. He had not called Joan to let her know he would be late. He hoped she would understand.

The report was put in an envelope and placed in the out tray for delivery. Nothing more could be accomplished at work. Marc cleaned off his desk, locked the files up, and departed the office. Not much else was happening, fortunately. A quiet night for the evening shift would be a great relief. He entered his car and headed for home. Lack of dinner haunted his body, but he figured food mercifully would be waiting for him.

Marc went through his mental routine in the garage, but tensed when Joan came out to meet him. "You received a call from a Victoria Johnson. Who is she?"

"Mary Waite's sister. Did she want me to call her this evening?"

"No, the message said it could wait until morning." Joan wrapped her arm in Marc's. They strolled into the house together. Marc relaxed. Joan was serene for now. Dinner, as predicted, awaited his troubled body. Satisfaction guaranteed in this household, thought Marc. *I really do need to come home at a more reasonable hour.* He ate.

With his appetite sated, he visited his children in the family room and retired to the bedroom for much needed sleep. The day had been 'curiouser and curiouser', to steal a phrase. The call from Victoria just added to the curiousness of it all. Roger opened up, but not to everything. Mary was an enigma. A call to the sister in the morning and contacting the girl's parents should clear up the teenage incident. Medical records for that time might be important, as well.

Marc climbed into bed while Joan made herself ready. They kissed and held each other until sleep overcame Marc's active mind. Please, he thought, as he drifted off, no dreams tonight.

CHAPTER 13

M ary floated over the ground. He ran to get away. There was nowhere to hide. The sky filled with rain, but the drops were large and shaped like pills. Marc entered a bedroom bright red and smoky. It smelled of cordite. Roger came in, "I didn't mean to. I didn't mean to."

The sky in the room cleared. Victoria appeared, "My sister is crazy. Roger where are you going?" Roger left. Victoria followed him. Marc began to spin around as Mary remarked that no one understood her. "You are not solving this fast enough, Marc. Where have you been?" Marc stopped and stared at her.

"I don't even know you. Stop floating." Roger reentered the room, "why did you do it?"

"Mary, honey it means nothing to me. Please don't do it. Come home with me."

"I will be with you forever, Roger. You can't escape me. Killing me doesn't free you from me. You are mine."

Marc walked around the red room, clouds billowing over his head. A fog formed and his vision deteriorated. He heard gunshots, but no one was nearby. The room cleared and Mary held the gun in her hand. Part of her head was missing, but Roger lay on the floor gasping for air. "You're suffocating me, you unworthy bitch."

Mary laughed wickedly, "I will be with you forever. Nothing can separate us. Not a gun, not my sister, not even death. You are mine."

Suddenly the room quieted and Joan was talking, mumbling. The room vanished and the sheriff's office materialized. Joan continued to mumble something about waking to the truth. He slowly gained consciousness as Joan's voice cleared. She now spoke about dreaming. Marc realized a different world, a world of the truth. He opened his eyes and found a room that was a pale yellow, the bedroom of his house. Marc woke from a fitful sleep with Joan looking concerned, "You were babbling. What was going on?"

Marc explained dreaming but remembering nothing of it. Joan listened. "I can't prove anything yet about Roger Waite. I'm thinking he might be an unfaithful husband." Marc sat up in the bed. The dream left him tired. Wednesday would be another busy day. "I hope this case ends quickly or you will be living with a blithering idiot."

"This shooting is consuming too much of you. Let the rest of the team finish it," Joan pleaded. "It's just a suicide isn't it?"

"I'm not so sure. I think someone other than Mary Waite pulled the trigger. I don't know who but I suspect the husband has more information than he's letting out. I'm sorry it's not an open and shut case, but I have to finish it."

"Everyone suspects the husband. But now I question whether you want this more than you want me." Marc did not respond but contemplated Uncle Jerry's death and knew suicide was not the answer he sought.

Joan left the bedroom to check on the children and fix breakfast. Marc showered and dressed. He picked up his cell phone and dialed the number for Victoria who answered. Marc identified himself, listened and wrote an address on a piece of paper to meet her in Wendlesburg around noon. She told him she must confess to something. "Intriguing," reflected Marc. *Why meet in Wendlesburg? Why are you coming here?*

He headed down stairs. After breakfast he kissed the kids and Joan and left for the office. Another meeting with Victoria could be interesting. To what she would confess, he could only guess. But Marc had suspicions and these might be a giant reason for Roger Waite to want his wife out of the way. Ben Johnson knew more as well. Was there a solid motive for prosecution of murder? Opportunity existed. Enough proof of action was all that Marc and Duncan Patterson needed to convince a jury. Marc called Patterson. No one answered, so he headed to his own office.

Yesterday's news frenzy had evaporated. Tomorrow's hearing would be news enough for the weekend. Reporters seemed a strange breed. Nothing lasted for very long since the public's insatiable appetite for other people's problems was fleeting. He parked in his usual spot and entered the building without fanfare. Victoria Johnson was first on the list of tasks. Calls to the Johnson parents and brother were next. He thought about his conversation with Roger the previous evening. "We must get the medical reports," thought Marc. "Are there any other attempts we don't know about?"

A message from Patterson waited. The time stamp showed 7:30 AM. *Well, the early bird does get the worm.* He called Patterson again and filled the prosecutor in with the details of last night and enlightened him about the call from Victoria Johnson.

Pulling out the files, he reviewed the details of each report and took notes for his discussion with Miss Johnson. If she confessed to what he thought might be the indiscretion he speculated, a new twist to the case would require another meeting with Roger and his attorney. The lineup of reasons for dispatching Mary Waite was lengthening. Roger had some explaining to do, and it could be at the office or on a witness stand.

If Roger Waite desired a separation from his wife, why not just divorce her? Maybe she wanted more than he was willing to part with. Maybe he just wanted her to leave him alone and she wouldn't do it. Maybe she threatened to expose him for the jerk he was.

Marc looked at his watch. It was nearly 10:30. He picked up the phone to call the Waite house wanting to speak with the Johnsons. Looking in his notes, he found the number, and dialed. Nancy Waite answered. The Johnsons were at the coroner's office finalizing the paperwork for transporting their daughter's remains to a mortuary they had contacted. He would try again later.

He called Patterson again. "Do you need particular questions answered for the hearing in the morning?"

Patterson answered, "No, I'm letting Atherton handle it. But have Victoria Johnson come to the hearing, if possible, to explain her version of events when Mary was a teenager."

"Alright," Marc promised. "I'll glean as much detail of the time period at the very least." *Ben Johnson has more to relate,* thought Marc as he disconnected. He picked up the phone again and called the work number he had in his notes.

Ben had called in sick and could be reached at home. Marc asked for the number. The receptionist explained, as a policy, the company did not release home addresses or numbers without clearance from the HR department. He asked to be transferred. Explaining who he was and the necessity to speak with Ben Johnson and the requirement to not impede a lawful investigation, he obtained the number and address.

He reset the phone and dialed Ben's home number. No one answered. Marc did not leave a message. If Ben felt threatened, he might vanish until this matter blew over. Victoria could be the better source, he surmised. It was time to leave.

Arriving at the restaurant address given by Victoria, Marc parked his car, picked up his memo pad, and exited the car. Entering the building, he found her sitting at a corner booth, alone. Her halter-top plunged at the neck. The light from the window cast a halo around her head. Her beauty intrigued Marc's sense of intrigue. Oh, to be young again and meet someone like her. Marc suppressed feelings which betrayed his love for Joan. He sat down with her, and they exchanged pleasantries for a few minutes. They ordered some coffee and lunchtime food.

"Mr. Jefferson, did Roger do something bad last Sunday? I haven't slept well since I found out about Mary's death."

"He says he witnessed her shoot herself. Do you know of any reason he would want to make sure she finished the suicide?"

Victoria hesitated for a moment. Slowly, she breathed in, then out, reluctant to speak. He watched her breasts rise and fall. Finally, "I don't think he's capable of violence. I've known him since he first met Mary. He's gentle and kind. I really admire him as a man and a parent. He and Mary were so cute together."

"You are not very convincing. Why are we here?"

"Alright, I really shouldn't say anything because I am not so innocent myself. Roger and Mary's marriage began fine. They seemed very happy for the first couple of years. I was glad for Mary."

"Why?"

"Well, she didn't have a great life growing up, and I didn't think she was a very happy adult. When she met Roger in college and they seemed to hit it off, I was ecstatic."

"How long did their marriage remain happy?"

"What do you mean 'remain happy'? They were happy until the end."

"Look, you're wasting my time. You said you had to confess something and I think I know what it is. Will you tell me or shall I just speculate?" His eyes narrowed and he glared at her with disdain.

"My family is not stable, Mr. Jefferson. I admired Roger because his family seemed so normal. My brother and sister had problems I somehow avoided, probably because I'm so much younger. Maybe I shouldn't say this, but my father can be difficult. Mary told me about times she and Ben were disciplined for things most people would think were nothing. Mom always acquiesces to my father. Behind his back she talked with us about how to get along with him. Generally, as I grew up, I did not have to deal with Dad's angry tirades, but once, I heard Mom and Dad talking. My sister and brother weren't home. He confessed that he really didn't want children and he could hardly wait until we were all gone. He was sorry I had been born. I was about 10 at the time. I knew he was sorry because I was still home and my sister and brother were in college. He didn't have much to do with me as I grew up. My father is not what you would call affectionate." Victoria paused.

Marc interjected, "Did your father ever abuse you or your sister, physically?"

"No, it was more emotional than anything."

"How did Mary and Ben handle it?"

"My brother can be very much like my father at times. Mary just withdrew from life. She would find a friend and cling to her. When she met Roger, she seemed more open, less clingy. I don't know. She just seemed to ignore anything from her past."

"So what's this confession of yours?"

Victoria looked away, blushing. A moment of silence passed. "About three years ago, right after Rebecca's birth, I noticed Mary was sad a lot, you know, post-partum blues. She just never seemed to get out of it. When Sam was born her mental state really seemed to plummet. Roger called me several times and we talked about her. My brother didn't approve, so we kept quiet about the calls."

"Is this your confession? I think maybe there's more to it."

"I began to think my sister would never recover from her psychoses. I believed she was becoming mentally unstable." Victoria reached across the table and held Marc's hand. He didn't resist. "I wanted her to die so she could be whole again. I feel badly now, because what I wanted came true and I feel responsible for it."

"Why? You didn't pull the trigger did you?"

Victoria acted startled, then haltingly said, "No, of course not, but Mary and I talked regularly about her mental state and I think I may have convinced her that it was hopeless. I'm not a bad person." She removed her hand from his and continued. "Look at me. I know what people say. How I look like Mary and how pretty we are… ah…were. I don't date, however, and don't have a boyfriend. I believe in Roger's innocence and hope you do as well."

Marc scowled, "Why tell me this? Was Mary hard to live with?"

"No," Victoria winced noticeably. "Well, at times, yes. And that's why I feel so conflicted. I know she and Roger fought at times for no apparent reason. He told about times when she just seemed to change moods in the middle of a conversation. I had seen it at home when we were growing up."

"So you assumed her mind was deteriorating and you wanted her to have comfort by dying? That doesn't make sense to me." He hesitated. "Tell me about these conversations with Roger."

"Roger and I started when I was in high school. He wanted help for Mary and her funk. I liked Roger a lot and I felt sorry for him. He asked about Mary's life growing up and I explained what happened to her in our house."

"Did you and he develop a close relationship during these conversations?"

"What do you mean?" She blushed. "Did we have an affair? Is that what you mean?" Marc observed her countenance.

"Well, it's a possibility. You think your sister was unstable and Roger may have been lonely for companionship."

"I am attracted to Roger. I have been since I first met him, but to interfere with my sister's marriage seems a terrible thing to do."

"Yet, you've not denied it."

Victoria stood up as if to leave, then stopped. "I think I should go." Marc looked at her face then scanned down to her short skirt which exposed shapely tanned legs.

"Sit down. I'm not here to condemn you. I need to know what Roger and Mary's life was like. If she committed suicide, Roger is in the clear. If he had motive to want out of the marriage without divorcing her, then he needs to pay for his crime."

Victoria scooted in next to Marc. He shifted to let her sit. She placed a leg on the bench exposing more of her tan. Marc sensed a twinge of youthfulness. "Marc, may I call you Marc?" He nodded. "Mary shot herself and Roger is guilty of loving a crazy woman. If you think anything else took place, you're wrong."

"I admire your sense of dedication to Mary and Roger. What do you get out of her death? Maybe you pulled the trigger."

"Oh, come on now. Like, I have the guts to do such a horrendous thing. Besides I don't own a gun and I was home when she died."

"Do you feel remorse for your confessed sin?"

"That's a funny question to ask. I feel responsible and that's all. If Mary and I had not been discussing her mental state maybe this would never have happened. Now I want comforting and have no one to give it to me."

"You still have a family, a brother, and a mother. Maybe you can seek solace from Roger now."

She grimaced. "Do you find me attractive?"

"Yes, but my wife isn't much for sharing. So you and Roger had these intimate conversations and nothing happened between you two. Watching you work here I find that hard to believe."

"Well, who knows what will happen now."

Marc decided enough had been discussed. His suspicions remained. As Victoria slid out of the seat, Marc glimpsed her bared hip. A deliberate move on her part, he guessed. *What's her motive in this?* He wondered.

"I'll be in touch." Marc stood up and picked up the bill which the waitress had deposited on the table long before. "I'll get this. Next time you can give me what I want." Marc laid a twenty on the table and departed. He looked back to see Victoria head to the bathroom. Her shapely legs created a swirl of her hips as she walked. *She's quite an enticement,* he thought. He imagined Roger and her in more than a mere conversational tryst. Could she have been more intimately involved in her sister's death?

CHAPTER 14

Marc explained Victoria Johnson's confession to Duncan Patterson who laughed audibly through the phone. He had not anticipated the little sister and Roger as a possible item. This piece of information cemented in his mind that Roger indeed had decided to kill his wife and make it appear to be a suicide. Victoria's presence was not vital at the hearing, but she could shed light on the early years. He would call her later in the day.

Marc's presenting his findings, if needed, to the court, made Thursday a bust for interviewing any of the families. He reset the phone and called Waite's business office. Asking for Roger he discovered Roger was out at an open house sales interview. Marc requested the address and drove to the location.

At the address, Marc parked across the street and slowly walked to the front door, opened it and entered. Two people, an obvious couple, spoke with a professionally dressed woman with a clipboard, a sales representative. She looked at him and said, "My associate is in the kitchen through this door. He can help you with any questions you have and show you around the house." She went back to talking with the couple.

Marc walked through the designated door and found Roger at a table, writing. His face paled when he noticed the intruder. He stood and approached. "What do you want?" he said indignantly.

"I would like to ask you some questions about information related to me this morning by your sister in-law." Roger looked away.

"Oh," he turned to face Marc. "What did Vickie say to you?" His demeanor calmed but his face looked worried. His brow furrowed as he spoke.

"Maybe we should go somewhere a little more private. Can you let your associate know you are leaving?"

Roger nodded and left the room. He returned shortly saying, "We can go next door. The house is also part of this showing. Maddie will keep everyone out." He led Marc out through the back door and across the yard to the next house. The door by the patio led into a family room. Roger directed Marc to a chair. They sat and remained quiet for a moment. "What did Vickie have to say?" he repeated. The fear on his face was clear.

Marc pulled out his notepad. He read for a short time wanting Roger's anxiety level to increase. Looking at Roger he said, "Miss Johnson related to me that you and she began a series of intimate meetings while she was in high school. These intimate meetings were about your wife and her mental state. What did you two talk about?"

Roger looked like a dead man walking. "We saw each other at family things. You know dinners, parties, and such. She and I talked, of course. I began to think that she sought me out because she didn't fit in with her family. I opened up to her about Mary's mental state and we just kept talking. It helped me to unload about the fighting and yelling. I'm not even sure how some of our fights started. Mary and I would be talking and all of a sudden I was on the receiving end of a tirade about what a loser I was."

"So, you and Victoria talked about Mary's changing attitudes. Did you two get tired of these tantrums and decide to do something about them?"

"Are you accusing me of killing my wife?"

"A jury may be convinced you had ulterior motives and took advantage of the situation. You're a smart man, how do you see it?"

"Yeah, I get it, but for me to shoot Mary? I'm not capable of that."

"I don't know. You were the one present at the time."

"But I didn't shoot her. I wouldn't. I did love my wife, despite all of the rough times we were going through. You've got to believe me. It was a suicide."

Marc nodded. "Victoria told me she was attracted to you. Do you find her attractive? After all, from what I have ascertained, she is very much like her sister."

Roger hesitated in his answer. "Yeah, she does look like Mary, and I knew she was attracted to me. That was apparent soon after Mary brought me to meet her family."

"How so?"

"Oh, you know the usual things a teenager does."

"No I don't think I do. Please elaborate."

"Well, as I said before, she seemed to seek me out when I was at her parents' house for dinner or parties. When Mary and I announced our engagement, she showed a bit of resentment toward me. I knew then she thought we could possibly be a couple. But she was just fourteen and I was in love with her sister."

"When did you and she begin your intimate conversations about Mary?"

Roger moved away from Marc and spoke. "She came to me one evening and asked to speak with me alone. I asked her about what and she said 'About Mary'. We went outside and walked in her parents' garden. She said she noticed Mary being emotionally distant with me and told me about her conversations with her sister."

"So, how old was she?"

"She was in high school. We had been married a couple of years and had a new baby. Mary was depressed."

"Are these conversations still going on?"

"Listen, I have to get back to work. I'm taking the rest of the week off as well as next week. Call me if you need me. I'll cooperate with you and I will instruct my attorney to help when appropriate." Roger looked like a constrained puppy. He wasn't relaxed as if a heavy weight was on his shoulders. Marc didn't inform him that a heavier weight was coming soon.

"Thank you for your time." Marc wasn't sure why he had sympathy for Roger. The guy probably didn't deserve any. "I'll be in touch with you later. Will you be at the hearing tomorrow?" Marc asked out of curiosity.

"Yes, will I see you there?"

"Yes."

They walked out together. Roger went back to the first house, while Marc walked around the house to his car. The neighborhood seemed like an upscale place, probably out of Joan and his price range. He felt he had evidence leading him to believe Roger probably finished what Mary Waite had started. He understood the temptations of a young, beautiful girl, but Roger may have strayed. *Conversations, my foot.*

Marc drove back to the office. Mr. and Mrs. Johnson were waiting for him. They had arrived about 10 minutes before. Fortunately, he had called in to report his return. They decided to wait.

Marc greeted the parents. "Good afternoon. I'm Detective Marc Jefferson." Mr. Johnson was a shorter than average man with piercing steel blue eyes. He was dressed in a charcoal suit, with a light blue shirt and dark blue tie. His hair had begun to gray. Marc could see Ben in the father's face. He was a fairly good looking man who had passed some of his features on to his daughters, as well. "Would you like some coffee, water, or juice?" Marc directed them to chairs by his desk. He sat down and placed his notepad in the drawer.

"No, thank you." Mr. Johnson directed his wife to a chair. She sat down meekly. She was a little taller than her husband and wore flat shoes as a result. Her graying hair sat in a bun atop her head. She was a very attractive woman and Marc realized where Mary and Victoria received their good looks. She said nothing.

She was dressed in an attractive but plain outfit that said to Marc, 'Don't outshine the husband.' He found it interesting the strong female in the family to be the youngest. "I am interested in knowing what happened to my daughter on Sunday."

Marc reflected for a moment. *Shouldn't these people already have an idea of the events?* "We received a call from your son-in-law that your daughter had shot herself. We investigated the scene and concluded that indeed she had a gunshot wound to the head which was the cause of her death. We are still gathering evidence for a final summation of the events."

"My daughter would not shoot herself. She would not embarrass her family in such a way." *The father certainly is strong willed.* "Have you spoken with Roger yet?"

Marc wondered if they suspected him. "We have spoken. He insisted she did the shooting."

"Can you tell us what happened?" Mr. Johnson asked.

"He said while he was at church he received a call from Mary to come home without the children. His parents, who were also at church, took your grandchildren home with them. He went to the house to find Mary with a gun and wanting to end it all. He took the gun from her and laid it on the dresser. As he looked around the bedroom, he claims, she picked it up and shot herself." Marc remembered Roger had called his in-laws before calling 911. They must have known all of this before coming in here. Or they knew a version Roger had told them.

"Thank you for your forthrightness. Roger had called us as I am sure you already know. I just wanted to hear your take on it. We will be going now." Mr. Johnson touched his wife's arm and she stood. "By the way, I am going to ask that Mary's medical records be kept confidential. No good can come from having them exposed to the world. Her life is finished and I would like for this to end today." He and his wife left the office.

Marc shook his head in disbelief. Mr. Johnson's gruff demeanor seemed to be a compensation for something. Another deputy, Tom Wilkins, sat nearby and remarked, "That guy is some piece of work. Who is he?"

Marc turned, "He's the father of the lady who was shot on Sunday. I think he may not want to have his daughter's dirty laundry aired in public."

Officer Tom interposed, "Maybe he thinks it will reflect on him."

"Maybe, but the hearing about her medical records is tomorrow and Patterson says he's ready for it." Marc picked up the phone to call Patterson and relate the details about the intimate conversations, changed his mind and went to the Prosecutor's office.

"Does this guy know what he's done?" Duncan asked incredulously. He shook his head and continued, "I don't have sympathy for this guy. If he was unhappy with the conditions of his marriage, he needed to get counseling or a divorce. Having intimate meetings, as you call them, with the sister leads me to believe there's more to it."

"Roger Waite is going to be at the hearing tomorrow. Did you get to ask Victoria Johnson to be there?"

"My staff called, but we did not connect with her. We're still trying. This Waite guy's losing any credibility with me. What's the girl like?"

"I'll admit it. She's extremely attractive and nicely put together. She exudes a sensuality to which I'm sure Roger may have succumbed. Why she found her brother-in-law attractive, I'll never know. She's intelligent and probably invites a lot of attention from guys her own age. She and her sister look a lot alike, but the personality traits are on opposite poles."

"Motive for wanting her out of the way has presented itself. Do you think this Victoria might have had something to do with her sister's death?"

"We're checking her alibi about being home."

Patterson swirled his desk around. "I wasn't sure we had much of a case. No clear motive seemed present. Now, I'm convinced this was not a suicide."

"Fellington gave me to end of the week to clear this up."

"Get me what you can. I'll call your boss."

"Alright, I had a meeting with Mary Waite's parents just before coming over here. The father is adamant about the medical records being kept away from us."

Patterson replied. "Yeah, but I am pretty sure we can get them. We're going for the evidentiary support for the suicide angle. We will use what we need to support a case against Roger Waite, if possible."

Marc stood up from the chair he had occupied since coming in. "Then, I'll see you tomorrow."

Patterson said, "This guy may not be such a clean upstanding citizen after all. Do you believe he succumbed to the wiles of a young girl, who herself is not as innocent as one might expect? Mr. Waite has more evidence piling up against him than for him."

"I don't know what to believe." Marc left the office. The day was waning. Nothing more could be done, so he went home to his family.

CHAPTER 15

At home, Marc followed his usual pattern. The children were watching a television show about some movie star, or so he thought. Joan greeted him with a hug and kiss, and asked him about the day. He responded about the Waite case becoming more bizarre than he could have expected. After a friendly parental 'Hello' to his children, he and Joan ascended the stairs to their bedroom. Marc removed his suit anticipating the comfort of a looser set of clothing. As he stood in his boxers, Joan came to him and kissed his lips. He returned the favor and unbuttoned her blouse. She did not often surprise Marc with an after work dalliance, but he did not resist. The afternoon revelations had left their marks and distracting them now was welcomed. Joan often just seemed to perceive his needs. *People probably are correct. She is the brains of the outfit.*

The afternoon interlude finished, Joan left him alone. After resting his eyes for a few minutes, Marc rose and put on his comfortable clothing. He wanted to be with his family and the stability he appreciated compared to these other families crossing his path. All was well with the Jefferson household and he felt a pull to keep it that way. Joan was right. The investigation was intruding on family cohesion.

He trusted his children; however, wisdom-filled lectures surely wouldn't hurt them. They, of course, would whine a bit and pretend to listen. Marc hoped the words would be seeds growing and producing fruit. No need for his children to be screwed up and dysfunctional.

Marc entered the kitchen. He paused to admire his wife, busily preparing dinner. "Need any help?"

"Yes," she answered. "You can set the table and pour milk for the children. Thank you," Joan smiled. "I appreciate your help." She returned to cutting vegetables. Marc did as requested. He reflected on the afternoon interactions with Waite and his sister-in-law and marveled at the sanity in this home. Normal to him certainly was not normal in other homes. His mind wandered from his chore. "Marc, what are you doing?" Jerked back to reality, he realized that he over filled a glass of milk. The counter was awash.

"Oops," was his only response.

Joan threw a towel to Marc. "I'm sorry," he said as he sopped up the spill. 'I was thinking of something I found out today that really confounds me." She laughed.

"I don't think I've ever seen you so possessed by a case. You've only been on it three days and it's beginning to consume you." She helped clean the counter and floor with more paper towels. Her concern was genuine.

"Thanks for caring. I don't mean to be obsessed with it, but I am beginning to see a pattern that points to murder and I don't know if there's enough evidence to put the guilty party away." He returned to pouring milk. Putting the glasses on the table, he turned to Joan again and asked a hypothetical question. "What would you do if you thought I might be somewhat crazy or at least bordering on a bi-polar type of mentality? I'm asking because I am not sure what I would do if you were to become unstable and unresponsive."

"Wow! That's quite a question. I do hope you aren't thinking of me as crazy."

"No, but Mary Waite had incidences in her life that may have been suicide attempts. And this last one may have been as well.

However, if her husband felt his life was spiraling into oblivion and he had a way to get out of it without too many encumbrances, he may have staged it."

"I don't think like that so it's hard for me to grasp the concept. If he felt his life with her was not going anywhere, why wouldn't he divorce her?" Joan looked puzzled.

"Good question for which I don't have an answer. But that brings up a point. I think I'll look into whether or not either of them filed for divorce or sought information from an attorney about one. You really are beautiful and smart. People are right. You're the brains of this outfit." They laughed.

Continuing the conversation Joan asked, "Did he have any wealth that would complicate a divorce?"

"Roger? I don't know of any, but his parents are well off and I think the younger Waite was getting to be successful. Maybe he didn't want to give up his future by having a messy divorce. Her parents are assertive. Well, actually, her father is really aggressive, more than just assertive. I'm sure they would be very supportive of their daughter in a divorce, probably pushing the support angle to the end."

"As to your question, I'm not sure what I would do. I guess it would depend on the type of crazy you became. If I felt any danger to me or the children, I would be out of here in a heartbeat. If you were injured and lost cognitive abilities or were physically impaired, I would stay with you and care for you. Sex is great, but loving you is even greater. What did this guy do?"

"No one has admitted to anything, but I think he and his sister-in-law may have started an affair. She is quite a bit younger than her sister, better looking, well built, and I guess hungry for her brother-in-law's attention. She admitted she had a crush on him when he and her sister married. After a while, with the sister becoming less stable and unresponsive, Waite could have turned to her to satisfy his sexual desires. They admit to talking about the sister's mental decline, which both of them state they started a few years ago. I think it may have become something more and now is akin to a motive for murder."

"Can you prove it?"

"I don't know. I'll try and play one against the other and see what happens. If they cop to the affair, I'll let Patterson sort it out. There's a hearing tomorrow to release the deceased woman's medical records and that should help us to understand her mental state throughout her life. Waite must have known what he was getting into when he married her, but it may have gotten to a point where he couldn't take it anymore." They continued to finalize the evening meal as they conversed. This conversation was unusual for Marc and Joan. Keeping the job at work made his life better at home. However, he sought help from the one person he trusted most and with whom he could exchange ideas and strategies. Joan always seemed to know the best way to approach things.

Marc called the children into the kitchen and they sat at the table and ate. Conversations were about the day's events in the lives of the children. Nothing of the case was mentioned.

Tomorrow would be another busy day. After cleaning the kitchen with the help of the children, Joan and Marc sat down in the family room and enjoyed a couple hours of television with the children. They all went to bed before ten to rest for the next day's onslaught. Marc's mind imagined different scenarios as he drifted into sleep.

CHAPTER 16

"I want you to know that I'm leaving you and I'm taking the children with me," Joan screamed at Marc. "You are nothing but a slimy, mean person. I want nothing to do with you ever again."

Marc faced Joan with an angry look on his face. "What did I do to make you act crazy?" he screamed in return.

"That woman is not to step foot in this house ever again. If you want her then you can have her." Marc looked surprised.

"But I haven't done anything with her. She came on to me and I rejected her. You're acting crazy!" he repeated.

"I know what you're thinking even when you don't. So don't tell me nothing has happened. I know you want to have sex with her." Joan turned away and vanished. Marc was alone in a hotel room.

"Victoria, I can't do this." She stood in front of Marc with nothing on. "I need to go home and explain to my wife." He stared at the supple body, nicely shaped breasts and trimmed pubis. She reminded him of Joan but with the advantage of youth. She reached for him.

"Come on, Marc, you know you want me. I want you. Ever since I met you after he killed my sister, I've wanted you. Roger means nothing to me anymore." She moved closer and unbuttoned his shirt. He did not resist.

Yes, he thought, *no one will find out*. Aloud he said, "No, I can't do this." Joan came into the room with a gun in her hand. He turned to her and pleaded, "Help me." Joan fired the gun in the air. The loudness shocked her and Victoria. Marc was alone again with Joan. He had the gun in his hand. "You're crazy," he muttered. Turning the gun on Joan he fired. She slumped to the floor.

Victoria returned again, "See, that wasn't so hard, now was it?" Marc began to cry softly. "I want you." Her voice trailed off and she faded away. Joan arose from the floor and said something. He didn't understand.

Marc stood statue-like looking at Joan's bloody face. "You think it's that easy to get rid of me? I'll haunt you to the very end of time for this."

"I haven't done anything! Leave me alone! Leave me alone…" his voice melted into a blur of words that meant nothing.

Victoria turned to Joan and said, "I know he loved you, but he can't resist me. We'll take good care of the children. I want him for myself. See how easy it was for him to get rid of you? What can you do now?"

Joan smiled, "I'm sorry. What are you talking about?"

"The gun in Marc's hand. He shot you as easily as if he were getting rid of a pesky mosquito. I'll seduce him now."

"What about Roger?"

"Roger is great, but Marc is a real man. You wanted to kill yourself." Victoria laughed an evil cackle.

No, I haven't done anything," Marc interjected. He looked at Joan again who no longer had any blood on her. The gun was in her hand again and she pointed it at Victoria and fired. Marc yelled, "No…"

He was sitting up in his bed. Sweat trickled from his forehead. He breathed heavily and had to settle his mind. Looking at the clock on the side table, he sighed. The time was early, a little past three. Sleep would elude him from now on, so he rose and went to the bathroom, closing the door so as not to disturb Joan. After turning on the light, he looked at himself in the mirror. A tired face reflected back. The dream had left its effect. He remembered it vividly but he'd never act toward Joan the way he did in the dream. Well, he hoped he'd never be that deceptive. In actuality Victoria Johnson offered him nothing. He thought it amusing how dreams mix up all kinds of facts into psychologically strange stories.

Leaving the bathroom, he glanced at Joan still sleeping. He smiled happily because he had not awakened her. He could not be sure if he had yelled aloud in reality or within the confines of the dream. He guessed that it was in the dream. Putting on his robe, he left the bedroom and went downstairs. Entering the kitchen, he turned on a light and got a glass out of the cupboard. After retrieving the milk from the refrigerator, and being careful to not spill it again, Marc sat at the kitchen table and pondered his next move. What if Victoria and Roger had contemplated ridding the world of a crazy lady? Dreams can give one ideas to ponder.

He finished the milk and went to his home office. He had access to his office computer and decided to do some work. *Might as well put the time to good use,* he thought. He activated the computer and searched Walter Waite. Over 50,000 hits showed. Many of the first sites were about real estate and his company. Marc dug deeper into the list. He clicked on a link and found a family history. Another link connected to a photo gallery of Roger and Mary's wedding pictures. He scrolled through them. "Nothing much here," he mused. Mary looked very happy. Another showed Roger and Mary with his family. Another showed them with her family. Marc found a picture with all of the siblings. Victoria looked very young, but she seemed older than Marc knew she had to be. Another shot of her with Roger showed something of a flirtatious look in her eye. Or was it just his imagination. A picture of Ben, Mary, and Victoria showed three very normal siblings. Marc could see a clear resemblance between Mary and Victoria. *Nothing out of line in any of the pictures,* Marc's thoughts continued. *Ben must have been the originator of this site.*

Marc continued his searching, this time for Garrett Johnson. Not much came up. He discovered an old newspaper article. Amazed that pre-online news would show, he read the article. It was about a local girl headed to New York for an art show. The article praised the work of the young lady and wished her the best. The girl's name was Mary Johnson. The girl's parents were traveling with her and the three of them wanted to see some shows and experience the Big Apple. The gallery had expressed an interest in new talent and had advertised for people to apply for an interview. Agents of the gallery had been in Seattle and Mary had submitted some of her work. Upon being accepted, her parents praised her work and expressed their pride in their daughter. Marc thought, *this doesn't sound like what Victoria told me.*

I need to interview Ben and his parents again. "I'll separate the father and mother next time," he spoke aloud.

Marc heard noise in the kitchen and looked at the clock on the monitor screen. It was nearly seven o'clock. The time slipped by quietly. He printed the article as a reference piece. The Johnson family hid a mysterious past and Marc meant to uncover it. After the article printed, Marc closed the connection and locked his computer, left the room and found Joan in the kitchen. Slowly the children arrived for breakfast. They ate with little conversation and departed for each of their rooms to dress and prepare for the daily chores of school and work.

When Joan and Marc entered their bedroom, Joan inquired about his night's sleep. "You had another dream, didn't you? I rolled over and you were gone, but your pillow was damp with moisture. It was not warm, so I guessed you had been up for a while. It must have been quite a dream."

"I didn't want to disturb you. I woke about three from a dream in which Victoria Johnson, Roger's sister-in-law, was trying to seduce me. You were going to leave me. You had a gun. I somehow got it and shot you, but you didn't die or you became a ghost. Victoria hinted that she and Roger had planned Mary's death. Then you had the gun again and shot it at Victoria. That's when I awoke. There are a few more details but that is the gist of it."

"Are you attracted to her?"

"Who, Victoria? No, but I can see how a person would fall for her wiles."

"I hope you get through this case soon. I don't need a crazy husband right now. I think I should meet this Victoria who can seduce men in their dreams."

"Believe me. I'm not interested in her. I do think, however, the idea of the two of them planning something sinister is probable."

"I trust you, but this is bothersome. Can someone else take over? I love you too much to have you suffer this way."

"I want to finish this." Marc dressed, kissed his wife, and left for work. He felt Joan had a right to know his dreams. They shared most things and trusted each other implicitly. No woman must interfere with his marriage or cause any kind of doubt about how he felt regarding Joan. As for telling her about his thoughts about Uncle Jerry's death, he felt no compunction to confuse the issue. Uncle Jerry could wait until he had time to investigate the report.

* * *

The drive to the office became a mental trial as ideas flooded his brain. Fortunately, few cars were on the roads and streets this early in the morning. He had now been awake nearly 5 hours and the day had not yet fully begun. Hopefully, the court session would be short and Patterson would get what he wanted. At the office Marc planned to call in the elder Waite and Johnson family members for interviews. If they refused, he would talk to Patterson about applying more leverage to compel their cooperation. Medical records and interviews made the day busy.

Arriving at the office, Marc parked in his usual spot. Funny how the media frenzy dies an ignoble death. Maybe the frenzy wasn't dead but had just moved. Being early in the morning the personnel of the various media groups probably were in radio and television stations beginning their broadcasts. Marc, wanting only to avoid any vulture ready to pounce for an interview, vacated his car and entered the sheriff's office.

CHAPTER 17

Patterson left a message for Marc, "arrive early for the hearing." He expected nothing to interfere with a beneficial outcome and the information in the medical records held the secrets of an enigma. Let it clear up who she was and what she was capable of doing. Even if capable of self-inflicting a mortal wound, would the information reveal a troubled person driving another person to want to end her life? Marc picked up the phone and called Roger.

"Would you come to the office this afternoon after the court hearing and discuss the information you gave me yesterday?" Marc listened to Roger's response. A meeting at the office about three was arranged. Marc wanted to hash out the possibility of an affair and Mary's death. Marc then called the Johnson's and asked for Mrs. Johnson. Garret Johnson answered the call not allowing his wife to speak. Marc requested they come to the office around one. He agreed. Marc would separate them after their arrival, interested in what Marion Johnson might have to say without her husband present. Marc gathered his notes and file folders about the case and left for the courthouse.

He entered through a door without any media, glad to avoid their insipid questions. There would be enough time later for information hounds and their incessant barking. He hunted for Patterson and Atherton and a preliminary review of what he needed to do. The dream haunted him, but new ideas encouraged him to interview Roger and Victoria with vigor.

"Marc, over here," Patterson was sitting on a bench outside of a courtroom with a folder in his hand. Atherton stood nearby talking on her cell. Marc sat with him awaiting instructions. "I don't anticipate this taking very long. Let's go over the focus of our goals for today. We want to have copies of all of Mary Waite's medical records from childhood to adult. Simple enough request. And I understand Roger's not protesting this?"

"He's not, but Mary Waite's father is. He wants to hide his daughter's history for some reason." Marc looked directly at Duncan and added, "I think he feels revealing anything about her reflects badly on him. He's aggressive and angers easily."

"Okay. If he comes with an attorney and enters an objection, we'll deal with it then." Duncan continued staring at a folder, "We shouldn't have much of a problem since Roger is willing to release her records." He placed the folder into his typically oversized attaché case and stood up. Marc likewise stood and together they entered the appointed courtroom. Monica followed shortly after.

The day's docket included several cases of DUI, a divorce settlement case, and one reckless driving violation challenge as well as the medical record release for Mary Johnson Waite. Marc made a note to check divorce records. He sat quietly as people entered the small space of the county courtroom. If this case did go to trial, another courtroom would be needed for all of the people who might be interested. Murder was not a common occurrence but when it did happen, dark, sordid spectators seemed to crawl out of the hidden nooks and crannies of the city, interested in forgetting their own morose lives by observing the evil of others.

The room filled with people dressed unprofessionally in jeans, sweatshirts, and torn garments of varying color schemes. They were dirty, gritty people with little going for them. Judges faced so many people whose lives were a gathering storm of chaos and disorder. Marc knew these people repeatedly entered the legal system because of decisions for which seemingly sane humans would never opt. He felt some sorrow for them, but he and his fellow officers had dealt with the scum of society for years creating a mental attitude that they brought on their own problems. Drinking and drugs were used to escape unhappy existences and broken lives. Bad parenting was blamed as the environmental basis of these human failures, but Marc suspected that each one chose the easy way out and could then blame others for their choices. How different his job would be if only these people opted for other realities.

The court bailiff announced the judge's entrance and all stood as requested and required. After seating himself on his judicial throne, Anton Malicorne asked the audience to be seated. He requested the clerk announce the docket to begin proceedings. Patterson knew this judge as a fair-minded person who listened carefully and pondered deliberately. When matters came before him, he expected all to be ready with facts and evidence to support those facts. If anyone was not prepared, then nothing could be guaranteed. Patterson was prepared.

His hearing was listed fourth; expecting to be heard at nine thirty, as long as the first three cases moved quickly and without complications. Roger and his attorney, Jeff Woodbury, entered and seated themselves opposite Patterson and Atherton. Victoria came in, dressed conservatively, downplaying her figure as much as possible, and sat with Roger. Even with the attempted fashion deception she attracted lurid stares from the miscreants in attendance, as their girlfriends stared with obvious dislike of the competition to their affections. Marc observed the distraction with little interest. He now wanted to know how involved in planning a "suicide" she might be.

Her parents arrived and Garrett Johnson scanned the arena looking with great disdain at the riffraff seated around the room. He espied Roger and Victoria, but no room existed to sit with them. They found one chair against the wall and Marion sat down. No attorney was in attendance with them, and Marc assumed he would not challenge after all. Maybe Woodbury advised them against challenging because of how Roger felt. Maybe Victoria counseled her parents to be cooperative for Roger's sake. He wondered about the family dynamics at work in the jumble of people. Since Victoria and Roger had not declared they were engaged in an affair, Marc was curious how each family would handle finding out about it, if it did exist. If Roger had informed Woodbury, he certainly would be concerned because of the implications.

No need for uneasiness now. The first two DUI cases concluded with one guilty plea and one calendar scheduling for trial. The third case was now called to the bench, a family dissolving for unknown and indifferent reasons. Marc listened passively as the judge heard one attorney state an agreed partition of property and children supervision rules accomplished. The judge ordered the decree to be entered into the record and filed with the clerk. The divorce would be final in the required ninety days without any further proceedings. The antagonists and their attorneys packed up and left the court. Next up was the medical records request.

As the paperwork of the previous hearing was completed and filed, Atherton and Woodbury stood to position themselves in the appropriate chairs before the judge. Patterson sat beside Monica. They exchanged the usual pleasantries. Roger came up with Woodbury and sat down as directed. The clerk announced the docket number and Judge Malicorne called for the attorneys to present the case.

Atherton opened with a request to have the medical records released to the prosecutor's office for examination. "Your honor, we are concerned about the disposition of this matter as to why a seemingly successful and content young lady would commit such a heinous assault upon her person. We want to discharge any culpability on the part of the husband since he was present at the time of the shooting. Evidence is pointing to a disturbed woman who wanted on more than one occasion to end the pain and suffering of living a disturbed life. We ask for the medical records of her adult life to be released and her minor records to be unsealed for examination to determine the beginnings of this improper decline to an early death. Evidence will be presented as needed. Thank you, your honor."

Judge Malicorne turned his attention to Woodbury. "Mr. Woodbury, do you have any objections to this request?"

Before Jeff Woodbury could respond, Garrett Johnson interrupted, "Your honor, my name is Garrett Johnson. I am the father of Mary Waite. I would like to speak, if I may."

The judge spoke before either attorney could react. "Come forward, sir." Judge Malicorne was calm but looked somewhat surprised. "What do you want from this court?" Johnson left his spot by the wall and moved to the area where the attorneys stood. Marc observed Mrs. Johnson and noticed a distressed look on her face.

"Your honor, my daughter was a troubled girl and I would like to have her remain as I, uh we, my wife is here also, want to remember her. I am concerned that she will be vilified by these people if records are released and publically displayed."

"I understand your concern, Mr. Johnson. Your daughter's husband, however, is the closet relation with legal standing. His desired intention would normally be the court's rationale for a decision."

"I understand that, sir, but my wife and I live a quiet life and our daughter's death has shaken that life. We request she be left at peace. We are not arguing the fact that she apparently committed suicide. We just are not sure why this has to be dredged up."

"Your honor, Mr. Johnson's point is taken," interjected Atherton, "but our investigation into the death has questions that we want to clear up so that Mr. Waite and his family can continue their lives. Until we answer those questions, we can't finish our investigation. My office and that of the sheriff will have to spend many hours continuing an investigation that can be finished fairly quickly with the medical records. That is our intention. We will keep the honor of this young woman intact as best we can."

Jeff Woodbury entered the fray. "Your honor, Mr. Waite has requested that the records be released so that this matter can be concluded. We support the request of the prosecutor."

"I have enough, thank you." The judge then returned to Johnson, "Mr. Johnson, do you have an attorney right now?" The judge looked intently at Garrett and then looked at Marion Johnson as if looking for a sign from her.

"I am here representing myself and my wife." He pointed at Marion who stood up when she saw Garrett pointing. "I only want to have my daughter's life be kept out of the public. She deserves to have that, doesn't she?" He gazed at the judge like a lost soul.

Judge Malicorne grimaced but remained silent for a moment. He then cleared his throat and took a drink out a glass of water on his desk. The room had silenced as people realized the controversy rising between the attorneys and Garrett Johnson. No one had been overly concerned about medical records before this. Now the crowd understood something significant had actually entered the courtroom. This was not a mundane court proceeding.

The judge scanned the room as if to find a savior for his decision. Jefferson noticed an angel in the third row but recognized her as a part time prostitute whose boyfriend was present yet again for a reckless driving charge. No help from her and maybe jail for her boyfriend. She needs to get away from him, thought Marc. No hope for that, though.

The silence broke as Judge Malicorne began speaking. "I understand your concern for your daughter, Mr. Johnson. She has apparently committed an act leaving a scar on you and your family. However, you have not presented any material evidence that would have me question releasing the records to the prosecutor's office. I'm not going to rule on your request regarding your daughter's minor years. I am releasing all medical records of her adult life while married to Roger Waite. Mr. Johnson, I strongly suggest you get an attorney and return to this court with material evidence that would compel a decision favoring your request. You will have one week to do this." Looking over to the court clerk, Judge Malicorne picked up a calendar and said, "Put this on the calendar for next Thursday." She did as asked. "Miss Atherton, you may pick up the order at the court office. Use it wisely and try to appeal to Mr. Johnson's desire for his daughter."

"Thank you, your Honor. I will." Monica rotated to return to the table for other materials as Woodbury sauntered to his table. Garrett Johnson looked dejected but left quickly with his wife. Marc did not think he would return to the court especially if any of the information about his living daughter was revealed to him. Victoria came over to Marc with a look of concern.

"Mr. Jefferson, what happens now?" The few incorrigible men in the room watched her every move with lust in their eyes. Marc supposed she attracted attention wherever she went.

"The DA will get the order releasing your sister's medical records. If your father comes back to court with material evidence about her younger years, then a hearing will proceed. I still want to talk with you about that other thing between you and Roger. He's coming in early this afternoon. Can I speak with you after that?"

"I really don't know how much more I can explain about Roger and me that I haven't told you, but I guess I can. When?"

"Come in at three." Marc wanted to have the two possible lovers to question what each was saying. Maybe then he could crack open a confession to an affair. At the same time Roger might alert Woodbury something was happening about which he knew nothing. Curiosity about Woodbury's reaction heightened his interest in Victoria's arrival at the office. "I'll see you then."

Victoria left the courtroom with an abundance of leers. She exited unaware of the attention. Roger came up to Marc and asked, "What did Victoria want?"

"She was curious about what her father wanted. I explained about the procedures. She seemed interested in whether her father was right in doing what he did."

"Do you think that my father-in-law is right in what he wants?" Marc felt badly for Roger but still wanted his conviction for killing his wife.

"I don't know about your father-in-law. I'll see you later." Roger thanked him, returned to Woodbury's side glancing back at Marc with a look of concern, and left with his attorney. The afternoon would be exciting and informative with these people crossing paths.

Marc waited for Patterson and Atherton, and they walked out together. "Well, that went better than I expected," Patterson said. "Nice job in there, Monica." He smiled all the way back to his office.

The three of them walked quietly as they set off to formulate their next move.

CHAPTER 18

"I'm meeting with Roger and his attorney this afternoon. What other information might you want?" Marc sat in Duncan's office. The outcome gave the prosecutor and his team a chance to secure details of Mary Waite's life. Morning had not yet passed, but Marc thought only of how to handle his afternoon guests. Lunch would be postponed for now.

"Well, can you get Waite to confess to killing his wife?"

Marc grinned. "Ah, if only I could. I'm sure Woodbury wants to give him up so easily. An affair, as an ace-in-the-hole, will certainly shake up this case."

"Yeah, maybe we can bribe the truth from him about last Sunday. Were you talking with the sister in the courtroom?"

"She wanted to know what her father was up to. By the way, she's coming in this afternoon around the same time as her boy toy. If we can get them to sing a separate tune from each other we could crack this thing open a bit. Mary's parents are also coming in. I'll separate them to get a shot at the mother. She doesn't speak much when hubby is close by. His aggressive attitude shuts her up."

"Good luck and happy hunting." Marc stood, picking up the case folders from a side table, and left for his own office. Lunchtime had come and gone by the time he settled into his chair in the office. The victims' of his covert assault would arrive soon to reveal their tainted little secrets. The Johnsons' hid their little girl's sordid teen years to protect themselves, not her. Roger Waite knew the truth about last Sunday, but was what he had already verbalized truly the script that had been performed? Victoria Johnson involved herself in a most intriguing and meaningful way that implicated not only Roger, but her, as well. Yes, the afternoon would be very interesting indeed.

Marc's stomach complained about the lack of sustenance, so he reached for his stash of snacks, which would upset Joan, if she knew about it. Oh well, the stomach speaks and the body needs fueling. He grabbed a Butterfinger and munched greedily. The clock on the wall indicated the Johnson's imminent arrival. Calling to Tom at the next desk, he asked him to place each Johnson in a separate room. He had made up his mind that Garrett Johnson was not a person destined to be likable. Johnson cared more for his own personality than for anyone else. Truly, no other person existed around him except to enhance his own character.

Marc still felt hunger, but he would have to wait until dinner. As punctual as a clock, the Johnson's arrived and Tom offered them separate rooms with great argument from Garrett the belligerent. However, the deed was accomplished and Marc met with Marion first. No argument with Garrett Johnson was worth losing all the possible information awaiting. He asked Tom to keep Garrett occupied with anything that seemed relevant to the satisfaction of the case. Tom agreed.

Marc rose from his chair to glean the truth about Mary's youthful indiscretion and just how she had collapsed to such a depth of despair and forlornness as to attempt to end her life so many times. Did mother know more about her daughter than she allowed anyone to know?

"Mrs. Johnson, thank you for coming in this afternoon. I'm so sorry for your loss, but I have some questions about Mary." Marc kept the interview friendly and stress free; Marion might relax enough to cooperate. He expected resistance with her husband in the next room. Hopefully, Tom would not be stonewalled by Mr. Johnson. The questions from Marion began as Marc sat down.

"Why am I here? Where is my husband? What do you want from me? How much trouble am I in? Did Roger do something he shouldn't have? Oh God, what has happened to my family? I miss my daughter so much. She was so fragile and needed so much help. Roger couldn't do it all by himself. I helped whenever I could. Oh Mary, what have you done?" Tears flowed freely from her eyes, down her cheeks to her blouse. Marion did not hold back any grief while she sat with Marc.

"Mrs. Johnson, I am very sorry about what happened to your daughter. No parent should have to endure what you have gone through these last few days." He truly did understand. In his business he had seen many others who endured unfathomable loss at the hands of unscrupulous people. "You are not in any trouble." He handed her a box of tissues which she accepted. She daubed her eyes and then unceremoniously emptied her nasal passages. "Please explain to me what Mary was like as a child." He positioned himself to write, but nothing presented itself for notation. Slowly, as Mary slackened her crying, she began to relate the early years of Mary's life.

"Mary was a good girl growing up, no problems. She was a good student and people liked her. She seemed to show a propensity for drawing pictures. I thought they were good, but her father did not want her wasting her time. She had to study and learn to be a success in life. The drawing continued in secret. She kept up her grades and made friends, but she seemed to only keep them for a short while. As she grew into adolescence, her art talent improved, so I got her lessons. Then the break came when she entered the contest and was asked to come to New York. Garrett did not want to go and a family battle began. Ben became very sullen and stayed away from home for longer and longer periods of time. Little Victoria did not understand and stayed in her room. After a while, Garrett just gave in and we made plans to travel to New York for the show."

Marc wrote furiously trying to keep up as Marion spilled her guts. In an attempt to slow her down Marc said, "Let's take a break?" He needed to catch his breath and stood up. "Do you want anything to drink?"

"Thank you, I could use some coffee, if you please."

"I'll get it for you right away." He left the room and asked one of office personnel to take coffee into Mrs. Johnson. He went to the bathroom and completed his break from the one-sided interview. All the pent-up anguish of years of sublimation of emotions had exploded in a cavalcade of information. As he returned to the room, he stopped by the other interview room to see how things were progressing. Garrett Johnson angrily asked for his wife to be brought in. "Mr. Johnson, I will bring your wife in as soon as we have finished." Marc left the room so Tom could continue with the interrogation.

Not one piece of information that Marc had heard increased his real understanding of Mary or her mental state. He pressed for more details. As he sat Marc inquired, "What happened in New York?"

"We had been there about two days, the show was going well. Mary's artwork seemed well received and she was feeling ecstatic about all of the attention. My husband relaxed for the first time in a long time. He did not have to pay for much of the trip, but he still complained that it was a waste of time. Mary was so happy on the trip and then she fell and broke her hand. Garrett thought this was an opportunity to come home. Mary argued that she was fine and wanted to continue with the trip, but we left New York and came home. The situation at home deteriorated and Mary became sullen."

Marc looked directly at Marion and asked, "When did Mary attempt her first suicide?" He expected Mrs. Johnson to sidestep the issue, but she came forward with information.

"Mary cried often. We spoke about the trip and how her father felt. She resented his attitude and became very distant with him. He did not understand any of it. Then one day, Mary cut herself. She did not cut deeply enough. I found her in the bathroom and after being taken to the hospital for treatment, we got her psychiatric help. Dr. Baxter Conley, her doctor, helped a great deal. She gained stability and finished high school. She seemed happy at college, met Roger, and married him. Life seemed very good for her. I don't understand what happened this last week. I know she was sad after the birth of Samuel, but I thought she seemed happier, lately." Marion hung her head.

"Maybe, she was happier because she had made up her mind about ending her life. People can appear better when they have made up their minds. Well, anyway I really am sorry for your loss. Mrs. Johnson, do you think that Roger knew about Mary's problems when he was dating her?"

Oblivious to the question she rambled on. "I don't understand. Mary was happy with Roger. She had gotten over her difficulties. Roger and she were very happy together. Pregnancy changed their relationship as with any marriage and the birth of babies. But they were working through it. Mary and I spoke regularly and I never felt she wanted to do this awful thing. I loved my daughter and I love Roger like my own son. The children are great and I love seeing them. I sure hope that Roger didn't do anything wrong. I feel so badly that he witnessed this." She looked at Marc with lonely eyes that exposed her sadness.

"Mrs. Johnson, I want you to know we are investigating everything to be sure events happened as they have been stated to us. We're pretty sure Roger had nothing to do with her death, but we still have to find out." Marc closed his notebook and stood. "I am going to get your husband now."

"Could you wait for a few minutes? I just want to sit here for a while."

"Alright, I'll leave you alone." Marc left the room. He had more to find out, Marion did not or could not believe negative information about her daughter. She was imperceptive to the events of Mary's life. Nothing would come from any more questions. Marc went down the hall to the next room to see how Tom had been doing. As he approached, he could hear shouting from the room, and it wasn't Tom. He entered to see Garrett Johnson standing near the window-mirror. He gave the impression of being truly mad at Tom. "Mr. Johnson, are you okay?"

"Where's my wife?" He started toward Marc with angry eyes and fists. Tom rose to intervene.

Marc prepared to defend himself. "Be careful, Mr. Johnson. What you do here can be expensive. This is not a place from which you can easily escape." Garrett stopped immediately.

He calmed quickly and the look in his eyes lost their rage. "I'm sorry. Where's my wife?"

"She's next door. She wanted some time alone. We've finished." Turning to Tom he continued, "How did it go in here?"

"We're finished here, as well, but Mr. Johnson wanted to leave to get to his wife and I stopped him as requested."

"You ordered him to keep me from my wife?" Anger returned.

"Calm yourself Mr. Johnson. We're done here and you're free to go." Garrett left the room, storming next door to his wife with Marc and Tom following intrigued by his behavior. Gathering his emotionally exhausted wife, he glared angrily at the sheriff's deputies, and then they departed the office. Turning back to Tom, Marc gleefully inquired, "What did you find out from him?"

"That guy is self-centered and insecure. He admitted to being happy after Mary got hurt in New York; her useless ideas of being an artist finished. I asked him about his relationship with her and he said she was close to him. But I don't believe it. He did not come across as credible and if I had to live with that guy, I might have wanted to kill myself. What did you find out from the mother?"

"She released a lot of pent-up emotion. Mary Johnson was a normal child until living with daddy turned her into Jell-O. I imagine the marriage is held together only by a sense of duty on the part of Mrs. Johnson. She admitted she and Mary connived behind daddy before the New York gig. That must have really irritated the old man. Roger was a saving grace for Mary when she was in college, and the marriage may have been good at first. However, I think she couldn't overcome the damage done, so I do hope the medical reports help clarify her status."

"How soon are the others coming?" Tom asked knowing Marc set them up for a show. He interviewed several people who knew the Waite's, gleaning that not all was well in the family.

"They're coming in about three so we should get the interview rooms ready for them. Woodbury is coming with Roger so we aren't going to be going into any depth. I'll let you begin and I'll watch the show for any craziness."

"Alright, by the way, I found a police report of Mary Waite's first suicide as a teenager. It's on my desk for you to read later. I have some questions I can direct at Roger about what he knew regarding that history. If he knew anything at all and began to regret his decision to marry her, he may have planned to rid himself of her and the problems he was encountering. Anyway I'll work to get evidence he was inclined to want her out of the way."

"Thanks, Tom. You're one of the best. I'll push Victoria to see if she has any other information to impart regarding her and Roger's relationship that might have led to his killing his wife. She may have encouraged him to do the nasty deed so they could be together. Have you met her? She could seduce a man without even being in the room. She's young, gorgeous, well-built and I can imagine, highly sexed."

Tom went to his desk and retrieved the folder with the information about Mary's first suicide. "This is an interesting read, but I don't think it will add any more to the investigation."

Marc took the folder and opened it to quickly peruse the information. Nothing stood out to him. He closed the folder and placed it with the other collected folders. He sat for a moment to gather his thoughts and prepare his mind.

Three o'clock came and went but no one showed. He began to think they had changed their minds about being interviewed again, when the doors to the office opened and Roger and his attorney entered. Marc stood to greet them. He gestured to Tom to join the group, asking him to lead them to an interview room. As they were heading to the room, Victoria entered. The players in this staged event noticed each other. Marc observed the faces of Roger and Victoria for telltale signs. Nothing seemed to show for the moment. He moved to greet Victoria.

"Thank you for coming in, Miss Johnson. Please, follow me."

"Why is Roger here?" Victoria whispered with indignation. She followed but watched as Roger and his attorney entered into an interview room. As she and Marc entered another room, she again asked angrily, "Why is Roger here? You think he's done something wrong."

"Why do you ask? Has he?" Marc felt a sense of glee that his ruse may have produced results.

"No, he hasn't." Victoria sat down when directed by Marc. "I came here, as you requested. But I don't want to be any part of your scheme to convict Roger of killing my sister. She wasn't stable and you know it."

"That may be true. Roger, however, may have been fed up with her and decided to simplify his life a bit." Marc sat opposite Victoria at the table. "Tell me again about your feelings for Roger and just what your plans for the future are."

"Do I need a lawyer?"

"If you wish, it's your option. I'm not interested in prosecuting Roger or you or anyone if the evidence clearly points to Mary having shot herself. Now, what are your plans with Roger?"

"We don't have any plans. We've no more to discuss since Mary is dead." She paused a moment and then continued. "I do still care about what happens to him, and I do not want him to go to jail for something he didn't do." Victoria stood and moved toward the window looking at nothing in particular. Suddenly she turned to Marc and blurted, "He couldn't have done it. He's not like that." Marc doubted her words.

"Miss Johnson, I'm sorry about your sister, but questions still need to be answered and events sorted out. Mr. Waite and his attorney are here to help answer those questions and to sort through the events so a clear picture of the tragedy last Sunday can be seen." Victoria returned to the table and sat. She looked distraught.

"Mr. Jefferson, do you really think Roger shot my sister? It seems so cold hearted for a person to do something like that." The doubt about Roger was now evident but she did not express it openly.

"If you'll wait here, I'll be right back. I wish to see Mr. Waite and ask him a few questions. Would you like anything to drink?" She shook her head slowly. Marc left.

"I am not going to let my client answer that." Marc heard Woodbury responding to a question from Tom. Closing the door behind him he presented his hand to Roger for shaking.

"Thank you for coming in, Mr. Waite." Turning to Tom he asked, "What was the question?"

"I asked Mr. Waite if his wife had tried to commit suicide before last Sunday."

"Is there something that you have to hide?" Marc stood next to the table and glowered at Roger.

Woodbury spoke. "You have access to the medical files, so Roger doesn't need to answer the question. I think we're done here." Woodbury stood and motioned for his client to stand, as well. "If you want anything else you will contact me directly. I will decide whether we talk with you again."

"Why is Victoria here?" Roger scrutinized Marc with angry eyes.

"Be quiet, Roger."

"No," turning back to Marc, "I want to know why you wanted her to come in." Marc did not answer but looked at Woodbury, who grabbed Roger's arm and dragged him away from the room and the inquisition. Roger did not fight back. Woodbury looked as though he didn't understand Roger's elusive question. Maybe he didn't know about the affair.

"Wow! I think something is rotten in Wendlesberg." Tom turned off the video machine, picked up his notebook saying, "I'll write this up and have it for you tonight. Roger did not fare well in this meeting. He is hiding things and his attorney is not sure what. You'll be interested in what was said and not said."

"Did you record this meeting?"

"Yes, on video, and Woodbury was not very happy, but he went along with it until that last question."

"I should get back to Miss Johnson. Want to come along?"

"Sure, I like to look at her. Sounds bad, doesn't it." Tom laughed a little and Marc grinned and shook his head.

Victoria was looking out of the window. She turned when she heard the men enter. "What have you done? Roger looks mad and Mr. Woodbury seemed to be yelling at him." She gathered her purse and coat and left.

CHAPTER 19

Marc and Tom returned to the squad room bewildered by Victoria's response. Tom went to work on his report, while Marc sat down to ponder the day's results. Marc revisited early medical examiner reports looking for anything that would support allegations against Waite. The evidence was inconclusive. Roger had touched the gun. He had GSR on him as did Mary. She was not positioned as one would expect for a shooting victim falling to the floor. Sure, Roger probably picked her up or moved her somehow. But if he had shot her, then he needed to be prosecuted and found guilty.

Marc looked at his watch and decided to leave for the evening. Nothing more could be done. He would talk with Patterson tomorrow after their office retrieved medical records. Toxicity reports would be available tomorrow and might reveal something. Blood spatter and bullet fragments, unknown finger prints, body position and GSR, suicide or murder, Marc's brain felt tired. Resting would be a welcome relief. He said goodbye to Tom, asking him to put the report on his desk for reading on the morrow, and left the building.

Driving home gave Marc time to contemplate ideas about substance and motive. He knew that the motive existed even if Roger did not act upon it. But acting upon the motive meant that Roger should be in jail. The Waite children already had enough changes in their life and sending their father to jail would create more chaos. Family was important to Marc and he wanted to be sure about Roger Waite before sending evidence to Patterson for conviction and incarceration. Fortunately, for the children, at least, grandparents and aunts and uncles were available to raise them.

Passing through a middle class area of the city, he decided to return to the scene of the crime to search again for any evidence of strangeness or oddities. Arriving at the house, Marc sat for a moment looking at the surroundings, the neighbors, and the house itself. Nothing seemed to indicate that any problems should have occurred inside. He exited his car and entered the house. He went to the bedroom where Mary had died. The scene remained the same as he remembered; nothing was out of place, except, of course, that unacceptable violence had occurred. The blood stains on the furniture and floor remained. Something must be in the room to help explain the events. Maybe other rooms of the home hid evidence of the history of this sad family. Only time would tell. Officers had inspected the home, but had they found everything needed to substantiate a criminal case against the man of the house?

Because Mary had allegedly killed herself, the search did not have the intensity of a murder investigation. Marc roamed around the house looking at the various rooms as though they were never explored. Nothing seemed out of place. The officers had been kind in their hunt for evidence. He entered a room, clearly the office for Roger's work when at home, looking around to see if anything could be suspicious. He approached the desk and open drawers looking for anything. The investigative reports had not mentioned any significant findings. Had they missed something? Folders in one drawer were real estate records and personal family expense records. Income tax files indicated a growing income over the years of marriage with deductions to charities around town including the church his family attended.

Marc made a note to speak with the pastor or priest of the church. He mentally beat himself for not thinking about the connection between the family and church last Sunday. Had Mary been attending regularly before last week? If not, then the shooting might have been premeditated by Roger. If she regularly attended and had deliberately decided to remain home, then maybe she truly wanted to commit this heinous act. Opening another drawer, Marc found another folder that seemed hidden from view under a pile of papers and a couple of books. Someone looking quickly in the drawer might have missed it. Marc cleared the drawer of its contents and opened the folder. The first paper, a letter dated three months earlier from Jeff Woodbury's office, explained the processes of obtaining a divorce. This had been in the back of Marc's mind but nothing had pointed to anything being done about it. So, here was evidence that Roger investigated dissolving his marriage. Did anyone know what he was doing, especially Victoria? If they planned to be together, despite their earlier communications, then what would have prevented them from contemplating the unthinkable?

Marc removed the letter to find a preliminary divorce decree with red inscriptions making changes to the document. The date on the cover page was two months past. Well then, Roger and Jeff had been conversing long before Mary's death. Mary probably did not know; except, if she did know, she may have become depressed enough to want to end it all. So many options within this case pointed to an unhappy husband who wanted to break out of the malaise of a depressing union.

Marc replaced the papers in the folder to take them to his house and then to the office tomorrow. He inspected the other drawers but found nothing of interest. The computer on the desk was turned off, so he pushed the power button to turn it on. Waiting for the computer to boot up, he remembered the photo albums in the living room and left to retrieve them. There were three of them plus the wedding album. Other loose pictures might be available, but Marc decided to wait. He returned to Roger's office to see what was on the computer. The login screen indicated the need for a name and password. Marc decided to get a warrant to inspect the computer. Pictures, e-mails, files, etc. could be informative. He pushed the power button again to power down the computer. He decided to take the box with him so that the contents could not be compromised. Of course, Roger may have deleted incriminating files already. The computer techs should be able decode anything that had been deleted recently.

Unplugging all of the peripherals, Marc carried the box out to his car, and then returned to collect the folders containing the divorce papers and the tax returns. He made a note to check the Waite's phone records for a call to the church from home. No call and Roger was lying. A call could mean Mary was serious about the suicide. This was enough for tonight. He picked up the folders and left the house. Seating himself in his car, Marc pulled out his cell phone and called Patterson's office, expecting to leave a message.

"Hello, Duncan Patterson, here."" he heard on the end of the other line.

"Duncan, Marc Jefferson, I'm at the Waite house and have found a folder indicating Waite investigated a divorce. I'm bringing it to the office tomorrow along with tax files and his computer. Do you think we should have a warrant to look at the contents of the computer?"

"Yes, a divorce, huh, that sure makes this case more interesting. What about the tax records, did you see anything pointing to Roger needing to rid himself of his wife instead of divorcing her?"

"Well, he kept making more money each year for the five years of the marriage, but I don't know what their total assets are. I am going to check phone records for that call last Sunday."

"Good idea, Marc," Duncan sounded a bit giddy about the news. "I'm headed home myself. I'll talk to you tomorrow." The phone line went dead. Marc replaced his phone in his pocket. He had what he needed and drove to his house and his wonderful, happy family. It was late and he had not consumed anything for a while. Although the family had probably eaten, he hoped Joan had put aside a dinner for him.

At the house, he opened the garage door remotely, drove into the garage and sat for a moment as usual. He left the folders and computer in the car for the night, closed the garage door with the wall button and went into the house to his family.

CHAPTER 20

J oan sat at the table reading the newspaper. The kitchen did not reflect any of the remnants of a dinner. She looked up as Marc came in. "Well, hello stranger." She smiled at him and stood up to retrieve the anticipated dinner.

"What a day! I've been to court, listened to some wild testimony, and watched two people look so confused about being in the same place that I know they thought we were going to have them rat each other out. I then discovered another surprising piece to my puzzle." Joan placed the reheated meal in front of him, kissed him on his head, and sat with him while he ate. Marc explained the some of the events of the day as he ate. Joan listened with affection, knowing he needed to vent.

With the meal consumed, Marc helped clean up and went to the family room to see the children. They were watching television. He sat with them and relaxed for the first time of the day. Little conversation passed between them and soon Marc nodded off to sleep.

"Hey, Dad, are you asleep?" Marc twitched awake and smiled.

"I was just resting my eyes." The children laughed having heard this many times before; all of them hugged their father tightly. "Alright, you guys, I think I need to get some real rest before tomorrow." Standing up he kissed each of them, said 'good night' and departed for his bedroom. Joan stayed with the children until they went to bed for the evening, and then she joined Marc.

Arriving she found Marc lying on their bed. "Do you want to tell me anything more about your day or do you need to think things through?" She lay with him, wrapped her arms around the man she adored, and kissed him gently on the lips. He accepted gratefully.

"I love you so much." He smiled and then explained, "Nothing really new came up other than I found a folder containing documents about a divorce from Mary. If he was to divorce her it might lessen the idea of his killing her. And, if she found out about it, that knowledge may have pushed her to suicide. However, he may also have discovered a divorce would be too expensive and so he wanted to rid himself of her. I just hate this case. It demonstrates the ugliness of humanity."

"Well, take solace in the fact not everyone is a bad, unscrupulous person. You work with honorable people and I like to think your family is honorable as well." She stood and undressed to get ready for bed. Marc, no longer transfixed on this troubling case, stirred from his spot. The week was nearly over but the case had much more investigation ahead. A divorce, now a possibility, changed the dynamics. The medical records of the distressed young mother could reveal a motive for murder. A suicide history could support allegations Roger was truly innocent. Only time and a probable trial would answer the question "Who killed Mary Waite".

The evening slid eagerly into sleep for Marc Jefferson. Another series of nightmares notwithstanding, rest was welcome.

No nightmares but Marc dreamed nonetheless. In the morning he tried to remember his dreams, but only remnants remained. He felt refreshed and ready to assault the day, so he dressed quickly and joined his wife who had risen earlier leaving him to sleep.

His children were up and dressed for the last day of school for the week and each was eating a breakfast of cereal, toast, and juice. Joan prepared a bowl for Marc and placed a glass of orange juice on the table for him, as well. He approached her and gently kissed her to the delight of the children, who declared a knowing 'Ooooh' not of embarrassment but exclaiming their joy of the parents' closeness. They smiled and Joan and Marc sat with the family to consume a family breakfast.

After the ritual goodbyes, the children left for school while Joan and Marc enjoyed a moment alone before leaving for the work that differed so greatly from each other. Marc drove directly to the office to begin sorting through the information gathered so far. He assumed the medical records would be turned over to the prosecutor soon, hopefully today. He decided to contact the pastor at the church the Waite's attended to find out what he knew about the family and to uncover any information he might have about the events of last Sunday. The coroner's office planned to release Mary's body to the family today so that a funeral could be held over the weekend. Marc figured the pastor would be at his office.

Ben Johnson was another person of interest from whom to glean information about Mary. Marc made a mental note to call him soon. As he came into the office Officer Tom approached with a folder, "I have compiled the interviews from yesterday into a file. I think the Johnson family is dysfunctional." He handed the folder to Marc and returned to his desk. Marc appreciated the professional attitude and work ethic that Tom projected. His investigations would be very useful in any prosecution.

Marc proceeded to his desk and sat down to read the report but discovered another folder from the medical examiner's office. Picking it up and reading, he quickly perused through it to find anything new, but most of the information was updates from earlier reports. The toxicity report indicated that Mary Waite was taking drugs for mood alteration, but no indication of DMSO use. Marc guessed that she must have been a handful to be married to and that Roger was growing tired of it. "Time to contact the families again," he thought out loud.

Another trip to the house of horror seemed appropriate, but Marc contacted Patterson first to find out the timeline for the medical records. Duncan's secretary connected the call to his desk. A short conversation ensued and Marc had what he needed. He hung up his phone, collected his various items of investigation and left to search for the truth.

"Tom, I'm leaving for a while. Would you go to the store where Mary Waite purchased the gun and interview the store clerk. I'm interested in knowing what transpired and how Mary seemed that day."

"Okay. Do you want me to bring him here?"

"If you want, but I think that we can get what we need there."

Marc left to rummage through the crime scene again. What hidden treasures lurked underneath the veil of family secrets? As his car approached the house a man in the next door yard stopped his work and came up to the cruiser. Marc got out and asked the man what he wanted.

"You're investigating the suicide last Sunday, aren't you?"

"Yes."

"Well, I got to thinking about what the officer asked me earlier this week and I think maybe I left something out." Marc nodded as if to say continue. "About six months ago they had a real donnybrook of a fight and I noticed that Roger was torn up a bit when I saw him next. You know, face scratched and wearing long sleeves, which he doesn't normally do." The man looked down embarrassed. "I asked him if everything was alright and he mumbled something I didn't quite understand. I didn't want to get involved so I just left it alone. "Did he kill her? 'Cuz I thought she killed herself?"

"We're still investigating. What was the fight about?"

"I'm not really sure, but they had been going at it for an hour before I saw Roger come out of the house. My wife and I didn't have much to do with the Waite's since we thought her odd. Roger's nice enough, but his wife could go off halfcocked in a matter of minutes if you crossed her. A couple of years ago the cops were all over that house. She overdosed on something, I think. Well, I'm sorry for butting in, but I think he needs to be looked into, although I'm not sure what he would do with the kids. I know he has family in the area. I met them once when they came over. I think he's in real estate or something."

"Thanks for your information." Marc shook hands when offered and walked up to the door and entered. He turned and watched the man return to his yard work. Interesting no one mentioned fighting in the family. Another secret exposed. Entering the den, Marc surveyed the shelves of books and albums. Noticing a misplaced book, he walked over to the shelf and removed other books. Behind some of them was a recessed safe missed by the officers earlier in the week. No reason to suspect anything then. The safe was closed, but Marc figured someone had been here and removed the contents.

He returned the books to their former place and began a more thorough hunt for secrets. Moving slowly around the room, moving a picture here, opening a drawer there, nothing seemed to be out of place. Marc approached the desk and studied it. Nothing fancy about it, just an ordinary desk from an office supply company. He opened the drawers one at a time as he had done when he discovered the divorce papers. This time he sorted more carefully. Old tax records, bank statements, and business accounts were all he discovered. Everything neatly filed and in place where it should be. A man like Roger kept an orderly life, probably disordered by a crazy wife. "I'll bet he hated her for messing up his neat little plan." Marc conjured up an image of Roger at his desk devising ways of eliminating the disorder without incriminating himself.

Secrets are hard to keep for any length of time. Something in this office should tip the scales in favor of a guilty verdict. Marc pulled out the drawers looking for any sign of a secret compartment. He felt under each drawer and within the slide areas, wanting to find something of value. Nothing materialized at first, but he kept searching. Under the lower left drawer he found a paper taped to it. Removing it, Marc discovered the paper had numbers on it that seemed like a combination and a bank account. He returned to the bookcase, studied the numbers and tried the lock. The safe opened with ease.

Motive

Inside Marc found insurance documents, a quantity of money, and property titles to three houses. "I wonder if Mary knew about these?" he thought aloud. The properties were located in Wendlesburg and Seattle. Was he hiding property ownership? If so, why would he? A divorce might cost him these, another reason to eliminate any encumbrances. Marc noted the information and replaced everything. This evidence would more than likely need a warrant. Searching public records would not. He counted the money and wrote the insurance policy numbers and benefit amounts. The policies were on Roger, Mary, and the house and car. He closed the safe, and again placed the books as he had found them. He put all of the drawers back in the desk having returned the paper to its hiding spot.

Marc left the house to go to their church on this Friday morning. Barton Hancock met Marc in the hallway near his office. The two men went in the office and sat down to talk.

"Pastor Barton, I have delayed coming to you because I needed to understand the situation within the Waite's family. I understand they were active members of your parish."

"Yes, Roger and his family have been members of our church for a long time. When Roger and Mary wed, they continued attending fairly regularly."

"Last week, Roger claims that a call came in to him at church from Mary. I am seeking confirmation of the call."

"I was talking with Roger when the call came in. Mary had stayed home and Roger was here with the children."

"What time was the call?"

"If I remember correctly, about 11:30."

"Did Roger say anything to you about the call?"

"No, next thing I knew he had gone home and the children were with his parents. I went on with my business and heard about Mary's death that evening when Walker called me to let me know what had happened."

"Did you have any interaction with the Waite's because of problems with Mary's mental stability?"

130

"I did counsel them on occasion, but I really can't talk about anything we have discussed. I will say that I was concerned about Mary."

"What concerned you?"

"I didn't think she was a very happy person. I've known her for the last five years and lately she seemed very depressed most of the time."

"How has Roger reacted to her depression?"

"He has been very supportive of her. He genuinely loves her and has been a great father." Barton shifted his position.

"I know that church finance is another sacred area, but did the Waite's support the church well? I only ask as a matter of understanding their financial status, which seems to be fairly well to do."

"They have pledged every year. Roger was also generous with his time. Are you concerned Roger may have done something wrong that drove Mary to commit suicide?"

"Possibly, but I am also investigating whether Roger may have wanted to extricate himself from his marriage and found a way to do it." Marc watched Barton's reaction to his statement. Nothing of note seemed to emanate from him.

"I would be surprised if he did anything to Mary. He always was so kind to her and to the children."

"Did you help them when they had problems? I understand they had been fighting lately and that Mary did have suicide attempts in the past."

"As I said before I am unwilling to discuss our conversations."

"Okay, then tell me about Walker and Nancy Waite."

"What do you want to know?"

"How did they feel about Roger's marriage?"

"They were very supportive and loving. Mary became a member of the family. Her parents also were very happy to see their daughter marry a fine upstanding person. We hosted a reception for the newlyweds when they returned from their honeymoon. Everyone had a wonderful time."

"Did you speak with Walker or Nancy after Roger left for home?"

Pastor Barton, uneasy for a moment, said, "I spoke with Nancy briefly. She told me Roger had to go home and that Mary requested they watch the children. She and Walker left church afterward with their grandchildren." Barton stood up and moved from behind his desk. "I must get to an appointment. Please contact me if you have any more questions, although I don't know how I'm of much help."

Marc stood as well and shook hands with Barton. "Thank you for your time. I'll be in touch." Marc left the church thinking that Barton might be holding out on him. Privilege or not, he wanted Barton to come clean with the Waite's relationship as he knew it.

Marc returned to his office to read the accumulated information again, reviewing all the data. What hadn't been uncovered which compelled a man to murder his wife? Was enough gathered to convict? Marc called Patterson about the medical records.

"Sorry to bother you again," Marc said when connected with Patterson. "I was curious to know if you have Mary Waite's medical records."

"They came in about an hour ago. Why don't you come over and look at them with me. I think there is some interesting information about her relationship with her parents and her brother."

"I'll be right over." Marc hung up. As he left for the prosecutor's office the chief medical examiner came in.

"You might want to see this." Perry Andrews usually didn't come to the sheriff's office. He expected people to come to him, a minor arrogance considering what he uncovered with his autopsies. Marc greeted him. "I just received the final toxicity report and stomach content evaluation. She had taken a dose of anti-pain medication sometime in the morning. It hadn't fully digested into her system. Also, I hadn't looked for this before, because of the nature of this being a suicide case, but her hormone levels were high for progesterone, so I checked for pregnancy. She was about five weeks along. Examining the fetal DNA, she was having a boy."

"Pregnant? Would you care to guess about who shot her?"

"Well, the evidence points to a suicide being set up. But I still don't think that may be the final conclusion. With GSR on him as well as her, I couldn't say for sure. Also, we ran the prints on the revolver and found three sets. One set was Mary's. One was Roger's, and another set is, as yet, unidentified."

"A third person touched the gun?"

"Yes," Perry nodded. "The end of the bullet casings had unknown prints on them. Someone other than Mary or Roger Waite loaded the gun."

"Whose print is on the trigger?"

"Can't really tell. The print was smudged. Also, Mary Waite didn't have any need to use DMSO. Why it was on her is a question yet to be answered."

"Thanks, Perry, I'll let Patterson know."

Andrews handed a folder to Marc with the reports in it and they left the office for their respective destinations.

CHAPTER 21

"Marc, this family is seriously dysfunctional." Duncan spread out the contents of a large box which had arrived at his office.

Monica picked one of the files and read. "How can a father be so belligerent to his own children?

"As often as these cases come through this office, I'm still perplexed that family means so little to so many," Duncan replied.

Marc nodded, another instance of the vile behavior of mean, evil people. "Look at this," Marc interjected. "Mary was taken to the hospital after that call two years ago and tried to leave before the psych evaluation. They kept her there for two days to make sure she was stable. She was examined by a Doctor Conley who also saw her after she was ordered by the court to see a shrink. I'll contact Conley."

"Good, maybe he has more insight not written in here."

Monica said, "This is interesting; Mary stated her father abused her and her brother but says Victoria did not suffer the same thing."

"She hinted at the father being emotional when I interviewed her earlier this week. I'll dig out the type of abuse." Marc said.

"Could be a reason to off yourself or drive your husband crazy." Patterson continued, "She's seen an awful lot of doctors who prescribed an awful lot of drugs. This one for pain suppressants was only three days old. Sleeping pills from two different doctors and filled at two different pharmacies on the same day. I guess that slipped through the system." Duncan kept shuffling material. "I need her juvenile records. This stuff can help us next Thursday. Monica, get working on it right away." She looked up from her perusals and nodded.

"How old is that sleeping pill thing?" Marc asked.

"Three years ago. Are you thinking that she might have tried something then as well?" Duncan answered.

"Yeah, Roger hinted this was not the first time during their marriage and she cut herself as a teenager, according to Victoria," Marc said.

"Maybe he should come in here and tell the story again for clarity and understanding." Duncan moved to a phone in the room and called for his assistant to join them. He returned to the table. "I found no evidence on the court dockets of any divorce filing, so Roger has not yet put that into play. His tax records are pretty squared away."

"I found records of property holdings at the house. I replaced them. I'll get a warrant for his office." Marc turned as Monica looked as if to ask a question. He spoke first. "The items are in a safe hidden from view by books on his bookshelf."

Marc finished perusing the records and decided to call on Mrs. Johnson again without the husband. "Do you think Roger killed his wife?"

"Everything is circumstantial at best, but a case is emerging. The real question is the timing of Roger's call home and Mary's death. It's very tight."

"Sir, he still had time to shoot her," Monica said.

"The other tight timeline is the call to her parents and the 911. If she was shot before noon, then he only had a window of 15 minutes to hold a conversation with her and shoot her, according to his testimony. Of course, he says she shot herself," Marc said.

"I may want you to arrest him next week after we have the court hearing on Thursday. But we do not want to rush this and lose a conviction."

Marc nodded in agreement. "Oh, by the way, Andrews came to my office just before I came here."

"That's not like him."

"I know, but he had additional info about Mary Waite. Seems she was five weeks pregnant and had ingested a dose of pain suppressants a few hours before the shooting." Marc waited for a response. None came and he continued, "A third set of prints were located on the bullet casings. Someone other than Mary or Roger loaded the revolver. Also, she had traces of DMSO but he concluded she did not use it within herself for anything he could find."

"A third person was in the room?" Monica asked.

"I don't know about that. But a third person knew about the gun and may have been involved in the shooting."

"Any idea who?" Patterson sat at his desk.

"I might have an idea, but let me get a copy of prints from the person I suspect and compare them to the unknown casing prints."

"Ok. How did she get the pain pills?"

"I'm going to look into that as soon as I leave here." Marc packed up his gear, saluted Patterson lazily and left. Monica smiled invitingly and Marc envisioned Patterson involved in a sordid intra-office affair. *Good thing he's still unmarried.* The last event had cost him half his fortune and some of his personal reputation.

Marc pulled out his cell phone and punched in a number for Marion Johnson. "Mrs. Johnson, if you are available, I would like to meet with you about your daughter and son-in-law. Could I come over to your place?" He paused as she answered. "I see. Then I will meet you at your daughter's place in about two hours. Thank you." He clicked off the cell phone and walked to his car. He sat a for moment thinking and then called Ben Johnson, asking him to meet at his sister's place. Thus agreed, Marc began driving to Seattle.

* * *

"Thank you for coming. I'm curious. Why are we meeting here?" Marc asked.

Marion looked at him directly. "I didn't want Garrett to know we're meeting without him. He can be ... difficult."

"Mom uses Vickie's place as a sanctuary when Dad is on one of his tirades." Ben had been the first to arrive and had waited for his mother before exiting his car. Marc had parked away from the building but close enough to see who came and went. When they had gone into the building he left his car and followed them in. They were waiting in the apartment for him.

"Ben, I have evidence that you and Mary were abused as children. Please explain what happened." Ben squirmed and his mother lowered her eyes.

"I'm afraid I was not a very good mother," Marion cut in. She looked up at Marc. "We've not had the best family life. I know Garrett didn't mean to harm his children, but he didn't really understand how to treat them when they acted out. His method of discipline involved a belt."

"I tried to get him to stop hitting Mary, so I took the brunt of what happened." Ben seemed more relaxed than the last visit, as though a weight had been lifted.

"Did he abuse you, Mrs. Johnson?"

"Not physically, but he can be mean with words. I stayed with him because I don't believe in divorce." Marion anticipated the next question. "I knew he was strong willed when we married, but things became strained as he tried to protect his reputation and thought keeping the children in line was part of it. He had been raised by an abusive father himself."

"Was Victoria subjected to his abuse?"

"Not really, she came along later enough and I think he knew he'd been wrong. When Mary met Roger he felt vindicated that she turned out alright after all. Ben was another situation. They're pretty much estranged these days."

"I don't see my father much without other people around. I'm sure I'd hurt him if he came after me or Mom. I'm not putting up with any more."

"Has this interfered with your developing relationships with other people?" Marc thought that Ben might be hiding a disordered personality.

"I've been in counseling since leaving home so I can have normal relationships. I still fear having a companion, though. I'm not sure my father would understand my orientation." A revelation that Marc suspected now revealed.

"Did Garrett abuse Mary sexually?"

"No!" Marion responded angrily. Ben turned to his mother and held her hand gently.

"Mom doesn't know about it, but Dad did visit Mary occasionally. He never had sex with her from what she told me, but he touched her and told her she was to enjoy what a man could give her. She didn't fight back, but I know she didn't enjoy it. Sorry, Mom."

"I didn't want to know, but I suspected what Ben has said."

"Mrs. Johnson, your daughter had taken pain medication a few hours before she was shot. Did she tell you anything about suffering from pain?"

"No, but she had suffered from lower back pain from time to time."

"Did she tell you she was pregnant?"

"Yes, but she hadn't told Roger. She wanted to get an abortion. I told her to wait, talk to Roger, and find out how he felt. Do you think she killed herself because of my advice?"

"She left no note, but I am curious as to when she told you."

"She told me about two weeks ago. Missing her period was unusual, so she took a home pregnancy test. She hadn't even been to the doctor, yet."

"Ben, did you know she was pregnant?"

"This is the first I've heard of it."

Marc decided to open Pandora's Box. "Mrs. Johnson, we are not sure that Mary took her own life. Did she ever explain to you how she and Roger got along?"

Shocked she answered, "Roger killed Mary?" Then a serious look fell over her. Ben did not exhibit surprise. "Mary said she and Roger were having trouble. She suspected another woman and maybe he wanted out of the marriage. She didn't have any proof of infidelity and did not want any. But I think she feared Roger might hurt her. I thought she felt this way because of her father. I never thought of Roger as a violent person."

"We're gathering evidence right now, but nothing points to him, so please, don't jump to conclusions. I simply asked to get an idea of how they related with each other." What better way to know the true marriage than ask the mother of the wife. "Would Mary have contemplated leaving Roger?"

"We talked about it, but I told her I didn't think it was right. We talked about why I stayed with her father. She really tried to make it work. I guess that conversation didn't work. I miss her so much." Marion began crying softly, Ben held her as she mourned.

"Ben, how do you and Roger get along?"

"We're ok. We don't have a lot in common."

"Would you be surprised if Roger killed your sister?"

Ben shook his head, "I don't know... I mean ... I don't think he could have done it. But then I was surprised to hear my sister shot herself. I felt her other tries had really been cries for help." He released his mother's hand and stood up. "What's going to happen to Roger? If he did shoot Mary, how are you going to prove it?" He turned to Marc with an inquisitive, almost a pleading look. The door opened and Victoria joined the trio.

"What's going on here?" She looked at her mother and then Ben. "Mr. Jefferson?" She put her backpack on the floor by the door and came into the room to sit with her mother. "Mom, why are you here?"

"Mr. Jefferson wanted to talk with us without your father. I suggested here. I hope you're not upset." She hugged her daughter and tears welled up in her eyes.

"It's ok, Mom." She returned the hug, looking at Marc suspiciously. "What are you talking about?"

"Miss Johnson, we are talking about your sister and her relationship with her husband. You indicated that she was unhappy as a teenager. Did you know about the abusive activity your father had with her?"

"She and I talked about it." She looked intently at Marc.

"What did she tell you?"

Victoria fidgeted. "Dad started coming into her room when she turned 14. According to Mary, he said he was teaching her about men, but she didn't like it. I asked her what he was doing. She told me I wouldn't understand. I didn't get it out of her until I turned 12 and she warned me about Dad. Nothing ever happened to me, though."

"Did you and she ever discuss her suicide attempts?"

"She explained about the suicide when she was 14 and how she felt about going away to school. We talked about guys and neither of us wanted to be abused by them. We made a pact to stay away from them until we could take care of ourselves. In college she met Roger and seemed very happy."

"Did your father have sex with her?"

Victoria scrunched her face. "I asked her about that once. She said he just touched her. She didn't think he ever got any gratification from it, but it was still wrong."

"Could this have led to her depression as an adult?"

"I don't know; I'm not a psychologist."

Marion looked intently at her daughter, "Vickie, Roger may have killed Mary." She paused. "I miss her so much. Please don't let anything happen to you. Or you, Ben." Victoria blushed.

"Oh, Mom, he didn't kill her. He loved her. He told me so." Her face drained of color. Marc observed these changes with interest. "I love Roger, and he me. I sure hope he didn't do something stupid."

"What do you mean, Miss Johnson?" Marc pressed her.

She glared, "Roger is my brother-in-law. I simply love him as a brother. Did he kill Mary?"

"We're investigating, Miss Johnson." Marc checked his notebook. "Tell me again where you were Sunday morning."

"I was here."

"When did you find out about your sister?"

"Mom called me."

"What time was it?"

Vickie looked at her mother. "I think it was about 1:30."

"You said you and your sister were close. Did she tell you about her suicide attempt as a teenager?"

"Yes." Vickie stood up and moved toward her kitchen. "Can I get anyone something to drink?"

"Miss Johnson, please answer the question." Vickie turned toward Marc.

"Well, after she came home from New York, she was mad at Mom and Dad because everything seemed to have gone so wrong. She thought Dad was very insensitive to what happened. I tried to get her to forget about it, but she just kept harping on it. A couple of weeks later, she tried cutting herself."

"Mrs. Johnson, how much did your daughter talk to you about this?"

"She talked mostly with Vickie. I didn't talk with her very much since Garrett thought that she was just being a whiney teenager." She squirmed a little.

"Do you need anything more from us?" Ben chimed in. Moving to his mother, he helped her stand. "Let's go, Mom." Victoria and Marc stood, as well.

"Thanks for coming over. I'll be in touch." They left the room. Marc turned to Victoria. "I'm sorry about pushing you regarding Roger. Are ready to give me the truth about you and Roger? I realize this is difficult for you, but I suspect you and Roger are entangled in an affair. How long have you two been having sexual relations?"

Victoria's expression of surprise did not reflect disavowal. "I beg your pardon. What evidence do you have about an affair?"

"I have no direct evidence, but you are very attractive and both of you admit to what you call intimate meetings, so one can assume the meetings were more than just talk."

"I know Mom suspected Roger was seeing someone."

"Is it you?"

"Why would I? I love Roger, but I…" She ceased talking.

Marc asked another question. "Did you know about the divorce papers he had in his office?"

Victoria turned away. "He told me he was going to leave her. He confessed he wanted to be with me." Turning back, "I told him he was crazy. He couldn't leave my sister and the kids." She sat down. "I didn't want him to." Marc sat across from her. "I asked you once before if I had given him a reason to kill Mary. You seem to be doing an awful lot of investigating trying to convict Roger. He wouldn't kill her, but then I didn't think Mary could kill herself."

"I'm not sure what to say to you. If you have any ideas that Roger found an opportunity to rid himself of his wife, I would appreciate it. This may not end up in court, but I think it's more likely it will. There's a lot of evidence to follow, including your affair with him."

"I never said I was having an affair with him." Moving next to Marc she continued, "We're not meeting each other anymore. Being with him would be weird."

"You don't think it was weird before?"

Victoria giggled, "Yeah, you're right. Well, when this all comes out, I fear people will convict us of killing her without ever understanding the situation."

"What situation is that?" Marc stood up.

Victoria stood as well. "You know, how Roger and I might have plotted her death to be together. Mary was unstable and wanted the depression to stop." She laced her hands in his. "I know you won't believe this, but I don't think Roger wants to be with me anymore." Marc unhooked himself and walked to the door. "You're leaving?" Victoria contrived disappointment. Marc paused. He turned and examined her a moment too long. She grinned.

"I have to get back to the office and read some reports on my desk. I'll see you later." He left for the safety of his car and his home.

CHAPTER 22

Monday came and went. A warrant to search the rest of the house, including the office and safe, had been obtained. An appeal by Woodbury was to no avail. On Tuesday Marc and two other detectives went to the house, still marked as a crime scene. Roger had been allowed to retrieve clothes for himself and the children, but they were staying at his parents for the time being.

"What are we looking for?" Tom Wiggins carried the evidence box as they approached the house.

Roger Waite and Jeff Woodbury met them before they could get to the front door. "What are you looking for?" Woodbury asked when they stopped near Marc.

"We are after anything supporting the idea that Mary was depressed enough to commit suicide. We are also interested in any evidence that helps clear Mr. Waite of any intention that he may have wanted to eliminate his wife." Marc handed Woodbury the warrant.

"That's preposterous!" Roger interjected "I didn't do anything to her." He leaned over to Woodbury and whispered to him. Marc continued into the house with the other detectives followed by Waite and Woodbury.

Marc went to the office desk and opened drawers. He removed all of the contents pretending he was finding new material. When he came to the paper with the combination, he asked, "Where's this safe?" Roger hesitated but Woodbury directed him to show it.

"It's behind some books over here."

"What's in it?"

"Some insurance papers."

"Open it, please." Roger looked at Woodbury who nodded approval. Waite moved the books, which Marc noticed were not as he had left them, and unlocked the safe. "Please step away," Marc commanded. He removed the contents for examination.

"Are you satisfied, Mr. Jefferson?" Woodbury sounded smug knowing a secret had been kept. Marc let nothing of his previous inspection escape, but the real estate titles and cash were not among the contents.

"Mr. Waite, do you have any other secret alcoves or safes? We can stay here all day and tear this house apart or you can help us and yourself by disclosing everything you have that pertains to your business and your family."

"What are you looking for?" Woodbury inquired again looking angry and perplexed. "My client has nothing to hide. You're acting as if you actually suspect him of killing his wife. This is a matter of suicide and nothing more. I request that you stop haranguing Mr. Waite so he can get on with his life."

"Mr. Woodbury, we want nothing more than to complete our investigation and close this case. But if Mr. Waite had anything to do with his wife's death the prosecutor's office will prosecute. I'm just doing my job." Turning to Roger, "Well, do you have anywhere else you keep files and important documents?"

"Don't answer that. We have nothing more to say." Roger and his attorney left the room.

Guilty, thought Marc. Nothing more would be gained from looking here. He packed up the documents and papers gleaned from the desk and safe. He joined Waite and Woodbury in the living room. "Mr. Waite, I am going to examine these insurance papers, but do they contain any suicide waivers?"

"Why don't you just do your job, as you put it," Woodbury retorted. The battle had been joined. Marc would get nothing from Roger with Jeff Woodbury around. He would dig in other fertile ground. The plausibility of an affair could be confronted at a later time.

* * *

The inspection of the property came to a close and all participants exited. Marc watched as Roger and Woodbury left. He suspected Woodbury knew what had happened and would protect Roger from self-incrimination.

"We didn't get the real estate titles and a substantial amount of cash was missing from the safe as well." Marc explained the previous inspection to Duncan and Monica. "The insurance papers are here, but I don't know about any suicide waivers." Monica took the papers from Jeff to examine. He smiled as he handed them to her.

"Let's get real about this." Duncan sat at his desk. "We know that Roger and Mary were having difficulty. He is... or was... possibly involved with the sister-in-law, had property holdings which he may have hidden from his wife, stockpiled cash, investigated divorcing her, and had the opportunity to shoot her. I think we have a case. Monica, what is the payout on those policies?" He stood and moved toward her.

"One policy is on Roger for a million. Another is on her for half a million. Both have child riders. They were issued three years ago. Each has a two year suicide indemnity clause, which has passed. So he stands to receive the payout. Too bad it wasn't an accident. There's a double indemnity for it." He took the papers in hand and turned to Jefferson.

"Well, the literal smoking gun now has a brother." Patterson smiled "We have another motive. Find out how in debt Waite is. He might need this money to cover mortgages on those properties."

"I'll interview the neighbors again. What was the name of her psychiatrist?"

Monica answered, "Dr. Baxter Conley, here is the address and phone number." She handed him a paper on which she had written it. Marc thought, *efficient as well as attractive.*

"I'll get right on this." He left the office.

Tom Wiggins intercepted Marc as he entered the sheriff's office. "I followed up as you asked and spoke with neighbors. Three of them corroborated Roger and Mary had some real donnybrooks and on one occasion Roger looked to have been mauled by a bear, you know scratches and such. They seemed afraid of her and did not have much to do with her. They all stated that Roger was friendly, but Mary kept to herself and didn't talk with them much. She was a wacko, as one person put it."

"Thanks, Tom. I'm going out to talk with a Dr. Conley. Would you get these reports to Patterson? He thinks we have a case."

"Sure thing, boss."

Marc sat at his desk and looked at the phone number Monica had given him. "Nice handwriting," he whispered, picked up the phone and dialed the number. He asked to speak with the doctor who agreed to meet with him immediately. Marc packed up his gear and left.

In the office of Dr. Conley, Marc read each of the certificates and diplomas exhibited on the walls. The office décor expressed a modern motif with pale blue walls and soft creamy mocha carpet. The chairs and couches seemed better suited to a living room of an expensive home. The usual display of arrogance thought Marc who also had an extensive educational background but chose not the show it. He understood the need for a doctor to quell any patient anxiety as to competence, hence the wall adornments. The receptionist hailed him. "Dr. Conley will see you now. Please follow me."

"Thank you." They moved down a hall with muted flowery wallpaper to a large opulent office space. Psych work sure paid well. "Dr. Conley, I'm Detective Marc Jefferson of the sheriff's department." He reached out to shake hands. "I appreciate your time, today."

"What can I do for you? You indicated this is about Mary Waite?"

"Yes, I understand you saw her two years ago regarding an alleged suicide attempt which landed her in the hospital."

"That is correct."

"We have her medical records, as you know, and I have studied what you wrote in those records. Do you feel that her attempt was really a cry for help, as you wrote, or more likely a true death wish? I ask this because she died a week ago last Sunday from a self-inflicted gunshot."

"I read about it in the papers. I was sorry to hear of her death. However, I don't reveal patient confidentialities."

'Would it be helpful to have a court order for that to happen?"

"It wouldn't make any difference. The law protects me." Marc nodded.

"What I am trying to ascertain is her willingness to actually pull a trigger and end her life. If she was not truly capable of that then her husband may have used the opportunity to shoot her."

Dr. Conley moved from behind his desk. "Mr. Jefferson, the only thing I can give you is information when both of them were here. She was my patient, but Mr. Waite is not. He did not seem very sympathetic to her trials and tribulations. When we spoke he gave me the impression he wanted to be rid of her. He did not say that directly, but I could tell he felt frustrated and trapped because of her mental state at the time."

"Would you be willing to state that in a court of law?"

"I have been to court regarding many things. I will testify about anything that does not constitute a patient, doctor confidentiality breech. I can say from a professional point of view, Roger Waite might be willing to rid himself of an encumbrance such as a mentally fragile wife. I am not willing to state Mary Waite was that fragile wife. You have my records of our sessions with my notes. I leave it at that."

"Thank you very much, doctor. I'll be in touch." Marc left the office with a bit of a lift in his step. He stopped by the elder care facility to see his wife and let her know that he would be home for dinner.

Back at the office he called Patterson to inform him of the doctor's thoughts. The day had been productive. He wrote his notes into formal documents for Patterson. He formulated a hypothesis that Waite killed his wife for the money and the sister. Motive enough for a trial. Evidence enough for a conviction?

CHAPTER 23

Another day came and went. Thursday's court hearing was the next stop on the journey about this broken family. Nothing more could be done today. Marc packed up his evidence and locked it in the desk. He promised Joan an early return home. He kept his promise.

Sleep came easily for Marc, as did dreaming.

"Do you believe I am capable of murder? She was whacko. Can't you see that? I had no choice. She had to die." Roger sat at a table in a nondescript little room with a table and one chair. He was alone talking to no one in particular. Marc felt present and yet far away in another universe.

"Why did she have to die?" Marc's hollow voice demanded.

"I couldn't take it anymore. She was draining my soul from me. She had no personality of her own. I was becoming a 'nobody'. She had to die. I'm glad she died."

"Did you shoot her?" The voice questioned.

"She shot herself. No... she killed the wall. I killed her." Marc's absent voice watched a smile crawl across Roger's face.

"Yeah, I killed her. I don't have to hide any more. Victoria ....
Vickie ... we can be together, now."

"You can't have her," another voice cried.

"She wants me. I want her. We're matched."

"I miss my sister." Victoria suddenly is sitting with Roger.
"I don't want you any more, Roger. You killed my sister." She
stands and moves to the absent voice.

Roger cringes, "Then you are my next victim. Do what I ask
and you can have me for all eternity."

Speaking to the faceless voice, "No...I don't want that. I want
Roger to be punished for not being a good husband." Marc now
appeared "I'm a good husband!"

"Mary? Mary? Mary, where are you?"

"I'm here, Roger, behind you. Victoria, leave."

Marc watched the macabre scene dance around him. Victoria
came to him. "Roger can't have me anymore. I want to be with
you, now." She wrapped her arms around his disembodied entity
and kissed him on the mouth. "I want you to want me. I must be
wanted by someone. My sister doesn't love me."

The scene morphed into another spectacle of Marc's uninhib-
ited subconscious. He now sat with Joan in his house. "Why do
you love me? She is so much younger and wants you. I'm old and
worn out. She can give you more than I can. Go to her."

"No, I don't love her. Please, forgive me. I can forget her. I
will forget her. She only wants sex with us." Marc turned and
saw Joan and Victoria embracing, kissing, fondling. "What? No,
Joan I need you."

"Come join us." Both entities smirked and wagged fingers of
enticement.

"No, this isn't right. I only want to be with you, Joan." Marc
stood, floated to them. They gathered him in to their countenance and he observed them meld into one body with features of both, contorted and twisted into someone... something
unattractive and repulsive. Escape. Run. Nowhere to go. Marc
pushed it away but was increasingly absorbed into its being.
He heard its thoughts, felt its desires, until he was reassured
of the pleasure awaiting him. "No, you can't have me. You

cannot have Joan. You only want what you can't have. Leave me, now."

"Resistance is futile." Laughter strained the darkness. "You are mine. We are one with each other. Do not resist. Enjoy."

"Roger, you need to come here and get her away from us."

"I can't. I killed all I ever wanted. I might as well kill myself and the children."

"No...no....no......" Silence! Marc sat alone with Mary.

"He didn't mean to shoot me. I drove him to it. He loved me and I loved him. Why did Vickie interfere? We had a good thing. She messed it up. I want her dead. Stay with me, she has your wife. I'll be your wife."

"But you're dead."

"That's alright." Mary caressed Marc's hair and kissed his forehead. He felt a sense of reckless abandon. Roger whimpered alone in the distance. Marc and Mary's passion amplified the recklessness of his actions. "But you're dead," he repeated.

The room swirled and morphed into another room. Court had begun. The jury consisted of several of Joan's and Victoria's melded amorphous beings. The judge was Mary with half a head.

"Have you come to a decision?"

"We have, your honor. These men are guilty!" The sound echoed and trailed away.

"Of, what?" Marc tried to scream but nothing emerged. "I didn't shoot her."

"Guilty... Guilty... Guilty..." The chant arose from the jurors and the judge. Only the three of them were now separated and recognizable, young and healthy. Roger and Marc stood naked to the verdict. The scene darkened.

Marc awoke in darkness, breathing heavily. His face felt moist as did his pillow. He checked the clock which read 2:35, and whispered, "No more. Please, no more." Sleep evaded him, so he rose and descended the staircase to his den. He sat on the couch and just listened to the deafening silence. He recalled the dream, an alternate, vivid reality. He would not share this dream with Joan. Lying down he succumbed to a disquieting sleep.

"Marc? Are you okay?" Joan knelt by the couch stroking his hair. "I didn't know where you were. I found you asleep here." Marc stirred as she spoke.

"I'm alright. I woke up early, came down here. I guess I fell asleep again. I don't know." He was awake but not really aware of his surroundings. "What time is it?"

"A little past 6."

"I've got to get to the office. I think I know what happened, but I still have to prove it." She kissed him and they went upstairs to begin the day.

"Did you have another dream?"

"Yeah, but it was weird. Maybe I'll tell you about it later. I don't want to recall it now."

Marc dressed, ate some breakfast, and stated lunch was on him. He drove to the office and pulled out the files to review timelines. Thinking about the dream, he wondered if Victoria had more involvement in her sister's death. What motive did she have? Wanting Roger for herself? Wanting to raise Roger's kids? Sharing his money? Did she resent her sister? Was jealousy part of the scheme? Nothing seemed right about her complicity to murder. No, this still pointed at Roger and his desire for freedom from a crazy person. A jury could believe it. The facts were there. The proof relied on the amount of facts, and Roger had opportunity. Did he have state of mind? Marc reread his material. What was the order of events? What timeline was followed? "Think, Jefferson, think." His mind roiled as he read through the pages. The interviews provided much, but something was missing, something that could push a person to commit a most egregious act.

Picking up the phone, he called Patterson and set up a time to meet. The court hearing for Garrett Johnson was later in the morning and although he was not attending, Marc felt it important to talk about what may have compelled Roger to such extreme action. He packed up his evidence and left the office.

"I think her crazy enough to drive him over the edge," Patterson speculated. "But I agree with you. Something is not right yet. The timing of his coming home and the call to his in-laws and 911 is really tight. That third set of prints points to another person possibly at the house."

Marc nodded. "What about the Johnson girl? Do you think she had anything to do with it?"

"Possibly, she sure has the looks to drive a man wild. But then Mary was no ugly duckling. Investigate who her friends are. Maybe they have something to add. Can they vouch for her on that Sunday?"

"What are you thinking?"

"Well, at trial Woodbury will throw a lot of doubt into Roger being the perpetrator. That way the jury might not convict. I just want all the doubt dismissed because there is no other solution. I'm working the angle that Mary wanted to kill herself, decided not to, and Roger finished the job. Maybe he wanted out so he could be with Victoria. Maybe he just was tired of Mary. Either way, I have to be sure that nothing else can cloud the jury's deliberations."

"Alright, I'll find out who her friends are and build a case for Victoria." A crazy idea entered Marc's mind. He didn't dismiss it, but it probably had nothing to do with this at all. He would check on it. Monica Atherton entered the room with folders in hand. She also could drive a man to unreasonable action and he smiled as he left. *Hope Patterson is focused.*

The drive to Seattle was a pleasant one. Traffic remained light as he sped along Interstate 5. No reason to hurry, but Marc enjoyed a little speed when driving. Common courtesy had erased more than one stop by law enforcement. He drove directly to the university and parked. He had an idea the Student Union Building might be a classic place to hang around and ask questions. He figured the word would eventually get back to Victoria but that didn't really matter. He settled in to watch for a while, just to get a feel for the place. Students milled about as though no one had any classes.

"Time to work." Marc pulled out a picture of Victoria taken from her high school annual. He stepped toward a couple of girls and asked, "Do you know this girl?" They responded negatively. He continued inquiring for the next twenty minutes becoming frustrated a bit. Three girls came into the SUB as Marc was leaving. *Time for one more try* he thought. "Do you know this girl?"

"Sure, that's Vickie Johnson. Who are you?" An attractive blond responded.

"I'm Detective Marc Jefferson of the Wendlesburg Sheriff's Department. How do you know Miss Johnson?"

"We have classes together. Has she done something wrong? I know her sister died last week. Is this about that?" The other two girls stood off from the conversation.

"What kind of girl is Miss Johnson?"

"Oh, she's very nice. I liked her right away when we met."

"Does she have a boyfriend?" Marc looked at the other girls.

"I don't think so, but I could be wrong. She keeps to herself a lot. Her family is in the area and I think she spends time with them."

"Have you met them?"

"I met her sister and brother-in-law last year."

Marc turned to the other girls and asked, "Do you know Vickie Johnson?"

"Yeah, she's in my math class." Another good-looking blond, where do they all come from?

"And you? Do you know her?" he directed the question at a tall brunette, also very attractive.

"No, but I've seen her around campus."

Back to the second blond, Marc asked, "What kind of student is she?"

"She's always answering questions in class. I think she's pretty smart."

"Do you know of any boyfriends?"

"Well, I'm not sure but I think she is seeing someone, but not here at school." The girl stepped back into the conversation repeating the earlier question. "Has she done something wrong?"

Marc looked intently at her and then her friend, "Why do you ask?"

"I don't know, I don't think she could do anything like kill someone."

"We are investigating the sister and just want some background on the family. Has Vickie ever talked with you about her sister?" He asked this of the first young lady.

"She was concerned about how her sister felt. She said her sister was vulnerable."

"To what?"

"You know, like emotional things, depression. Vickie told me once that she worried about how her sister would react to any kind of bad news. I think she suspected something might happen."

"Like what?"

"I'm not sure, but Vickie and her brother-in-law met occasionally. She told me they were trying to figure out how to help her sister."

"Is she capable of intrigue?"

"Like what? I know she's always thinking about stuff. I once heard her say she wanted to be rid of her family. Uh... you know... move away from them. She likes her brother and mom, but has nothing good to say about her dad. I guess he's kind of, like, mean or something. I know she's close to her brother-in-law and sister. She doesn't talk much about growing up, always thinking of the future."

"Has she ever said anything about her feelings for her brother-in-law?"

"She said he's very nice. I think she kind of likes him, if you know what I mean."

"No, what do you mean?"

"You know, if he weren't married to her sister, she might want him for a boyfriend. I know she wouldn't do anything about it, though. Well, I think she wouldn't, would she? He is good looking. I wouldn't mind going out with him."

"When you see her, tell her I said 'Hi'." Marc figured the girls would find Victoria soon after he left. He wrote their names and contact information in his notebook and excused himself. The three young ladies stood quietly as Marc left the building with a better feeling about what he theorized. After a few more inquiries, he drove back to Wendlesburg his emotions lifted. A phone message awaited him at the office. As he suspected, Victoria Johnson had been quickly informed and did not wait for an invitation.

CHAPTER 24

Victoria could wait. *The court hearing must be over,* Marc thought. He picked up the phone. Patterson had not yet returned. He left a message and hung up the receiver. *No news is good news,* supposedly. Looking through the interview with the store clerk, Marc decided to secure in his mind his earlier thought. He called the store and asked for the clerk who sold the revolver. "I want to be sure of the details of the sale," he stated. "Are you available right now?" Listening, he nodded at the invisible speaker. "I'll be right over." He did not hesitate to think an alternative idea about the acquisition of the fateful weapon.

Marc scanned the parking lot for cameras and hoped for a state-of-the-art system within. A backup plan to support a theory could only help. He entered the store and approached the counter, recognizing the clerk whom he sought. "I want you again to identify the lady who purchased a 9 millimeter caliber revolver about a month and a half ago."

The clerk hesitated remembering the beautiful blond who came to him on two occasions. "I gave that information to an officer last week."

"I know. I would like for you to look at these photographs and tell me which one is the lady who bought the gun." Marc placed the pictures on the counter. The clerk looked at them and then Marc with a perplexed countenance.

"Is this some kind of joke? They're the same lady, well, except in this picture she looks younger."

"Please, humor me, which one bought the gun?" Marc scanned the store and observed the cameras for which he hoped.

"Well, I guess I'd have to say this one. But if they are of the same lady what's the difference?" Marc picked up the pictures.

"Does your security system work?"

"Yeah."

"I'd like to see the archive of the date this lady purchased the gun. Do you still have it?"

"We keep the hard drive archived for a year." The clerk stepped away from the counter and retrieved his manager. "This is my store manager, Bob Crotchet."

"My clerk says you would like to see our security log."

"Thank you, I would. I'm investigating a shooting with a gun purchased here about a month ago. I would like to observe the time frame in which a young lady came to the store and made that purchase."

"Sure, come with me."

"How long do you retain sales receipts?" Marc prayed for a miracle.

"We send them to corporate each day for the accounting and auditing. Do you want something in particular?"

"Well, if I could obtain a sales receipt with a signature of the lady in question, it would be very beneficial to my investigation."

"I'll check our sales records to see how the purchase transpired." The two men made their way into a back room near the offices. Monitors clearly displayed the various parts of the store. The system indeed recorded to a hard drive and the digital display was excellent. No loss of magnetic imaging here as encountered often with VCR tape overly used by cheapskates.

The manager explained to Marc how the system worked, calling on another person to work with him to find the period of time in question. He then left the room to retrieve the requested information. Marc and the technician watched the retrieval proceed on a monitor separate from the others. "We can move forward and backward as needed, enhance particular frames, and print." He paused his conversing. "Ah, here we are. This angle is the lady entering the store. Not much to see with that hat she's wearing. Nice shape, though." They watched as she moved about the aisles appearing to shop. Then she approached the counter.

"Do you have audio?"

"No, most systems don't because of the complexity. Here's a better angle to see her face." Marc watched the lady as she inspected several handguns. It seemed to him she was aware of the camera's intrusion and made an effort not to be seen, not always successfully.

"Wait, go back about 5 seconds. Yeah, right there. Can you enlarge her face and enhance the picture? It's not the best look at her but I think it will work just fine." The tech completed the request and handed the print to Marc. "I would like a copy of this time frame on disk, please." The tech made a copy on a CD and gave it to him. "Thank you very much. You have been very helpful" Marc thanked the manager who expressed disappointment about not having a signature receipt. Marc left the store and decided to find the mall office and another state-of-the-art security system. Lady Luck played a cruel game, no system.

Returning to the office, he found a message from Patterson. No go on the early medical records. Well, a setback offset by a revelation. Patterson certainly could use some good news. He picked up the phone and dialed. "I have something that may be of interest to you." Pause. "Yes, I'll come right over."

"What a find. What made you think she might have been the one to buy the gun?"

"The third set of prints. We need to get hers and compare them to those unknowns. I still need to get a handwriting sample, but the clerk certainly wasn't as sure a second time around."

"Did the clerk know about the pictures you showed him?"

"I simply placed them on the counter and asked for him to pick out the lady who bought the gun. He thought they were all the same lady. It confused him at first. But he picked this one as the purchaser." Marc held up the yearbook picture of Victoria. The other pictures of Mary's high school senior photograph and individual family shots of the girls rounded out the montage.

"What photo had he been shown before?"

"The morgue shot. Not Mary's finest moment."

"Well, let's get her in here to explain."

"I also went through the security archive they have at the store and we printed this image of Victoria. Although, it's less than ideal, we can use it to press for a confession." The picture could have been of either sister. The clothing looked more like a younger person's apparel.

Patterson punched a button on his phone. "Monica, get in here. We have more info." He punched another button. "Call Seattle police for me, and then call Victoria Johnson, please." He picked up the three images of Victoria, studied them and then studied Mary's pictures. "Sure easy to confuse these two isn't it?" Monica entered the room. Marc noticed the change of appearance immediately, shorter hair and shorter skirt. Nice legs were still dressed in a professional suit. "We have Victoria buying the gun that killed her sister. What do you think about that?"

"Well, that certainly changes things, but it doesn't mean she shot her. We have no evidence of her being anywhere near the scene."

"True, but what if she and Roger were in cahoots?" Duncan smiled.

"I'll get right on that angle."

"No, I'm having Seattle pick her up and hold her. We'll go over and question her regarding this. Let's get going as soon as I hear from Seattle police."

The intercom clicked on and a receptionist said, "I have Seattle on line 2. Miss Johnson is on line 3."

"Thanks." Duncan picked up the receiver and pushed a button. "This is Duncan Patterson in Wendlesburg. I'm an assistant DA, and I need to have an officer sent to pick up a person of interest in a case over here." He gave the address to the other end of the line, said his thanks, and punched another button. "Hello, Miss

Johnson, Duncan Patterson in Wendlesburg. I need to speak with you about your sister. Are you at home right now?" He waited for a response. "Good, please stay there. A Seattle police officer is on the way to escort you to the precinct office nearest you. I will be there within the hour." He listened again. "No, there is no need to worry. We're just wrapping up our investigation." He paused again. "I know. He's here with me now. There is nothing to worry about." More listening occurred. "I know, it does seem strange, but I assure you that we are coming to conclusion." He listened for a while. "Thank you, we are on our way." He packed up materials, got his coat and the three intrepid legal hounds left to seek clarity.

The drive was brisk and the conversation centered on Victoria and Roger. Mary's ghost probably haunted the two of them for what they had been doing. The facts were coming together with increasing speed and it would be only a matter of time before this all fell into place. "I think Roger wanted out of his marriage," Marc said.

"He certainly looks guilty," Monica replied.

"Well, Victoria probably bought the gun so Roger could off her." They continued talking until their arrival at the Seattle precinct office. Marc parked the car and they exited to uncover the next intricacy of the case.

Patterson introduced himself to the desk sergeant who directed them to another part of the station. An officer met them and led them to an interrogation room where they found Victoria waiting. She stood as they entered. "What's this all about?" The worried countenance revealed an aura of confusion. "Why am I being rousted like some kind of criminal?"

"All is well, Miss Johnson. Please have a seat. We need to ask you a few questions about your sister's gun purchase, that's all." Her face bleached white as she understood what was transpiring. "What do you know about her buying the gun?" Marc placed a glass of water next to Victoria.

"I ... I don't know what you mean? She bought the gun for security. Isn't that why people arm themselves?"

"From whom did she need security?" Patterson pressed the issue.

"I don't know. Maybe she thought the neighborhood was not as safe as she wanted it to be."

"Did she need security from Roger?"

"Why would you ask that? Roger loved her and took great care of her. He really wanted her to be safe and healthy and … and why are you asking me this? Does this have to do with … ah…you know… ah …your belief that we had an affair?" Victoria dropped her eyes and then looked at Patterson as if guilty of "swallowing" the proverbial canary. She drank from the glass.

"Something like that. We don't know if she feared Roger or even you. We do know that the gun purchase is very interesting. Would you care to clarify it for us?" Victoria's face now reddened.

"I don't know how I can clarify it for you." She spoke slowly and deliberately.

"The clerk at the store where the gun was purchased was pretty sure the young lady who purchased the gun was the same lady he picked out of a montage of photos shown to him recently." Patterson placed the chosen picture on the table. "The picture was you, Miss Johnson. Would you be able to clarify it for us, now?" Patterson glared at her.

Victoria returned the glare spitting daggers from her eyes. She hesitated for a moment, breathing deeply. "What, you think I bought the gun for my sister so she could shoot herself? Are you crazy or do you get off on accusing people of things they haven't done?" She stood and moved to the window/mirror. Turning she raged on, "I loved my sister and I can't stand here and listen to you accuse me of wanting to help her kill herself."

"I have not accused you of anything. But unless I get some very credible answers to my questions, I might decide to charge you with filing a false report or impersonating someone and forging their name on an official document. For all I know, you and Roger have staged this whole thing and are planning to run away together. Did you know he had life insurance on her and will be able to collect as long as he didn't kill her?" Patterson had moved close to her.

"I think I need a lawyer."

"That certainly may be true. And when you do please explain to him why you were involved with your brother-in-law and bought a gun that killed your sister. I'm sure he will have a wonderful laugh at your expense. He can then advise you on the latest prison haute couture. I'm sure Roger will wait for you even as you turn forty or fifty before you get out. By the way, were you present when your sister died?"

"What? No! I found out about the shooting when Mom called me at home." Victoria sat down again. "Alright, I bought the gun. But Mary asked me to because she didn't want Roger to know about it. I took her ID and cash she gave me and I bought the gun. I waited the required time period and went back to get it." She faced Marc. "You know how it is, don't you? You want to help but it all turns out wrong." Marc shook his head from side to side. "Did Roger really kill my sister?"

"I'm beginning to think that you were in on the plan all along. Maybe you even fabricated it all by yourself. How did you ever convince Roger to go along with this scheme?"

"Are you charging me with murder?" Victoria rose again and moved toward the door. "I'm leaving now and I don't ever want to see you again."

"Wait. I just need to understand why Mary felt compelled to have a gun in her possession. Her life didn't seem so bad."

"You think her life was good? She had a husband who didn't love her anymore, two children she didn't know how to raise, and a family that didn't want her around. Well, except for me of course."

"Of course, and you still loved her but wanted to sleep with her husband. Maybe you wanted her husband for yourself and figured she could commit suicide and that would be that. Did you encourage her to end it all?"

"You're mean. No, I didn't encourage her at all." Victoria opened the door. "She decided on her own to do it. And you have no evidence of any affair." The door closed loudly as she left.

Marc moved to the door, "Shall I stop her?"

"No, let her go. I have someone tailing her to see what she does." Patterson turned to Monica, "Make sure to have her whereabouts verified for that Sunday. If she's lying about being with her sister, I want to know about it." Turning to Marc, he said, "Marc, find out how she and Roger communicate with each other without using their own phones. Get their phone records out and scan them with a fine tooth comb. We're missing something." He packed his valise to go, then hesitated, "Marc, get a search warrant issued for Miss Johnson's place. Maybe she has something of interest in the apartment."

Monica made a note in her notebook and said, "Mary's death makes it somewhat easier for Mr. Waite and that little bimbo. I really think we can convict him."

"Let's not get hasty. The timeline is really tight, but if Miss Johnson was at the house that morning, she may be the key that unlocks this case."

Marc picked up the glass with a paper towel. "I'll get this printed right away."

The three sleuths felt good about the information they had compelled from Victoria. It didn't mean a conspiracy was afoot, but the intrigue of this family's dynamics certainly increased. Who else was a part of the master plan? Another day finished and more twists than a New York pretzel. Monica effused enthusiasm for convicting Roger, or did Victoria really commit this heinous crime?

CHAPTER 25

arc sealed the glass in an evidence bag and carried it to
a Seattle crime lab for processing. Monica decided to
stay in Seattle with Marc while he attained the warrant.
Analysis of the fingerprints would be available on the morrow.
Comparison to the unknown prints on the gun and around the
Waite's house might prove Victoria's presence when Mary died.
It was becoming clear to Marc that Roger was not the trigger man.
His morning timeline provided little or no room for the ability to
clean up after shooting his wife. He had to have come home to
discover what Victoria refused to admit. Now the case needed a
motive for murder by the sister and what better one than the age
old one of jealousy.

Marc clicked on his laptop and began a search of types of
communications devices other than cell phones that had range
enough for use between Seattle and Wendlesburg. Although the
distance was not more than 20 miles by straight line direction, he
uncovered only a few walkie-talkie devices. Other than using pre-
paid cell phones which are difficult, but not impossible, to trace,

a walkie-talkie provided more security because of the range of channels which were free. Marc surmised that these conspirators used some kind of high end, long range handheld transmitter. Amazon sold them for less than $100.

He picked up his phone and called the one judge in Seattle he anticipated would accept an explanation as feeble as the one he was about to provide. But a search of Victoria's apartment for communications only was not a total loss. Motive was the bigger problem for convicting the young beautiful siren who must have compelled Roger into a situation as untenable as he must have found himself embroiled. Roger, who knew what his mistress had done, who then had to reconstruct a scene of suicide to protect her, who was ready to face the consequences of murder if his scheme failed, now was more conflicted than ever. Marc presumed Roger's children would need years of therapy to understand how three people they were supposed to trust could be so messed up. These two children would feel the abandonment of parents and possible rejection by other family members, overburdened with raising them.

Marc was not going to let this happen to his family. Joan was correct; he needed to heed the separation from his children and wife because of his drive to crush criminal activity. Crime invaded families without direct contact when one became an officer of the law.

Having explained the need for a warrant to the judge's clerk, he was connected. Fortunately, a lull in court proceedings made the judge available for a conversation. "Good morning, Mr. Jefferson. What can I do to aid your battle with nefarious individuals?" he heard the judge say.

"Sir, I would like to have a warrant issued to search one Victoria Johnson's apartment in Seattle. She is the sister of Mary Waite, who died a week ago on Sunday in Wendlesburg. We believe she was present in the house when her sister was shot. The husband is the current suspect, but it appears that he is covering for someone. We believe that someone to be this younger sister with whom we suspect he's having an affair. Assistant District Attorney Duncan Patterson wants to uncover how they

are communicating with each other without the use of cell phones since we find no records of cell phone use."

Marc listened as the judge questioned the fairness for a search. In the end one was granted, and as anticipated, it was limited to communications only. He could send an officer to pick it up within the hour. Marc called Patterson to apprise him of the issuance. "Good work, Marc. Monica is to accompany you for legal situations which might arise. I don't want evidence compromised if anything else surfaces outside the warrant."

Marc said, "I'll retrieve the document and we can head out as soon as possible."

A Seattle patrol officer left for the judge's office to get the warrant once it was issued. Monica and Marc waited in the office where they had interviewed Victoria. Upon the officer's return, Marc said, "We are looking for communication devices. Let's move it. We're burning daylight." The troop of investigators departed for Victoria's apartment in Seattle with the interagency warrant. Seattle police would meet them to help oversee the work. The drive took less time than expected.

"Is Victoria going to be present while we search?" Monica asked, although she was sure she would be.

"As far as I know she'll be there. She left this office after we spoke with her. Seattle will keep her at bay so we can do our work."

At the scene the crew delivered the warrant to Victoria and entered her residence. As expected, Seattle police kept unwanted intruders out, including the renter of the apartment. Marc approached Victoria, "We would like to make this as easy as possible, Miss Johnson. Specifically, we are looking for any communication devices you have to contact Roger without creating a record. Do you have anything of this kind in your possession?"

Tears welled up in Victoria's eyes. "Roger gave me a walkie-talkie with a long range so we could talk. It's in my bedroom in my dresser's bottom drawer. I'm sorry, Mr. Jefferson, I didn't mean to cause so much trouble." She moved to embrace him, but he prohibited her advance, seizing her shoulders, glaring into her moist expression.

"Miss Johnson, you are very attractive, and I do appreciate your beauty, but your seductive nature will not influence me. You and Mr. Waite have involved yourselves in an unscrupulous affair. It appears you did not love your sister as much as would be deemed appropriate. You are in deep and dangerous waters. Seattle Police are going to detain you this evening until Mr. Patterson decides what to do with you." Marc removed his hands and stepped back. A Seattle officer led her to a squad car for transport to the downtown headquarters. "Please think about what has happened and tell the truth about your involvement."

"She didn't want to live any more. Did you know that? I miss her so much. Can you understand what happened? I know Roger didn't kill her. I'm not sure why she wanted to die. I know we wanted to get her help, but I guess we were too late." Victoria cried a truthful cry for what Marc considered to be the first time. "Who's going to raise my niece and nephew if Roger goes to jail for something he didn't do?" The officer placed her in the car and closed the door.

Marc entered the apartment building moving directly to the room containing the dresser. He found what he wanted. Frustrated with family degeneracy, he preferred to toss it across the room. Instead he gave the item to Wilkins, "Here, bag this," and departed.

Monica approached him, "What's with you?"

"Have you never experienced frustration before? I guess it might be hard for you to understand, but this is a mess." After sealing the apartment as a crime scene, the two of them, with evidence in hand, returned to Wendlesburg. Another day of research ended, but how was Joan going to react to another late return home? He braced himself for another unpleasant encounter with a wife he knew was justified in her growing displeasure with his obsessive fixation on proving a suicide had not occurred.

CHAPTER 26

After reclaiming Victoria from the Seattle police, Monica and Marc returned to Wendlesburg and deposited her in the county lockup for the evening. Patterson had contacted Monica about possibly filing charges of obstruction, hence the need to detain her a day or two. Marc returned to his house not wanting to be confronted with the lateness of the day.

He sat for his usual moment in the garage and bolstered enough courage to face the onslaught. As he entered the kitchen, an aroma of Italian cooking penetrated his brooding emotional muddle. Nobody entered the kitchen to greet him and a quick scan uncovered no remnants of the aromatic meal which must have been served. He walked into the family room and found his children watching the latest version of a talent search. "Where's your mother?" he asked. The countenance of three young faces spoke volumes as if of doomsday tomes written by so many authors over the years.

Marc Junior replied first, "She's upstairs." He looked like he wanted to say more but hesitated.

Sarah finished his unspoken message. "She's not very happy with you right now."

Marc nodded an acknowledgment and said, "I'm sorry I'm so late, but I guess you had a nice dinner." Three sets of eyes glanced back and forth to each other and then to their father.

"Mom says you're on your own for dinner." Sarah responded. She returned her attention to the television and Marc left the room more sullen than when he entered. He hung his coat in the closet and ascended the stairs to face disappointment once again.

"Joan," he said as he entered his bedroom, "I'm sorry about being late." He found her sitting on the edge of the bed with her back to him. She stood when he spoke. As she turned her green eyes streaked with mascara displayed the disappointment which he knew he initiated. "I'm so sorry," he restated.

"Why do you even bother?" Joan said. "You don't even call to say you'll be late. It seems to me that you take us for granted, that you know we'll be here regardless of what happens in your life. I want more from you than you seem willing to give. Am I so unimportant to you that I don't even rate a phone call?" She whispered her tirade, Marc supposing that she did not want prying ears to hear a fight. He closed the door and moved toward her. "No, I don't want you to touch me right now. I'm angry."

"What can I do to make it up to you, then?" he said. "I have to do my job, but I know I should have called while I was in Seattle. We were running late and I had business to finish before coming home." Then Marc defended himself and regretted his next comment. "Look, am I to report to you everything I do so you can keep tabs on me? I don't question what you do."

"No, but I need to know that you still care for me more than your job. What's your priority? Me and the kids or solving this stupid crime?"

"You're right. This particular case has befuddled me more than I anticipated. Each time I feel good about the evidence trail, I end up changing course. It's taking more time than I had figured it would. Please forgive me. I do love you and you and the children are more important than any criminal case, but they do need to be solved. I can let Tom take more of the frontline if that will help us."

"I'm not asking you to give up solving crimes. I just want to know where I stand in your life." Joan slipped out of her nursing uniform and continued. "Am I still a desirable person or does that young Johnson girl hold your attention now?" Marc smiled and then clasped Joan's hands in his.

"Victoria Johnson can captivate other men, but she's a suspect to me. You are my life and I only want you." He attempted a hug and felt the initial resistance but her acceptance was the reality for him. He relaxed and kissed her neck.

Joan then pushed away. "I didn't save you any spaghetti, but there's garlic bread in the fridge. I wasn't sure when you were coming home and I was mad at you."

"I deserve that. I'm not very hungry now anyway." He hoped his empty stomach would not betray him. "What I need right now is sleep. Tomorrow, we question that vixen you should not be jealous of because she has more involvement than previously thought." He prepared for bed and then decided that garlic bread could help him sleep more peacefully.

Joan followed him downstairs. As they entered the family room the children looked apprehensive as though a gloom of doom had entered. Sarah asked, "Are you two going to get a divorce?"

In unison Marc and Joan retorted, "No!"

"Get ready for bed and we'll come up and say goodnight," Marc said as he disappeared into the kitchen. He found some salad leftovers and the bread, which he removed from the refrigerator. Joan opened a cupboard and got him a plate. He picked a clean glass out of the dishwasher and poured wine which he offered to Joan. She accepted and he took another glass out and filled it. They sat quietly while he ate his meager ration. "I guess I was hungry after all," he said when he finished. He put his dishes in the sink.

The evening time approached ten-thirty which Marc recognized as a probable cause for Joan's anger. He had not comprehended the lateness of his return home. "Joan, time got away from me today. I must be more careful about squandering our time together because of this case. I don't think much is left, but I think it best to keep you apprised of what's transpiring." She wrapped her arm in his as they climbed the stairs to say goodnight to their children and to sleep a more peaceful night than originally anticipated by Marc. At least he hoped it would be.

CHAPTER 27

"Marc," Joan said. "I realize you have a job to do. I realize your schedule is not as cut and dried as mine." They had tucked in the three children and were changing for bed. "But if you cannot place some emphasis in your life for us… for me, I don't know what's going to happen."

"I'm sorry." Marc looked at Joan begging for compassion and expecting none. "I guess a phone call home could help, if I'm going to be later than expected."

"It's not just a phone call. I don't feel you're here when you are home. Is this Johnson girl so enticing that you forget about me?"

Marc moved closer to Joan and reached out to hold her hands. "No one can replace you in my life. I think she killed her sister and I can't find enough evidence yet to convict her." He raised her hands and kissed them. "I love you and if something comes up to upset our timeline together, I'll call." The atmosphere wasn't any warmer as they climbed into bed. Sleep for Marc was evasive at best.

As morning arrived, Marc finally passed into Morpheus's arms only to be rudely snatched back by an incessant buzzing. He reached out to the bedside table and slapped the alarm clock button. Looking toward his wife's side of the bed, he discovered it empty.

The annoying clock read 6:32, so Marc arose and did his normal routine for morning.

"Do you ever sleep?" He asked when he entered the kitchen. Joan often awoke earlier than others in the household. He sat at the kitchen table as Joan placed a mug of coffee near him, but he received no answer to his inquiry. Sarah and James wandered in shortly after. "Where's your brother?" he directed his question to his youngest who shared bedroom space with Marc Junior.

"He's in the bathroom," James answered.

Joan then said, "Would one of you get the newspaper, please." She directed the question to both children knowing neither wanted to get it. Sarah shrugged her shoulders and left the room. James sat in his usual seat. "I am not a slave in this house. You can get your own cereal." James rose from the spot and opened the pantry looking for his Cheerios. Marc wondered if Joan's snippiness had something to do with yesterday. He rose from his seat and got bowls out of the cupboard, spoons from the drawer, and milk from the refrigerator.

Joan continued with lunch preparations for her three students. School lunches did not provide the correct dietary needs she insisted the children have. Marc was beyond help when it came to lunch, and although she often fixed something for him, nothing was forthcoming that he could see. Marc Junior entered the room as Sarah came in with the paper.

With juice poured and cereals gathered, the family ate silently, each person fearing any word which could ignite the tinderbox that permeated the atmosphere. After breakfast the children placed dishes in the dishwasher and cleared the cereal boxes from the table. Marc sat and watched Joan wipe the counters. "Are you still mad at me?" he asked.

"No, disappointed." She turned toward him. "How will this day end? Will you call or do we just guess?" She stared at him awaiting an answer.

Marc felt most vulnerable whenever he messed with family expectations. She knew his life was frenzied because of criminal pursuits, and he understood her current anger for not including her in his timeline. Telling her about the case might help, but was not the usual order of conversation. Still he needed to keep her in the loop, so to speak.

"I'll call you and let you know." He kissed her cheek, her only offering, and left for the office.

* * *

Friday found Patterson eager for a fight. "Roger must have a walkie-talkie too. Find it." Marc arrived at Duncan's office when he received the message at home. "That guy is going to sing a new song with that little piece of evidence in the fold."

"We did not find it at his home, so it has to be at his place of business. We haven't searched it, yet."

"Another warrant! Our judges are going to think we've gone crazy. Alright, get right on it. I'll have Monica accompany you like last night so that we can keep everything neat. That girl is amazing."

"Are you and she…" Marc hesitated.

"What makes you ask that?" He cut Marc off.

Marc smiled, "I've observed a few things, lately."

"We've had a few drinks together, nothing more. I'm a bit older than she if you hadn't noticed." Patterson smirked. "Back to our business, though. Find the other walkie-talkie. Bail hearing is scheduled for Monday. Victoria Johnson has been transferred to our custody. She's downstairs. Let's have a talk with her about their communications over the last few weeks. I think they planned everything, right down to Mary's death." He moved from behind his desk. Marc rose from the chair in which he sat and the two of them left to ask pointed questions of the little vixen.

* * *

"Miss Johnson, I hope your accommodations have been satisfactory." Victoria sneered. "Have you contacted anyone?" Patterson knew the answer.

"I called Jeff Woodbury. He'll be here soon."

"We'll wait for him. Meanwhile, I want to talk to you and you listen." Patterson sat in a chair on the opposite side of the table. Marc sat next to him. "I have worked to prosecute criminals for twenty years. Some have been easily identifiable; some have been a challenge. As I worked to convict each and every one of them, I knew the evidence had to be conclusive. I realized that only by having all of the information could I get the conviction needed. But in all my years of convicting people for their nefarious activities, I have never come across two people who have so confounded their lives more than you and Roger. You have cheated on your sister with her husband, lied about purchasing a gun, kept information hidden, and now I discover you've continued communications when you have stated the affair is over. Roger has lied about you, his relationship with his wife, and many other things. I want you to understand something very clearly. If Roger did not actually kill your sister, I believe you and he conspired to drive her to this so called suicide. You're not an innocent youth. You're a conniving wench who wants all for herself. If I can't get Roger for the crime of killing his wife, then I will come after you. When your attorney arrives, please have him explain what is going to happen." Patterson stood up and moved to the door. Marc followed. "Remember what I said."

Outside of the room Marc and Duncan saw Jeff Woodbury coming toward them. "Are you two out of your minds?" He fumed. "First you arrest an innocent man, and now you interrogate a young lady without me present and with nothing to hide." He entered the room without asking. Duncan and Marc followed him in, but he turned and said, "I want to speak with my client without you. Get out!" They nodded and left the room.

As the door closed, Duncan asked, "Do you think he's uptight?"

"Maybe a little." Marc responded. They sat in a couple of chairs waiting their turn for questioning. "I think he's feeling in over his head. These two people created a complex, almost impossible, situation and set it into motion." They sat silently until Woodbury came out.

"You threatened my client?" Woodberry screamed. "What are you up to? They are not guilty of any crime, and you want to prosecute them?" He was still fuming.

"Yeah, it kind of looks like that." Patterson stood as Woodbury raged. "Let's talk in here." He opened the door to the interrogation room containing Victoria and entered. Woodbury and Jefferson followed. "Miss Johnson, I do hope you and Mr. Woodbury had a pleasant talk. I would like you to explain to me, with Mr. Woodbury present, why you purchased a gun for your sister, lied about your communications with Mr. Waite, and conspired to have your sister killed."

Victoria looked at the three men, pleading with her eyes. "I don't think I should say anything."

"Well, in that case, Mr. Jefferson, arrest her for filing a false document."

"Just a minute," Woodbury intoned. "What do you have in mind?"

"I want the truth. I want Miss Johnson to tell me the truth."

"Go ahead, tell them about the walkie-talkies." Addressing Patterson, "She did not conspire to kill her sister. The gun purchase was done at Mary's request."

"But why did you comply with such a strange request?"

"My sister feared Roger. She said he threatened to hurt her if she didn't just leave. She wanted to leave but not without her children. Roger came at her with a knife. When she told me about what was happening, I felt I had to help her. After all, she is … was my sister. As for the walkie-talkies, Roger and I haven't used them for the last eight days."

"What did you use them for?"

Like you said before, we wanted to communicate without leaving a record. We set up a schedule of times to call each other."

"How long have you had these radios?"

"Roger bought them soon after we began meeting. He figured we could set up our rendezvous, and no one would be suspicious. It worked, too."

179

"Did you use them the day of the shooting?"

"You don't have to answer that," Woodbury said.

"It's okay. No, he called my parents and they called me, just like I told you. I'm not lying about that."

"Oh, so you are lying about other things?" Tears formed in Victoria's eyes.

"Alright, I've lied to you. I didn't want anything to happen to my sister, but things were getting very bad. She was getting worse and Roger suffered because of it. I love Roger very much, and now I think nothing can come of it. I don't think Roger shot her, but I can see why you think it."

"So does this mean you are confessing to having an affair with Roger?"

"You still harp on that piece of tabloid shit? No, I did not have an affair with Roger."

'Strange. He confessed to having one with you. Now why would he do that?"

"I knew he wanted me. He told me how much he loved me and that we would be better off together, but I told him I wouldn't break up his marriage to my sister just so he could fuck me. If he told you we were involved, he's living in a fantasy world of his own creation."

"Miss Johnson, I do sympathize with your position. But you can't hide the truth or I will prosecute you for any number of things."

"Are you charging my client with any crime?" Woodbury asked.

"Not today, but Miss Johnson, don't leave home without first letting me know where you're going. It 'll look bad if I think you are trying to run away." Woodbury and Victoria stood and left. Patterson looked at Marc. "That little bitch, she's still lying. She has to have been sleeping with her brother-in-law, and that's motive enough for me to think she's the shooter."

CHAPTER 28

As Marc returned to his office, he clicked on his cell phone to attain the warrant for Roger Waite's real estate office. Although a warrant could have been issued earlier in the week, a simple suicide hadn't justified it. Now the case was on a collision course with some of the biggest crimes Marc had studied in his college psychology classes about illicit behaviors. He thought of Joan and how another weekend could be lost if he didn't get what he needed from Roger's office. He knew he should spend as much time with this family and quell the storm brewing at home.

After a brief conversation with an assistant in the judge's office, he hung up. Had he given enough reason so the assistant could convince the judge to issue a warrant? Only time would tell. An afternoon search was not guaranteed.

Investigating Roger's recent history had not revealed his early years as a college student. Each report only illuminated his married life with Mary. What was his life like before marrying her? Who was he as a teenager? Had he met his wife in college?

"Tom, do we have anything on Roger Waite before he got married?" Marc asked his partner.

Tom shuffled through some files on his desk. "I don't see anything here."

Marc frowned. "Let's find out where he went to school and see if he met Mary Johnson there."

"I can call the family and ask," Tom said.

"Do that, in the meantime I'm going to talk with Mrs. Johnson again about her daughter's college career."

The conversations of both detectives filled in information lacking from their investigation about the young couple's start down the road to marital bliss or in this case, death. However, Marc felt something was lacking from the discussion about their findings.

"I may have found something useful to our case." Tom said. "He had other girlfriends at WSU before Mary. But his mother wasn't very enlightened about who they were or how he conducted himself with them. I think it might be worthwhile to try and contact some of his former companions, if we can, to see how he behaved with them."

"Sounds good, you see what you can dig up. Mrs. Johnson claims Mary didn't date in college until she met Roger. I'll bet her sister knows more about this than she has let on. I don't really want to, but I need to speak with her again about what happened in the years before Roger." He picked up his phone and dialed the cell number now lodged in his head. Victoria answered almost immediately. Marc signaled Tom to connect with the conversation.

"Miss Johnson, this is Marc Jefferson. I am sorry to bother you again, but I have some questions about Mary's college life."

Tom muffled a snicker when he heard her response. "Great, can't you leave me alone or are you so in love with seeing me that you just can't stand being away from me. I already told you I'm not sleeping with Roger."

Marc grimaced at Tom. "No, this call is about when Mary was in college."

"What do you want to know?"

"How long had Mary known Roger before they decided to get married?"

"A few months, I guess. She hadn't gone out with anyone else, but decided she must chance it."

"What do you mean?" Marc frowned as Tom noted what she said.

"Well, she was afraid of intimacy … you know… because of what my father had done to her. She didn't feel ready." A pause which Marc refrained from filling, Victoria continued. "Mary saw him on campus and decided enough was enough. She introduced herself and they started dating."

"Did your sister ever tell you how she … did in this … dating?"

"You sound cryptic. Why don't you just say what you want from me?"

Marc smile at Tom. "Alright, how soon did she become ready to fix her fear of intimacy?"

"When did they start having sex? Is that what you want to know? Remember, I was barely thirteen at the time. Or are you some kind of pervert?"

"No, but it might help to understand whether Roger was interested in just having sex or whether he fell hard for your sister."

"Mary told me he was a perfect gentleman with her, which surprised her because of his reputation." Marc nodded at Tom who reciprocated. Victoria continued, "She said she wanted to get over her fear of closeness and basically seduced him."

"So you sister was more interested in a sexual liaison than becoming Mrs. Roger Waite."

"I guess. But he fell for her and they decided to get married. I had never seen my sister so happy."

"When did you fall for him?"

"You're incorrigible, you know that." Marc let the comment slide. "I didn't fall for him, but I was intrigued by him because he so enthralled Mary, and I wanted to know why. Who was this man who stopped all of his philandering and became a one woman man?"

"Until he wanted you. Or was it you wanted him?"

Marc could almost feel the heat of her blush through the phone. "I am not having an affair with Roger. Why do you think I am?"

"Miss Johnson, was Roger dating anyone else when he met Mary?"

"I don't think so." She pauses a moment. "But there was one girl who didn't like Roger hooking up with my sister. I guess there were some threats, or at least, that's what Mary told me."

"Do you know who this person was? Do you have a name?"

"No, I just know she approached Mary and said she couldn't have Roger. She told her that Roger was cheating on her or something like that. They broke up for a while."

Mary and Roger broke up?"

"Yeah, but not for long."

"So this young woman still wanted Roger for herself." Marc did not direct the statement at Victoria. "Thank you, Miss Johnson." He clicked off the conversation as did Tom. "So maybe Roger's affair was directed at someone else. He just said it was Victoria to throw us off."

Tom, you investigate whether Victoria really was home on that Sunday. I'll find out about this other girl and any others he dated. Roger might have reignited an old flame for fun and games. I wonder how Victoria liked having competition for his affection." Tom nodded agreement and left the office.

CHAPTER 29

"Nothing's going to surprise me," Marc thought aloud. He contacted the registrar's office at Washington State University asking about Roger's educational career. The office secretary put him on hold while she contacted someone who could help.

The tawdry elevator music prodded his memory of college days and how he acted toward women. Although he didn't feel he had created a reputation, he knew he had broken a couple of hearts. He wondered about them, but Joan had captivated him at a sorority dance and they dated for a while. He graduated and left school to find work, not fully comprehending she was a prize waiting to be accepted.

She was the daughter of a Wendlesburg political leader and business owner and two years younger. She graduated and started work for Doctor Zachariah Thomas in Wendlesburg. He met her again after being injured in a car chase that ended badly.

While the injuries were minor and Doctor Thomas happened upon the scene accidentally, Marc thought the nurse accompanying the doctor looked familiar. The long dark, wavy hair had been cut and the stylish glasses had been removed, but the same well shaped body could not be hidden by the scrubs she wore. The same radiant beauty still flashed that same endearing smile. He asked for a number by which she could be contacted and she stated she was dating and was not necessarily interested. Marc was disappointed but kept regular appointments with the doctor as a safe precautionary move.

Joan and her boyfriend broke off their relationship a year later and Marc pounced like a cat waiting for a mouse. He never regretted waiting because he somehow knew in his heart; Joan was to be his wife. He had been there when she needed help with a burglary. He had given her a couple of cautionary warnings about automobile speed in the city. He described for her how to protect her home from intruders. As much as the other guy had been around, he seemed to be around even more. Finally, Joan just gave up and started seeing him. They married a year and a half later. The rest, as they say, is history.

A voice returned him to reality. He explained who he was and what he needed from the university. He expected to receive the information in the coming week, but a quick computer search by the voice on the line retrieved what he wanted. Printing and a fax machine had the information in Marc's hands within a few minutes. Marc thanked the person for the prompt reply to his request and hung up the phone. He mused about the quickness of data retrieval in today's world and wondered if his information had been digitized as well.

He checked the time and whispered, "Shit." He pulled out his cell phone and called home. *Better late than never.* He explained his predicament to Joan and hoped for a reasonable response. He promised to arrive within the hour. He could bring some work home with him, not the usual procedure.

Roger's application to school, yearly courses taken, grades, and class standing were quickly perused and set aside. The next report sparked a curious interest, a complaint issued through the campus police department against him. Although nothing had happened to forestall a successful graduation, the timing of the event sure did pique his interest. A new trail opened before him and he knew not where it might lead.

He packed up the material he wanted to study at home over the weekend and left the office. So Victoria was correct about Roger's history. The name of the petitioner surprised him, but he now had another possible motive. Just how did this person fit into the equation, he had yet to figure out.

Arriving at home he broke his 'waiting in the garage' pattern and entered his house, not wanting to be any later. Joan smiled as he entered the kitchen. His children, sitting at the table for dinner, chimed in with 'hello' and 'dad'. He placed his work on a side table and joined them.

After dinner, he helped with clearing and cleaning the dishes. He knew Joan still held some animosity, but she appreciated the gesture by kissing him, caressing his hair, and running hands down his back enticing closeness lost since that Sunday tragedy. He mentally promised himself not to wander so deeply into a case again. A call to Pullman would wait until the morning. Another motivation swelled within him. As important as his career was, Joan and his children trumped it. When finished with the kitchen, he guided his wife past the children in the family room, up the stairs to their bedroom. He closed the door and faced Joan.

"I had a breakthrough today, which I need to investigate, but not tonight. I think I can wrap this case up in the next couple of weeks." He clasped her hands and sat her on the bed. She leaned into him and kissed his lips again. "I love you," he said. She released from his hold and began loosening his clothing. Mesmerized by her action, he stared at her with passion. Joan then began a slow strip-tease, unbuttoning her uniform and letting it fall lightly to the floor. She reached behind her back to unhook her bra. She then held the cups taunting her husband who removed his shirt and tie as he stood.

She relinquished the hold on her bra freeing her firm breasts from the enclosure endured for the last few hours. Gravity had yet to win its relentless battle. Marc placed one hand under her left breast and pressed his lips over the nipple. The response from it and Joan encouraged his oral fondling. Joan grabbed his hair encouraging a continuance of the kissing. He moved his head over the right breast and repeated his motions. Joan rocked her head backward and sighed. Her hands left his hair and slid down his back. She felt each muscle flexion as his hands explored her intimate parts …

Sleep came easily this night. His call to Pullman in the morning might divulge information which could ruin a career because of whose name he uncovered this afternoon.

CHAPTER 30

Marc awoke before Joan and watched her sleep. The rise and fall of her chest aroused him and he kissed her awake. "Good morning, sunshine. I hope you slept well." He brushed across her fit stomach and slid closer to her. Joan felt the passion of his penis and reached for it.

"You're a horny little bastard." She said as she massaged his erection. He kissed her lips and began fondling her breasts. "Make it a 'quickie'. I think our children might be rising soon." Marc rotated his body so his face met her privates. The taste from the previous evening aroused him more. Joan slipped her mouth over his organ. After a few seconds she pleaded for him to penetrate her. Marc rolled on to his back and Joan sat on him feeling the full pleasure of his penis as it slid slowly into her. The rhythmic motions of their bodies brought them to climax.

"I love you more than anything, Joan." They lay on the bed holding each other. "I'll get this case finished and then we can plan a trip away from here."

Joan kissed him and rose from the bed. "I hope you mean what you say." She entered the bathroom continuing her speech, "I love you, too. But I will not be ignored for the sake of your work."

Marc entered the bathroom. "Okay." he said and tapped her bottom. "A trip it is."

After dressing and eating a hearty breakfast, He bounced out of the house to retrieve the newspaper. His heart appeased, his mind clear for the moment, and a phone call to Pullman delayed. He was as relaxed as he could be. He picked up the morning paper and returned to read it. He placed it on his desk in his den and clicked open his cell phone. It buzzed before he dialed. "Shit." He clicked to answer. "Alright, but can't this wait until Monday?" he said after listening. "I'll see you in an hour, then." He clicked off and then dialed another number. The conversation was short but a visit by her set a trap.

"Tom called," he said to Joan. "He wants me to come in and see what he uncovered. I'm really sorry, but the sooner this is over the sooner we get it behind us. I'll be home as soon as possible."

Joan remained silent with a look of disgust. She turned and walked away, another Saturday ruined.

At the office, Tom approached him with a folder in hand. "I worked through most of the night, but these should interest you."

"You're single, aren't you?" Marc quipped, knowing the truth. "What do you have?" He reached for the folder and spread out the pictures in his hands. "Where did you get these?"

"Well, as I said, I worked through the night because no woman wants me since all I ever do is police work." Marc grimaced. "I couldn't find anything from Seattle or the State Patrol, but, as you can see, this shot of her car clearly shows a license plate which matches her car. And this picture from a parking lot surveillance camera shows the same car with her as driver."

"Great, now it's time for Miss Johnson to explain why she's lying to us." Marc closed the folder and handed it back to Tom. "First, though, I have a call to make. Roger Waite also needs to explain why he's lying about his sister-in-law not being at his house. You pick him up and bring him to us. Charge him with obstruction if he objects. And be sure to get his lawyer and an ADA here, as well." Tom returned to his desk.

Marc sat at his desk and picked up the phone. Office records had supplied the number for the WSU Campus police. He explained who he was, and what he was interested in obtaining. After a pause of several minutes he said, "Thank you, very much. This will be very helpful in my investigation. Please fax a copy of the report to me." He supplied the fax number and hung up. "So, you think you can get away with the perfect crime." He sat for a moment shaking his head. "I wonder. How did you do it?" he thought. He stood and retrieved the report from the fax machine. He folded it and placed in his jacket. Another call to the University of Washington allayed his concern of a closed campus office.

Tom walked toward Marc. "Woodbury yelled a few expletives about harassing his client, and Atherton will be here as soon as she can. I sent a patrol car to Waite's office. I'm going there to get him."

"Good, if I'm not here when you return, start without me. I think I have another key which might unlock this mystery." Marc left the office.

He drove the 60 miles to the University of Washington, parked his car near Schmitz Hall, and found a stairwell to the second floor. The information quest needed a little secrecy for now. What he sought was far away from the case as it existed, but could explain Roger's attitude about Mary's death.

The assistant returned from a data file search with the requested information. He read through it and smiled. "I need to know about another student." He said to the assistant. He gave a last name and explained the person was a medical student who graduated sometime in the late nineties or early 21st century. A search gave several names which fit the profile. He thanked the lady, who looked like a student, for her help. As he left Schmitz Hall, he called his sheriff's office to find out about Waite and the collection of attorneys who controlled the young man's future. No one had arrived as yet, so he packed his materials into his car and left campus for a return to Wendlesburg after picking up the young lady who he called earlier. A ferry ride left soon from Colman Dock and would cut his travel time by half an hour. He headed toward Puget Sound and the construction zone for the new tunnel.

The ferry ride gave time for reflection about his day. He conversed with his passenger only a little. He called home and left a message about another late arrival. After last night and this morning, he hoped for leniency about his communication.

Arriving at the precinct, he saw Monica Atherton enter the building. "Interesting woman," he thought. In the office he found Tom and asked about Waite and Woodbury.

"Waite is in room 2 and Woodbury has not arrived."

"Let's go see our man, then." He directed his traveler into an interrogation room and asked her to be patient. They came within reach of the mirror separating them from the room containing Roger Waite. Monica Atherton had entered so they flipped the sound switch and listened.

Roger's eyes widened with recognition. "What are you doing here?"

She slinked up to him and whispered, "I couldn't have planned a better revenge if I tried. You shoot your wife just when I get my first job as an assistant in the DA's office."

"Why, what have you got against me? What happened between us is old news. I chose Mary, so what?"

She stood away from him and turned. "I've been assigned the case."

He stood. "You can't do this. It's conflict of interest or something. I'll tell my attorney, the judge, anybody, that you're out to get me."

"Oh, I think I can explain anything you have to say. And maybe that bimbo little sister can go to jail with you. You know … a conspiracy. I've got you now, you bastard." Monica walked to the door. "Maybe I'll go easy on you. Don't say anything and I'll leave your girlfriend out of it." Roger sat and stared. She left the room grinning. Roger started to follow but sat again.

The two detectives waited a moment, curious about what developed, and then they entered the interrogation room. Marc said, "We have some good news. There's enough evidence which may exonerate you from killing your wife. You don't have to say anything, but we now know someone else was at the house, as well as you. So we're going after the real shooter." They turned to leave.

"No, I want to confess. I shot Mary."

Woodbury entered. "Say nothing, Roger. You two cannot interview him without me. What are you doing in here?"

"We came to inform him we have another person of interest and he is free to go. However, he just confessed to shooting his wife," Marc said.

"He's not confessing, and I'll make damn sure this so called confession is not admissible."

"Roger, if you're not confessing, you're protecting someone. Care to clear the air and tell us about your relationship with her?"

Woodbury nodded at Roger, "I … we're having an affair. I think she wanted to get Mary out of the way so we could be together. I was trying to protect her from you. I didn't think you'd find out."

"Yeah, didn't think is right. You know you can be charged with obstructing an investigation."

Woodbury responded, "You want the right person for this shooting then leave Roger alone so he can raise his children. Let me talk with him and I'll get back to you." Marc nodded and he and Tom left the room.

"That worked pretty well," Tom said. "Do you think the DA will let him off?"

"Maybe probation, if he cooperates, but I can't see him getting jail time." They entered the next interrogation room and as the door closed Marc said, "Miss Johnson, your boyfriend just confessed to killing your sister. What do you have to say?"

CHAPTER 31

"Is this why you came to my home and brought me here? Just so you could tell me this?" Victoria asked.

"We don't believe Mr. Waite was alone in the house after he found his wife," Marc answered.

Tom placed a picture on the table. "Do you recognize this person?" he asked.

Victoria turned her face away. A silence followed.

Tom asked again, "Do you know this person?"

"Yes, it's me, so what?"

"It's from a surveillance camera located about a mile from your sister and brother-in-law's house. The time stamp is the Sunday morning when your sister died and you are headed for the house."

Marc said, "You were at the house before he left for church, weren't you?" He picked up the picture. "The time stamp on the document is 8:14 AM. Care to explain?"

"Do I need a lawyer?"

"Woodbury is in the next room. Want me to get him?" Marc nodded at Tom who left. "What I need to know is why you both have lied to us about your relationship and Mary's death. You can take turns filling in the blanks."

Tom returned with Woodbury and Roger. Roger mouthed "I'm sorry." Woodbury directed him to a chair away from the table. "What do you want?" he asked.

Marc said, "Since we now know Miss Johnson was at the house when her sister died, we need to have some clarity about the actual events of the day."

"I need time with my clients."

"Okay, but Saturday is not a good day to lose to work. Let us know when you are ready." Marc and Tom left the room.

Tom said, "What was Atherton doing with Waite. They seem to know each other."

"I'll check into it. I hope Woodbury doesn't take too long. I need to get home since this is a family man's day off."

"Have you eaten anything today?"

"Nah, but I'll be alright." The door opened and Woodbury appeared. "My clients have a statement to make about that Sunday. They are not confessing to any murder."

Tom and Marc followed him into the room. Marc spoke first. "So, what happened?"

Roger said, "Vickie came over as she had done the previous three weeks to watch over her sister while I took the children to church. Mary had been acting more and more depressed and we thought it best to have someone here with her. I didn't want her to be alone. She arrived about 45 minutes before I left. Mary seemed happy to see her sister, so I wasn't worried. When I got the call at church from Vickie…"

"Your sister-in-law called you? Not your wife?"

"Yes, Vickie called. She told me to get right home without the children, so I did, just as I told you before." Roger shifted in the chair. "When I arrived, Vickie was so incoherent I figured she'd been drinking or something. She hadn't sounded bad on the phone, so finding her in the condition I did was confusing."

"Miss Johnson, was it you who called him?" Marc moved toward the table.

"I don't know, I guess. I don't remember."

"You either called him or you didn't, which is it?"

"I don't know. All I remember is coming to house and watching Roger and the kids leave. I was in the kitchen fixing some tea for Mary and me. I heard a noise and that's the last thing I remember until Roger was back and shaking me."

"You want us to believe that you lost your memory. Is it because you shot your sister and are claiming some kind of temporary amnesia?"

Woodbury broke in. "She has the right to claim it and I can get any number of specialists to corroborate her statement."

"So she did shoot her sister and this is your defense?"

"I'm not saying that. She is not confessing to killing anyone. She is simply stating she has a memory lapse for the period of time when Mary obviously was killed."

Turning back to Victoria, Marc asked, "What noise did you hear?"

"I'm not sure. It sounded like another person coming into the kitchen. I thought it was Mary, so I started down the hall. That's all I remember."

"You want us to accept as truth a person has a traumatic experience and forces it into the subconscious so deeply as to render it forgotten." Marc furrowed his brow. "Who would do such a thing?"

"Obviously, my client has."

"Nothing is obvious at all. This means your other client has altered a crime scene to benefit a suspect and himself. The only question I have is whether or not Miss Johnson pulled the trigger. Obviously, we cannot test her for GSR, but Tom can get a warrant to search her apartment for anything which she may have been wearing or possessed on the Sunday in question." He nodded to his counterpart who left to fulfill the request. "And if we find any evidence which supports her complicity in the death of her sister, you can be assured of her immediate arrest. I think we will be holding her for a moment while the search commences. What do you think, Mr. Woodbury, is that alright with you?"

Marc looked at the three other people in the room. No one spoke. Marc left the room presuming they would confer about the present circumstances. He asked another deputy to watch the door and make sure no one left too soon.

"Is Miss Atherton still here?" he asked the front desk clerk, who pointed at the foyer of the building. Monica paced the floor with cell phone active by her ear. Marc approached and smiled. She fumbled through a quick goodbye and clicked it shut.

She asked, "Have they confessed?"

"To what?"

"I guess to a murder conspiracy."

"I don't think so, but you might want to hear their story before a criminal case is pursued. It makes for an interesting mystery book." Marc turned and walked back to the interrogation room. Monica scurried to catch up.

He knocked before entering, alerting the residences of his impending entry. Upon opening the door, he eyed Roger for recognition of the young lady following him. Nothing subtle or overt occurred.

"Mr. Woodbury, Miss Atherton and I are fascinated with what you have decided regarding the innocence of these clients."

Roger spoke first. "I want it known Victoria had nothing to do with Mary's death. So if anything happened, Mary must have done it herself." Woodbury scowled.

Marc responded, "That very well maybe the case. However, I don't think you can prove it and the fact that you altered the scene implicates Miss Johnson, since she was the other person in the house."

"You have no evidence of her pulling the trigger," Woodbury said.

Monica said, "You mean other than her fingerprints on the bullets, her lying about being in the house, the discovery of the body by Mr. Waite, and his suspicion that she killed his wife?" She paused. "No, I guess not. I can say that if he has confessed then we can use that as evidence of conspiracy and prosecute both Miss Johnson and Mr. Waite for the death of his wife. I'm sure a jury will pick one of them. You and I both know enough evidence and the jury convicts."

Marc spoke next. "We will hold Miss Johnson for the week-end while a search warrant is executed on her apartment in Seattle. Mr. Waite, you are free to go home, but don't leave town. It wouldn't bode well for your sister-in-law."

"Let me have some time with them," Woodbury said.

Monica and Marc left the room. Tom returned with news of a search warrant issuance on Monday, if the judge agrees. Marc said, "I guess that's the best we're getting. I'm going home. Tom, you field this as I have a family to assuage. Monica can assist you." Pulling him aside Marc asked him not say anything about seeing her in the room with Roger. He then departed for home to determine whether he still had a family.

CHAPTER 32

Although the exertion of police work took several hours, enough daytime remained for family interaction. Marc called as he left the precinct to state his impending arrival. Joan spoke with understanding, seemingly happy for his return. Maybe the family remained intact after all.

Not yet dinner time, he suggested a night out for the evening meal. The unanimous choice was the local hot spot which had a bar for evening twenty-something's to gather, mingle, and hook up. The remainder of the establishment included an unobtrusive restaurant away from the noise of music and carousing.

Joan smiled at Marc and said quietly, "Thank you." He grinned as the waitress strolled over to take drink orders. Three soft drinks and a bottle of chardonnay began the dinner. Upon returning with the drinks, the college aged waitress asked if they were ready to order food. They asked for a few more minutes.

Marc thought about meeting Joan at school and imagined Roger and Mary. How different the results. He hoped the young waitress was fruitful in her search for education and career as well as companionship without catastrophe. She returned and took dinner requests. The children wanted the signature pizza and Joan ordered salmon in a lemon-dill sauce with red potatoes and squash. Marc wanted something different and asked for pork chops and a baked potato. Bottomless salad came with the meal.

Finally, Marc reveled in an evening without interruption. He toasted his family and their patience. "Here's to best family an undeserving man can have." Glasses were clicked and conversation commenced again.

Marc Junior asked the unmentionable. "Dad, I know we don't normally talk about your work, but this one seems a little more intense than others you've worked on." Joan began to speak, he continued. "Mom, we are concerned about you and Dad."

Sarah entered the conversation. "Yeah, we don't want you fighting because Dad has to solve this case."

Marc answered, "Your mother and I sometimes have differences of opinion. She's a very bright woman and I respect her opinions. I need to make more of an effort to put you guys first and that's all it is." Joan sat listening. Marc pondered her silence. The dinner conversation lagged for want of any desire to broach the whirlpool the family was in.

The remainder of the weekend included a trip to their local Episcopal Church on Sunday and a backyard barbeque. Marc worked for only a short period of time on the files he brought home. Joan was warm to his affectionate touches but he sensed an undertone of angst in her. He had to be proactive and push for a solution, which he thought to be elusive. Victoria Johnson's story had more holes in it than a sieve and yet a jury could believe she was traumatized.

Perry Andrews might be able to answer his questions and another shot at Conley about Mary and the family appeared appropriate. Monica looked as if bent on convicting Roger. He wanted nothing more than the truth about Mary Waite.

* * *

Monday came as usual. Marc felt a sense of calm before the storm but was not sure which storm brewed in his life. Joan stated she appreciated the finish to the weekend and hoped for no others lost unless absolutely necessary which, in the crime solving business, could happen anytime. He entered the sheriff's office with a sense of knowing the truth but realizing it was going to take a minor miracle to prove it. A follow-up on his weekend investigation might just provide the needed pieces. He picked up the phone and called Dr. Conley, Mary's psychiatrist. A meeting for late morning was set. Next he called a hospital in Bellingham, north of Seattle on I-5, another lead which could provide another piece to the puzzle.

He decided to go to the Coroner's office to speak with Perry about his conclusions. "Tom," he said, "have Miss Johnson released as soon as the search warrant arrives. Take her home and complete the search with her present. If she wants Woodbury there, call him. Don't let his inability to be there stop you, however." Tom nodded agreement. "I'm headed out to follow up on some leads we have about the garlic smell and other new one. I'll return hopefully, later this afternoon."

At the coroner's office he found Perry working on a hit and run victim. "Your life sure isn't dull," he said.

"Oh, I do alright. These people come to me for inspection like they never expected." He placed an instrument on the table next to the autopsy table. "Let me finish here and I'll join you in my office."

Marc left the room and went to Perry's cubicle. He studied the books on forensic science, anatomy, bugs, and soils. He figured all of this to be important for solving deaths from unknown causes. Samples of animals in formaldehyde and bugs stuck on pins on framed mattes lined the wall next to Perry's desk. Files of cases were stacked on the left side. On the right side he saw a pamphlet about women with interstitial cystitis. Marc picked it up and flipped through the contents.

Perry strolled in. "That's a piece of information for you. I think it might help with the Waite case."

"What's it about?"

203

'Some women contract a disease which is not fatal but can be debilitating. It is known as I.C. One of the treatments which have been used is to instill a cocktail of Dimethyl Sulfoxide or DMSO, Solu-cortef, and Bicarbonate of Soda in solution into the bladder. I.C. affects the lining of the bladder and the mixture has been helpful to many women who have been afflicted with it. Newer remedies for I.C. have been found, so this mixture is not as prevalent as before."

"So how does this fit into the Waite case?"

"I investigated Mary Waite for any I.C. and, as I told you before, she was not affected." Perry picked up a file from his stack and handed it to Marc. "This report explains about the uses of DMSO as a transmitter of other drugs. I'm thinking someone who uses this cocktail was at the scene and left a marker behind. I've checked with Mary's doctor and confirmed from his answers she is not the user."

"So how does a woman use it?"

"The procedure is usually done in a doctor's office, but a patient can be taught to self-instill the mixture. So I think we may be looking for a person who needs the procedure or knows someone who does."

"I'm still lost here, Doc. What does this have to do with Mary Waite?"

"When DMSO is applied to the skin of humans, it has a strange quality for many individuals of secreting on the tongue and causing a garlic-like taste. Other people have reported being able to smell it. I sensed its presence in the house on that Sunday."

"Perry, is there any evidence of it being present without anyone using it?"

"Not likely, since it is not something a person will carry around, unless they are using it when traveling or heading to some place where the moment of use coincides."

"Somebody must have brought it with them. So possibly Victoria brought it with her. But the question is, why?" Marc skimmed through the file. "Are there any uses for the DMSO which Mary might have a need?"

"We didn't find any DMSO in the house, so I'm thinking it came in from outside."

"If Victoria Johnson brought it to the house, can you speculate as to its use for Mary?"

"The only thing I can think of is to use it as a topical analgesic or to administer medications through the skin. It has a property of readily being absorbed without causing any damage."

"Anything in Mary's system which might suggest she was given something using DMSO?"

"Nothing I found."

"Thanks, Perry. I'll be in touch." Marc started to leave with the file but stopped. "Oh, is it alright to take this with me?"

"Yes, take it and this pamphlet as well."

Marc waved goodbye with the file and walked from the building to his car. It was time for his appointment with Dr. Andrew Conley. He drove to the address of the clinic, parked his car and entered the building. The receptionist led him to Conley's office.

"Good morning, Doctor. Thank you for seeing me."

"I do hope this isn't a professional matter of you needing help?"

"No, I'm here about Mary Waite. Some new evidence has come to my attention which might shine a light on how she died."

CHAPTER 33

"Come in then and have a seat." Marc sat in an overstuffed leather wing chair. "What can I do for you?"

"I want to understand how a young lady, who seemingly has everything, can become suicidal."

"As you know, I can't speak directly of Mrs. Waite's condition. However, hypothetically, a person can be depressed for any number of reasons. I suppose someone like Mary can suffer from post-partum blues, a condition brought on by separation of the fetus from the mother. Hormonal changes usually are a factor, but not always."

"Could a condition such as Mrs. Waite suffered be diagnosed; is there a name for what a woman like her might have?"

She might suffer from mixed anxiety-depressive disorder or MADD."

"Explain what that means."

"From a psychological point of view chronic anxiety can cause biochemical variations in the brain which reproduce the psycho-physiological conditions typical of depression."

Motive

"What typically leads to a person being diagnosed this way?"

"The diagnosis of an episode of depression is determined in subjects who have continuously complained of a sense of fatigue, lack of strength and energy, lack of concentration, worry about their health, and a total lack of interest in eating, work, leisure activities or sexual pursuits. When this happens one speaks of a depressive-anxiety disorder, which is a form of mild depression accompanied by the symptoms of anxiety. In this disturbance, the predominant symptom is anxiety."

"Can this lead to a person being difficult to live with?"

"Yes, another person living with someone who is suffering from anxiety and depression would have a tough time coping."

"Can it be controlled with medicines?"

"The first line of treatment is usually an anti-anxiety medication and after anxiety has lessened, the patient is treated with antidepressants as well."

"How well do patients respond to treatment?"

"People with MADD do not tend to respond to medications as well as someone with a single disorder. As a result, their social life is limited, work is difficult, and the quality of their life is bleak."

"From a professional opinion, could this disorder possibly drive another person to want to eliminate the disruption of their normal life?"

"By eliminate, do you mean to kill the sufferer?"

"Alright, is it possible a person would murder another person, because he either is sick and tired of her problems or he has decided to put a stop to her suffering?"

"It's been known to happen."

Marc leaned forward. "Dr. Conley, is there any way in which a person can be administered medication without using a needle or taking it orally or rectally?"

"Hum. I guess the only way would be for a topical transmitter, but I can't think of any medicines which can be transmitted which would allay these conditions. I'd have to do some research."

"Alright, is there any way a person can lose memory for short periods of time?"

Conley furrowed his brow. "There are conditions which can trigger a person's defense mechanisms, but Mary wasn't experiencing anything which might cause that to happen."

"I know. I'm curious about how it happens that a person witnesses a shocking event such as a shooting and does not recall one detail of it."

"Selective amnesia is a rare condition. But it does occur. Are you thinking Roger does not remember shooting his wife? I thought a suicide transpired."

"Thank you for your time." Marc stood to leave but turned. "Did you prescribe any medication which might leave a garlic-like odor residue on Mrs. Waite?"

"No, but that sounds like Dimethyl Sulfoxide." Conley frowned.

"Again, thank you." As he left, a smile coursed his face.

CHAPTER 34

A long drive north did not please Marc, but a phone call left him without a confirmation. If the information warranted a trip, it needed to be so. He called home and left a message about his possible lateness. He started the car and headed for the ferry in Kingston.

The trip through Edmonds reminded him of his uncle, a Snohomish County sheriff's deputy whose untimely death was an event of which his family rarely spoke. This case reminded him of the circumstances which he did not comprehend until high school and the taunts with which fellow students bullied him. He wanted nothing to do with suicide and now he had to prove Mary Waite incapable of committing such a heinous act. Somebody killed her and that was all there was to it.

Maybe Joan would understand more if he explained his feelings to her. But his family did not discuss it, so why should he. Leaving her in the dark about his uncle didn't change his obsession. Telling her wouldn't change it either. She just had to appreciate a necessity for closure on Mary Waite.

The drive to Bellingham relaxed him. He enjoyed driving as a way of escaping the stress of living. No one complained about where he was, or who he let down. He could listen to any music he wanted and figure out what was wrong in his life. As much as he loved Joan, at times he needed to be alone.

The hospital in Bellingham, St. Joseph Medical Center, compiled lists of medicines used by doctors during surgeries. The nurse, Adeline Hancock, RN, affiliated with the pharmacy which dispenses the drugs for hospital use, decided to cooperate with Marc only because of a problem she encountered regularly. She required complete identification and verification of his status with the county sheriff's office before he was allowed to speak with her about his concerns.

They talked about the procedure for procurement of drugs and the log book requisite. Each doctor signed for anesthetics to be used in surgery before the actual surgery. Each dose was monitored by the records nurse during the surgery. After the surgery was completed the records nurse accounts for all medications which remained and logged them into a book which was handed to the specific doctor accountable for each drug. After signing the book, remaining medicines were returned to the pharmacy for restocking.

This procedure was installed to keep misused and abuse of drugs by medical personnel at a minimum. Several cases of addiction had occurred in the hospital which involved doctors and high ranking nurses and the disappearance of drugs. A new administration investigated the misuse, concluding the pharmacy was the source and needed to be closely monitored. So the procedure of checks and balances was instituted. Although some complaints were registered, the vast majority of personnel accepted the policy change and abuse of medication dropped sharply.

"When you notice a discrepancy from the log book, what do you and your colleagues in the pharmacy do?" Marc asked. "Can a person account for every drug which leaves and returns? Is there a time when a drug is checked out and not logged as used, but is still missing?"

Hancock oversaw the operations of the pharmacy and the people who worked in it. She was a short, squat pugnacious person who ran her department with military precision. Nothing got by her, or so it seemed to Marc.

She looked at the log book for the week prior to Mary Waite's untimely death and found nothing alarming. "I do not see anything wrong with the time period you have requested." She closed the book and replaced it on the proper shelf, in the proper cupboard. "Let me look at the previous week." She retrieved the book and studied it for a moment. A puzzled look fixed itself on her face.

"Something is wrong here. I should have caught this at the time."

"What's the matter?"

"The log shows a neurologist checking out midazolam and another anesthetic for a surgery. The log shows the return of unused midazolam and anesthetic, but the daily count for drugs is short one bottle of midazolam. I need to track this down."

"Can I speak with the doctor who was responsible for not returning it?"

"Let me check something first. I have had incidences of medicines being logged in but the daily accounting shows a discrepancy. Sometimes the medical personnel involved will pocket medicines for return and forget to bring them in. They are busy, you know. Most times I give them a reminder and the medication is brought in." She wrote a note which she did not show to Marc. "Please wait for me outside and I'll contact you soon."

"Protecting your fellow medical staff," thought Marc. A little CYA kept order and collegiality. He opened his phone and sent text to Joan about his lateness. Although the day was young, he did not know how long his quest would be. It may be a wild goose chase, but suicide was not an acceptable explanation or option for Mary's death, or Uncle Jerry's.

Hancock returned. "It seems we've had a break-in." She opened a file and showed a picture of a person in scrubs opening a cupboard. "This is the place the midazolam is stored. This person is not a member of my staff and I do not recognize her as a member of the hospital staff."

The face was grainy and hard to see. The culprit was cautious about facing the camera, as if knowing the camera was there and working.

"How does one gain access to the pharmacy?"

"I can let them enter but usually we dispense through the window." She pointed at a slotted pane in the wall next to the door.

"Who has keys for this room?"

"Besides me, two other nurses oversee the pharmacy when I am not on call. We work in shifts with three sets of two techs who work with us. Only the supervisors have keys and they are responsible to me."

Marc looked at the picture again but could fathom only a guess as to who the person was. He recognized a female or person posing as a female. How Hancock knew the person was not a staff member was beyond him. He saw a grainy picture of someone opening a storage cabinet wearing hospital garb. The name badge was not decipherable to him, either.

"What makes you say this person is not hospital staff?"

"The hospital uniform is an older version of our current scrubs. Maybe they worked here before and still had it. The badge is older as well."

Marc thanked Nurse Hancock and left the pharmacy. He realized the midazolam was significant but could not connect the dots. He went to the main offices of the hospital to speak with the administrator. His next target was a doctor he did not know. She was to explain about a sister who graduated after her, who attended several schools to attain a degree and now may be implicated in a death which Marc was now positive to be murder. He only needed to connect the dots.

CHAPTER 35

Marc sat in the anteroom of the hospital administrator. A secretary informed Dr. Riannah Uldanisan of his presence, so he waited reading the hospital information guide. It explained the medical procedures which were specialties of the facility He wondered which ones Joan might be familiar with as an elder-care nurse.

A door opened and a woman who looked to be in her forties approached. "Good morning, doctor. I'm Marc Jefferson, a detective in Kitsap County. Thank you for seeing me." She stood a bit taller in her slight heeled sneakers. She wore a professional blue pant suit which accentuated her trim body. The ivory blouse was buttoned to show some cleavage, and the pants framed her hips and flowed loosely down her legs. Her page cut hair framed her face nicely. Marc thought her good-looking but not beautiful. He reached out a hand.

Dr. Uldanisan said, "Good morning; I understand you wish to speak with me regarding one of my staff." She gripped his hand, firm but not tight and then motioned for him to enter her office.

The room was utilitarian and small by private CEO standards. He noticed the myriad plaques and certificates hung on the walls. Pictures of any kind were missing. She motioned him to sit in a large leather chair. He sat, but she stood next to her wood and glass desk, turned slightly so as to face him. Her desk contrasted his with its neatness and order, a picture of two children and a dog displayed on the corner.

"I spoke with a Nurse Adeline Hancock about the pharmacy and how it is operated. She informed me that a bottle of midazolam is missing from it. I would like to question the doctor who ordered it."

"I know nothing of this. When did she say she discovered it missing? Why didn't you come directly to me?"

"She told me she just uncovered it. I don't know when the occurrence happened." Marc ignored the question.

"Alright, who's the person who signed out and in the medication?"

"Her name is Giselle Selandian. I think she's a neurologist or something."

"Yes, she's one of three who are affiliated with St. Joe."

"How long has she been here?"

"She did her internship and residency, so I guess about eight years."

"Have there been any problems?"

"With Ginny, no. Why do you suspect her of taking the medication?"

"I suspect no one and everyone. The case I'm working on in Kitsap is a death of a young woman and I think Dr. Selandian is the sister of someone involved with the case. I need to speak with her about it."

Dr. Uldanisan sat in a chair next to Marc. "I can't believe someone broke into the pharmacy and you suspect Ginny."

"I'm not saying that at all. I'm not sure of anything other than I would like to speak with this doctor."

"Normally, anesthesiologists check out midazolam, but I suppose a neurologist might need it in some situations."

"What does it do?" he asked.

"It's a receptor inhibitor. It causes a brain to not record what is happening while under the influence of the drug. It is helpful for surgery when a person needs to be alert but afterward not aware of what has happened."

Marc perked up at this revelation. Now the dots were connecting but not enough to answer his riddle. "Is Doctor Selandian available?" She rose from the chair and clicked on her computer on the desk.

"She's on call starting at 2 PM." Marc checked his watch. It was nearly 1 already. "But she's not going to be here. She comes only when paged."

"Have her paged then, so I can see her, please."

Dr. Uldanisan's eyes narrowed as she responded. "We don't normally page people just to question them like criminals."

Marc stood. "I never said she was a criminal, but I have come from Kitsap today to gain information which can close a case for me. I think it appropriate."

The doctor picked up her phone and dialed a number. She made the request and hung up. "There, she's been paged. She will get here when she picks up the page."

"Thank you; if I may I would like to wait for her where she checks in."

"That would be here, as I requested her to report to me. You may wait in the reception area. I'll let you know when she comes in."

"What dots will you connect?" Marc thought.

CHAPTER 36

Marc called Tom, filling him in on some of his accumulated information. Tom related how the search of Victoria's apartment turned up nothing unusual. She gave them the clothing she wore that day, but it had been laundered.

This trail opened new ideas as to who committed this murder. Roger seemed in the clear for killing his wife, but nothing was settled yet.

Dr. Uldanisan opened her office door and invited Marc to return. "I have heard from Dr. Selandian. She will be here within the next ten minutes. Before she arrives I would like to know what connection she has to your case."

"I appreciate your concern, but I'm not at liberty to discuss ongoing investigations. May I use your office while I speak with Dr. Selandian?"

"Yes," she answered reluctant to leave. He believed her oversight of the hospital might be a more micromanagement style than she first let on. The pharmacy concern probably had not escaped her knowing. Hancock had that evidence more speedily than his detective history would accept as possible. Was a conspiracy conceivable? And how might a conspiracy connect to a murder in Kitsap County?

The door opened and an older version of the woman in Kitsap County appeared. Victoria Johnson and Mary Waite were nine years apart in age but looked like twins. This lady was not a twin but face and body matched. He stood to introduce himself.

"Dr. Selandian, thank you for coming. My name is Marc Jefferson; I am a detective with the sheriff's department in Kitsap County." Dr. Uldanisan lingered longer than he felt comfort, but a look at her conveyed a message of get lost. She excused herself and left. "Please, have a seat." They sat in the leather chairs.

"What do you want?" she asked.

"I am investigating a death in Kitsap County and need to have some questions clarified."

"This seems like a long way to come just to answer questions."

"I suppose so, but if I can answer these questions then I may close the case sooner."

"Alright, ask away."

"Your sister is located in Kitsap County, isn't she?"

"I think you already know the answer to that."

"Yes, well then, do you or she have a need to use DMSO for medicinal purposes?"

"I'm not at liberty to say."

"And why is that?"

"My sister is a patient of mine and therefore I cannot answer any medical questions. Patient confidentiality laws prohibit it."

"I am aware of that. I didn't realize your sister had neurological problems. Let me ask you this then. Would you consider your sister to be a stable person?"

"What kind of question is that?"

"I understand your sister considered she was jilted while she attended college. Now the issue becomes one of exacting revenge upon the person who broke her heart."

"She left school because of that man, but I wouldn't say it destroyed her. She went to another school and finished her degree. So, no, I do not consider her to be unstable."

"Has she visited you recently or have you gone to see her?"

"We don't have a lot in common, but we talk often and visit each other every month or two."

"Your last name is not the same as hers. Are you married or is she a half-sister?"

"We have the same mother, but my father died in an automobile accident. Mom married her father about two years after that. My sister was born about a year and a half later."

"If your sister asked you to do something for her that might be on the edge of legal, would you do it?"

"I have no idea what you are saying. I cannot practice medicine and do illegal activities."

"Would you fudge medical records to help her?"

"I think you need to leave. I will not answer any more of your insane questions." She stood to leave.

Marc stood as well. "I apologize. I merely want to understand how your sister became intertwined in a case which she had no real reason to be implicated." He intervened between the doctor and the door. "One last question, if you please. Why is a bottle of midazolam missing from the hospital pharmacy and you are the doctor of record for the last withdrawal?"

"What? When did this happen? I hardly ever use it."

"According to Nurse Hancock a bottle went missing about three weeks ago and you checked out a bottle during that time period."

"I seriously doubt that. I am not a surgeon and I have little, if any, use for such a drug. What evidence is there that I checked it out?"

"The log books indicate you did and that it was returned. But a picture of a person entering the pharmacy shows a bottle being removed without proper authority. Do you have access to the pharmacy?"

Selandian sat down again, dismay radiated from her face. "I can't believe it. She wouldn't have. She couldn't have."

Marc sat and listened to a story of betrayal and conspiracy pour from a disappointed sister. Although she didn't connect all of the dots, enough now strung together so as to explain what happened on that Sunday morning three weeks ago. Marc had his answer, thanked the doctor for her help, asked another favor of her, and left for a rendezvous with the ADA in Kitsap County. He called Patterson to let him know he was coming and a meeting was set for early the next morning. No need to disappoint an already edgy wife.

CHAPTER 37

Marc arrived home as dinner appeared on the table. Joan stopped at a local diner and picked up an order she called in before leaving work. The children smiled and expressed their glee at having father home. He hugged them and greeted his wife affectionately.

"You seem to be in a happy mood today," she said. "I trust the trip north panned out well."

"I didn't get all I needed, but I can generate a confession with the information I have." They ate the pizza and salad from Maestroni's Pizzeria. The evening concluded with television and conversation about daily events. Marc asked Marc Junior if he might be interested in attending Western Washington University. Sarah intervened she had planned on it from her first day of high school.

"What happened in Bellingham which got you so excited?" Joan asked when everyone had gone to bed.

"I think I know what happened. I'll tell you the whole story after I meet with Duncan tomorrow. He's not going to believe what I have to say."

As they finished preparing for bed, Joan hugged her husband and said, "I appreciate your effort to get home today." Marc slept calmly without remembering any crazy dreams.

Morning came with a start since the phone rang at 5 AM. He answered groggy and not listening. The voice on the other end cursed at him which focused his hearing. "Who is this?" he said, but the line went dead.

Joan asked, "Who was that?"

"I don't know, but they were angry about something." Marc picked up the phone to call for a trace of his line. "That should tell us who called." Marc dressed and said, "I'll head to the office and follow up on this call. I think I know what it means." He headed to the kitchen for a quick bite to eat and then left for the office.

He arrived just before the shift change at 6 AM. He spoke with the night detectives who worked most of the nefarious crimes an evening can muster. The phone company report of his calls would arrive later in the day. He concentrated on researching DMSO and midazolam and how they might work together. If Victoria Johnson really didn't remember anything about that Sunday morning, maybe she had help with forgetting.

Tom came in shortly after seven. "Good morning," he said to Marc, "We found nothing exculpatory at Johnson's place. Woodbury took custody of her yesterday afternoon."

"Good work. I think I have something which can explain her loss of memory."

"I thought she was faking."

"So does Waite, I think. He changed the scene to be a suicide to protect her. He thinks she did it. And I wouldn't be surprised if she thinks she did it."

"So what did you find in Bellingham?"

"Did you know there's drug which can prevent memories from forming in the brain?"

"I've heard of something used in surgeries. I think they used it the last time I had ... well ... uh ... my colonoscopy."

Marc laughed. "Thanks for that information. Anyway, if Victoria was drugged, she might not know what took place."

"Could she have killed her sister and not remembered doing it?"

"Maybe, and Roger believes it."

"You don't think so, do you?"

Another person had to be in the house besides Mary, Victoria, and Roger."

"Who do you suspect?"

"If I told you, you wouldn't believe me. I need to connect a few dots before I reveal the person. Let's go see Roger and ask him a few questions about his past. That might help finish this case. Where did Woodbury take Victoria?"

"I think he simply escorted her from the station and let her leave."

"We should track her down and ask her another round of questions to see if she maintains a close resemblance of her tale of forgetfulness." Marc turned to depart. "Coming?" he asked.

Tom followed him to his car and they drove to Waite's parent's house, where Roger resided until the matter cleared. "I don't think he'll want to keep his house for a residence," Tom said.

"Probably not, and I wouldn't buy it considering what happened there." The drive was pleasant with a sun rising earlier each day. Summer was close to reality and the grayness of sky dampened not the spirits of the officers.

"What if Roger doesn't want to speak with us?"

"He can stay home or he can come to the station with us in handcuffs. Either way I want to clarify some facts and then find his vixen sister-in-law." They parked the car in front of the house and walked up the steps. The gray morning cast no shadows but daylight brightened the clouds. It was early and nothing stirred in the house. Marc rang the bell and stepped back from the door. A second ring aroused residents whose noises were heard from inside. Walker Waite peered out of the door curtain and frowned.

"You're here awfully early for a Tuesday. Don't you have better things to do than disturb our family this early?"

"I do apologize, but I must ask Roger some questions and help clear up this mess he's in."

Roger came to the door. "What do you want?"

"May Officer Watson and I come in? I want to clear up an issue that plagues this case. I think it might help you in your quest to get rid of us."

Walker stepped aside as Roger held the door open and gestured for the detectives to enter. He led them into the living room off to the left of the hallway. Walker retreated upstairs.

They sat in various chairs. "Maybe I should call my attorney."

"You certainly can, but I'm only here to gather answers which will free you from a burden I think you are carrying."

"Alright, you have my attention."

"Does Victoria know you think she killed her sister?"

Roger's eyes widened. "We've talked about it. But she says she doesn't remember anything."

"When you came home, what is the first thing you remember about Victoria? I need you to recall exactly what your first impression was." Marc leaned forward.

"She seemed disoriented, like she'd been drugged or something. I thought she was in shock when I found Mary."

"Is there anything about Victoria which seemed odd other than her being disoriented?"

"I don't know what you mean."

"Why didn't you believe her when she told you she didn't remember anything?"

"She was the only one in the house. She knew Mary and I were headed to a sanatorium to get Mary help for her depression." Roger shifted. "I figured she wanted Mary out of the way so we could be together. But I didn't want her going to jail."

"I understand that. Now please try and remember if you had any other senses come into play as you came to Victoria."

Roger sat silent for a moment. He turned his head and cocked it slightly creating creases on his forehead. He looked first at Tom and then at Marc. "She smelled like garlic."

Marc smiled and Tom narrowed his eyes. "Anything else which she said or did before you found your wife shot to death?"

"She handed me the gun and said I think I've done something terrible. I took the gun and went to find Mary."

"You believed her, didn't you?" Roger nodded. "She confessed to you and then told you she had no recollection of committing the murder." Roger nodded again.

"He tried to protect me." Victoria entered the room.

CHAPTER 38

"Miss Johnson, please join us. I am surprised, but glad to find you here. It makes my job so much easier." Marc said. "It's strange that you spent the night here with Roger."

Roger answered. "We have a spare bedroom downstairs."

"Oh, I'm not questioning your fidelity or your parents' motivation for aiding her. I'm simply interested in the truth."

"I heard what you asked Roger. He wanted to know why I killed my sister. I told him I didn't remember doing it. But you know all of this. I told you this at your station house."

"Tell me again, what do you remember after Roger left for church?"

"Mary and I were talking in her bedroom. She wanted some tea and I said I would get it for her. I went to the kitchen, as I told you; I heard a noise and the next thing I remember was Mary dead on the floor and the gun in my hand. Roger came home shortly after that and found me sitting in the living room."

"Roger, how much blood did you find on Victoria?"

"A little, why?"

"If she had fired the gun at her sister, she should have been close enough to have blood spatter on her. Was there enough blood on her to make you believe she did it?"

Roger cast his eyes downward. "Yes."

"Miss Johnson, do you have a need to use DMSO?"

"What's that?" she answered.

"It may be what caused the garlic smell Roger sensed on you when he first came near you."

"What garlic smell?" she asked.

"When we arrived at the scene a faint odor of garlic was present. Roger had sent you home so he could arrange the scene to protect you from what he believed was you murdering your sister. He remembered the garlic smell on you but said nothing to us. I believe someone else was in the house with you after Roger left or even before he took his children to church. You said you heard a noise in the hall and went to investigate. What happened then?"

"I thought Mary was coming into the kitchen. I wanted her to go back to bed. I don't remember anything after that until Roger came home. I don't even remember calling him."

"Listen, it's early and I have disturbed your day enough for now. I want both of you at ADA Patterson's office this afternoon. I think he should hear this story. It won't make any sense to him but I can clear it up with a little help." Tom and Marc thanked them for their time and left. An agreement for a meeting at 3 PM was arranged.

When the detectives drove back to the office, Tom said, "Now maybe you can let me in on your little secret." Marc smiled and filled in the missing parts. He swore his incredulous partner to secrecy and plotted the downfall of a clever killer.

CHAPTER 39

*II*I can't believe it." Tom and Marc sat in a room away from probing ears. "When did you suspect this other person?"

"I didn't like either Roger or Victoria's stories about the events of that day. I figured Roger didn't do it and was covering up for someone. When we found out about Victoria, naturally she became the prime suspect, but her story about not remembering anything was so lame as to be possible. As she continued relating it and still nothing came out that suggested she was guilty, I wondered whether Mary had actually killed herself and Victoria was in shock. Suicide is not an answer for me. I've never told anyone this, not even Joan. So keep it to yourself." Tom nodded.

"I had an uncle who was a Snohomish deputy. He had a rough go of it and was removed from the force for allegedly mishandling evidence in a drug case. The case was thrown out and so was he. He couldn't get over the fact they blamed him for the blown case, so he began to look into it. A few weeks later he ended up dead of a gunshot. Investigators said he committed suicide, but Uncle Jerry wasn't the kind to do such a heinous act. I know some people do die from their own hands, but I just couldn't believe Uncle Jerry committed suicide and I don't believe Mary Waite killed herself. So who was motivated enough to want her dead? Roger wasn't happy with her illness. That gave him motive. Victoria wanted Roger. That gave her motive. Neither one of their stories made any sense to me. Then I found out something about Roger's past which provided a motive for another person. All I had to do was figure out what happened and how this person was able to get the needed ingredients to knock out Victoria."

Tom said, "So we can finish this at Patterson's."

"Yes, I need to set up a few things before we go there."

They left the room. Marc called Perry Andrews, and then left to answer some questions he had.

CHAPTER 40

Perry met Marc as he came in the lab. He said, "So you have some information you want from me about using DMSO to transmit another medication into a body."

"That's what I need to know. Mary Waite's killer doesn't know I have uncovered a scheme which might have worked except for your investigative skills."

The two men walked into the autopsy lab and sat in chairs near a desk.

"Here's how it works. DMSO can penetrate the skin without causing any injury and it has the property to carry with it other medications. It has been used in a variety of purposes. But your question to me on the phone was about midazolam and how it can be transmitted into an unwary person."

"I have discovered that our perpetrator used DMSO to infiltrate Victoria Johnson and render her unconscious, so to speak."

"Yes, the midazolam will effectively block memory while operating in the body. Depending on the dose administered, she could lose a half hour or more."

"How would one administer a dose to a person without their knowing or understanding it happened?"

"I guess a person could have it on a cloth and rub it on the skin, but the victim would remember that being done. And the perpetrator would have to wear protective gear so as not to render themselves useless."

"How about using a spray bottle?"

"That would be more effective. It might not be as noticeable to the victim and it would take effect very soon after administration. If a person sprayed it onto the clothing and let it seep through, that might do it."

"Could Victoria function to, say, shoot her sister?"

"I don't know. I suspect that she would rebel at such an act. She still has the ability to think even if she won't remember it."

"What if another person coerced her into committing the act?" Marc asked

"My feeling is she would resist. Of course, if the other person pulled the trigger, Miss Johnson would not remember it later. She might think she was the person who did it. That kind of guilt could tear a mind apart."

"Perry, I think I know who pulled the trigger or at least forced Victoria Johnson to commit this crime. I'm meeting with Duncan this afternoon to discuss options and clear up this mess. He doesn't know what I have found, so it could be interesting."

"Does he have the lead on the case?"

"No, he turned it over to one of the new assistants, Monica Atherton."

"And she is unaware of any of this, also." Perry gleaned.

"She will hear what I have to say for the first time, as well. Could you be there to affirm the information I will deliver?"

Perry stood, "Sure, anything to help you out." Marc stood as well.

"Thanks, Perry; I'll see you at Duncan's office at 3."

They shook hands and Marc left for the next piece of his subterfuge.

At the office of Judge Bentley Ronderson, Marc explained in detail his need for a search warrant and the secrecy to go with it. The judge agreed enough information existed to process and expedite a search warrant. Marc called Tom to meet him at the address of the object of the search. He was to tell no one what he was doing. Tom agreed and left the office. Time was running short, and hopes for a solution depended deeply on finding the necessary pieces for cornering this despicable murderer.

At the address Marc explained to the superintendent of the apartment building the discretion required of this particular search. The superintendent frowned on opening a door without the lease holder present, but Marc appealed to his sense of justice and he relented.

"Tom, we are restricted to finding spray bottles, DMSO, and other medications. If we come across any other incriminating evidence, call Judge Ronderson and ask for an expansion warrant."

"Let's do this neatly," Tom said. "I think we can find our evidence without tearing up the place."

"Fine by me, I'll look in the bathroom. You go in the bedroom. Then we'll search in the other two rooms."

The exploration uncovered DMSO, two perfume sprayers, and an empty vial marked Versad, a brand name for midazolam. The Bellingham hospital name was on the vial. The two detectives thanked the superintendent and left the building. Hardly enough time remained for a preliminary examination of the materials before the meeting with Patterson. How could they stall the meeting and have the needed evidence examined and results delivered?

CHAPTER 41

Marc and Tom delivered the evidence to the crime lab and requested an expedited examination. The clock on the wall of the lab indicated the afternoon was passing. Neither man had eaten since early morning, but little time remained for them to design and execute a plan for cornering the killer. Fast food confined the beast within as they discussed the next move.

"Do you think we can get a confession?" Tom asked.

"It would make it easier, but a clever person won't be giving up. I was surprised to find the vial still present. I was sure it would have been disposed of long ago. Trophies are must for some people, I guess."

"Do you want me to get the evidence and bring it to Patterson's office? I can make sure nothing happens to it. I'd sure hate to lose it because of a careless messenger."

"Good idea, stay at the crime lab until we have a preliminary and bring all of the items to the office. Make sure to keep the evidence tracking intact. No need to have our suspect sneak out because of mishandling it. We're on close grounds as it is with our search warrant."

"I'll sign each tag and bag as required."

The two men split up to start the game. Marc entered the DA office and found Patterson. An explanation seemed appropriate before confronting Roger and Victoria with the truth.

"Duncan thanks for meeting with us this afternoon."

"This better be good. I rearranged my schedule for you. So what do you have which will crack this case open like a ripe melon?"

"Roger Waite and Victoria Johnson are coming in soon. They have little understanding about this meeting, but I plan to show all of you who the real killer is and how it was done. Will ADA Atherton be joining us?"

"She's the lead on this. I think she's in her office." He picked up the phone and called her. After hanging up he said, "She's on her way. So what can you tell me?"

"I prefer to wait until all are present. Tom Watson is bringing evidence over as soon as it is processed. I think it will answer your questions."

"Alright, I trust your judgment." A knocked on the door fixed attention to it as it opened and Monica entered the office.

Duncan said, "Marc has a line on the truth about Mary Waite's death. He has called this meeting and I will let him explain what he's doing."

"Monica, I have uncovered a conspiracy of sorts which involves another person who was present when Mary died. Hopefully, we can compel this person to admit to complicity and end this case as soon as possible."

"Is this person going to be at this meeting?" Monica asked.

"We will see what transpires as we go along. Roger Waite and Victoria Johnson will arrive soon. I imagine Woodbury will accompany them. I have spoken with them about a third person theory. What do you think about convicting either one of them?" Marc asked.

"I still hold with the idea that one of them is guilty and I plan to execute my duties and convict either or both of them. I don't see how a third person would have been present."

"I know. I was floored to find out about a possible third person, myself."

"Roger is guilty of tampering with evidence. He needs to be held accountable for that."

"I agree," Duncan said. "Marc, do you think he may be innocent of killing his wife?"

"I do. The timeline for him to get home and commit a murder is too tight according to Perry Andrews. So that leaves us with Victoria who claims no recollection of the events after Roger left with the children and his arrival home."

Monica huffed. "That is such a lame excuse. I can beat that defense in court. She killed her sister because she wanted Roger for her own."

Marc smiled, "That does seem to be the prevailing motive, but she may be telling the truth about not remembering. Let's wait until everyone is here and then we can sort through the evidence and find the truth."

A knock at the door alerted them to additional people joining the unearthing of the truth. Duncan opened his door and allowed Roger, Victoria, and Jeff Woodbury to enter.

Woodbury spoke before any greeting was given. "What's this all about? I get a call from these two that you, Marc, have uncovered some sort of scheme."

"Nice to see you, too," Duncan said. "Yes, it seems he thinks another person invaded the Waite domicile and committed the crime. Let's go to a conference room where we can be more comfortable."

As each person found a seat, Marc moved to the front which featured a white board. He began outlining the details of the case as had been currently established. He turned to the assemblage and asked, "Does anyone think I have left out anything?" Stalling for time never went as one desired. No one spoke. "Alright then, I guess I should add to the list of what I have uncovered so far." Hurry up, Tom, his mind conceded.

"I spoke with Perry Andrews about all of the trace elements found on Mary Waite to get a sense of who she was and what she did in her life. Nothing extraordinary came to light except for one element none of us could figure out. It seems someone had come into the house and left a garlic-like odor residue. Since Mary and Roger had not prepared any meal which incorporated garlic, another element had to be the source. Nothing came to mind for many days until a little remembered fact came to light. A by-product of the lumber industry has been developed for medicinal use. This product is dimethyl sulfoxide or DMSO." Marc watched for reactions, which did not follow. Tom had to appear soon.

"No one in the house had use for it and no trace of it other than the telltale odor first encountered by you, Roger, and then by the CSI team, was discovered. Detective Tom Watson smelled it and I caught a slight glimpse of it when I entered.

It was dismissed as a random odor from an unknown source. It could have been a lingering dinner preparation smell." Marc's cell buzzed in his pocket. "Excuse me while I find out where my partner is." He left the room.

"What's up?" he asked. He listened as Tom relayed the information he wanted. "Get here with it as soon as possible and bring a couple of deputies. They can wait outside the conference room until needed." He finished the call and returned.

"I do apologize for that. Tom is on his way." He moved to the front again. "Does anyone have any questions?"

Monica spoke. "Why are we talking about something you dismissed in your investigation as a random odor? Isn't the evidence pointing at Miss Johnson?"

Woodbury responded, "My client is not guilty of anything and you can't prove she is."

"She claims not to remember or has she forgotten that too? It's a lame excuse."

"Alright, let's not get into arguments prematurely," Marc said. "I know this will become clear when Tom arrives."

Duncan spoke, "I am interested in where this charade is headed, but I've a schedule to keep, so let's get on with it."

"Thank you, Duncan. I made a discovery about the alleged affair between Roger and Victoria. That's why I began delving deeper into Victoria's past and her relationship with Roger.

When I uncovered that she was at the house as well as Roger, then things got interesting. Now Victoria had motive and opportunity to kill her sister and have Roger for herself. The claim of memory loss made no sense to me or my partner. I just assumed she wanted him and he wanted to cover up her involvement." Marc moved behind the two people he referenced.

"This is getting us nowhere." Woodbury feigned anger. "Stop wasting time here."

"Oh, but it's such an intriguing story. Someone could write a book about this and maybe have a best seller. I could see it being a movie." Marc moved to the front again. "But I digress. I decided to prove Victoria was lying about her loss of memory, so I spoke with two people who showed me how a person could be drugged and not remember anything while under the influence of the drug." The door opened and Tom entered with Perry Andrews and a sealed evidence box marked Mary Waite.

CHAPTER 42

"Sorry we're late," Perry said. "We had to pick up the results before coming over."

"Results of what?" Monica asked.

"We'll get to that," Marc answered. "Perry Andrews pointed out to me a drug called midazolam is used in surgeries to influence memory without a person losing consciousness. Mary's psychiatrist, Dr. Conley confirmed what Perry had said. So now I had a dilemma on my hands. Was Victoria telling the truth, and if so, how was a drug administered to her that induced her lapse of memory? That was not easy to prove."

Marc picked up the evidence box and placed it on the table in front of the assemblage. "The real question for me became who else had motive to kill Mary Waite and place blame on Roger? I had to find another person who came to the house that Sunday, drugged Victoria, and killed Mary. I had no leads as to who would do such a thing. I now was convinced Mary didn't commit suicide. I was convinced Roger was covering for Victoria because he truly thought she killed Mary. I believed Victoria was not at all convinced she hadn't killed her sister. I believe she thought she had done this and it scared her. It scared her into forgetting what happened, so Victoria was prime suspect for murder."

"I agree," Monica said. "So let's arrest her for murder and arrest Roger for conspiracy to cover-up the murder."

"Good idea, Monica, except for one little detail which came to light quite by accident. We found the other person."

She leaned forward; a bead of moisture descending her forehead. "Who is it?" she asked.

"I'll get to that real soon."

Marc sliced open the evidence box watching for reactions. He pull out the folder marked 'test results' with today's date. "This is a record of tests we had run on some evidence we found only this morning. If you'll be patient just a little more, I would like to review it. Duncan, your office will be getting a copy of this after we are done here."

Duncan nodded. Monica regarded Marc as though he had lost his marbles. "Is any of this going to help with a conviction?" she asked.

"Oh, yes, quite so. You will be very interested in its use in court." He opened the folder and read. He looked at Roger and then Victoria. His eyes roamed the room stopping at each person. He was enjoying the hunt.

"Perry, explain to us what the lab found in these new pieces of evidence."

Perry stepped forward. "We found traces of DMSO and midazolam in a spray perfume bottle. If this concoction was sprayed on Victoria without her knowledge, she would have been unable to remember anything happening within minutes of spray application."

"So her story has validity?" Duncan asked.

"Yes." Perry answered.

"Thanks, Perry. I guess we need to know whose perfume bottle we found. But before we do that, let's uncover how I was able to ascertain the perpetrator. I came across a report from Roger's college days which indicated he was not a very nice person." Roger squirmed. "As a matter of fact, Roger, you dated girls only to have sex with them and throw them aside for the next conquest. Isn't that about right?"

Roger hung his head but said nothing. "He was attempting to bed as many girls as he could before graduation. I'm guessing mostly freshmen women, naïve young women who loved the attention of an older, handsome man who treated them nicely and got them to consent to sex, at least most of the time. Isn't that about right, Mr. Waite?"

"I wasn't being mean to them. They were as interested in having sex as I was."

"All of them? Weren't there some young ladies you forced your attentions on until they just stopped resisting?"

"Why are you asking him these questions?" Woodbury asked.

"Well, you see, his behavior could give a person motive to get revenge. He really pissed someone off and this person was the real killer of Mary Waite." Marc turned to Monica. "I hope you can help here, Monica." She sat back in her chair and folded her arms.

"How can I help?" she asked.

"You were one of his victims, weren't you? You probably know the person we discovered. I am hoping you can help us get a confession."

Monica remained silent. Marc continued. "Roger, you and Monica knew each other at Washington State and had a torrid affair. Didn't you?"

Roger looked at Monica. "If you know who killed my wife, Monica, please help get her killer. I'm sorry for the way it ended with us, but that doesn't mean you can't help." Monica sat forward and put her arms on the table.

Duncan spoke next. "Monica, you didn't tell me you knew Roger. You shouldn't … you can't try this case. Exculpatory as this is, you should have told me immediately when you found out who was being investigated."

"I'm sorry, sir, I guess I got caught up in the moment of seeking revenge for what happened in college. I wanted Roger to suffer."

"Woodbury, we need to talk about what occurs next," Duncan said.

Marc spoke again. "Well, that certainly puts a wrench in the machinery. Now for the next thing. I began to suspect Roger had returned to his old flame so he could weasel out of any responsibility for Mary's death. After all, if you are screwing the person who's going to prosecute you, it might make it difficult to seek a conviction. So Monica became a person of interest regarding how this case was coming together."

"I didn't kill anyone."

"Nobody has accused you. Anyway, a report came to light about a complaint filed against Roger at WSU for misconduct regarding a female student. I followed up on the report and found the person responsible for filing the complaint. Monica, this is where you can be of help. I think you know the person and can help us to get a confession from her."

"I'll do what I can," she answered.

"Good. I then uncovered another person related to the complainant. I interviewed this person who gave me the details I needed to connect all of the dots and finally figure out how the person disabled Victoria and then used Mary's own gun to kill her. I have a question for you, Victoria." She looked up. "Did you have the gun with you when you came to the house or did you retrieve it after you arrived?"

Victoria looked at Roger and then Marc. Woodbury placed his hand on her arm and said, "You don't have to answer that."

"That's okay; I think I know the answer anyway. Whether you brought it with you or retrieved it, it was on your person when you went to the kitchen, wasn't it?" Victoria nodded. "This noise you heard and thought was Mary; did you see anyone other than Mary in the house?"

"I didn't see anyone, but I sensed another person. I just can't remember anything. I don't remember going to Mary with tea or hearing any gunshot. I should have heard a gunshot, shouldn't I?"

"Maybe not, because the drug used to impair you works fairly quickly. Perry, explain what probably happened."

Perry stepped forward from his chair. "As far as I can ascertain, a concoction of DMSO and midazolam was placed into spray bottle and was used to spray Miss Johnson's clothing. As it soaked through the fabric and into the skin, it was absorbed into the body. The effects of the midazolam were transferred by the DMSO which easily penetrates the skin without any harmful properties. Miss Johnson probably didn't feel anything."

Marc said, "And the perpetrator then could control you, ask you questions, relieve you of the gun, have you call Roger, and you wouldn't remember any of it. She may even have had you pull the trigger, but I doubt that." He turned to Tom. "Has she arrived yet?" Tom left to check on the person referenced.

Upon returning he nodded. "Thanks, Tom. Let her know I'll be calling on her within the next few minutes. I think it time for us to get a confession, don't you, Monica?"

She appeared puzzled looking at the door as though a ghost was about to enter. "Is your suspect here?"

"Yes, Monica, she is."

CHAPTER 43

"Let's clear a few things away so that we don't confuse anyone. Monica, you dated Roger while in college at Wazzu, correct?" She sat stoic to the question. "Roger, you wanted sex with Monica but also kept hooking up with other coeds, correct?" Roger lowered his head. "You then met Mary and fell head over heels in love, probably for the first time in your life. Is that a fair assumption?" He raised his head and nodded.

"Victoria, when you met Roger, you developed a crush on him, didn't you?"

"Yes."

"And eventually, you pushed it to engaging in an affair with him while he was married to your sister." Tears flooded her eyes.

"Roger you did not have an affair with Monica, while married to Mary."

"No, I didn't know she was in town until she came to the sheriff's department last week and basically threatened me."

"I did not."

"Hold on," Marc interjected. "I'll get to that soon enough. Victoria bought a gun for protection of her sister from some unknown assailant. Roger had no understanding his wife was pregnant again until that Sunday morning. But, Roger, you and Mary had decided to seek help for her in a Seattle Sanatorium."

"Yes, we were headed there that day."

"Now comes the most exciting part for me. I abhor the idea anyone wants to commit suicide. I know some people do, but mostly I find a person has been murdered and it is made to look like suicide." Marc reached into the evidence box and removed a small parcel, sealed and marked as evidence. "Roger, I wish you hadn't changed the look of your bedroom. I understand why you did it. Victoria is probably glad you tried to help her, but it made my job and the job of the crime scene investigators more difficult. Had you believed Victoria's story of memory loss and kept her at the house, CSI would have found the evidence needed to start a trace on the real killer."

He reached in again and removed another small parcel marked and sealed. He picked up the folder again and read. "One of the bottles found at the residence of the person of interest contained dimethyl sulfoxide. Another bottle contained remnants of midazolam. A third container had traces of a cocktail of the two previously mentioned ingredients." He closed the folder.

"Victoria, when Tom searched your house, he found the clothing you wore the day of your sister's death. You had washed them and replaced them with other clothes in your closet. One item brought in for testing was a sweater you wore that day. Were you wearing it when you went to the kitchen to fix tea?"

Victoria transfixed a stare at the table and slowly raised her head. "I wore it over because the morning was chilly. I took it off when I came into the house and laid it on a table in the hall. I don't remember what I did with it, but it was at my apartment. Why?"

"Traces of DMSO were found on the sweater randomly spattered like an over splash of a spray. I'm guessing you were sprayed in the hall from behind, but you felt nothing because of your clothing. Is there a closet or a doorway of some sort in the hall?"

Roger answered, "Yes, a pantry connects with the kitchen and the dining room. It's at the end of the hall between them."

"Perry, in your estimation, how long would it take for a proper dose of a cocktail of DMSO and midazolam to take effect through a person's clothing?"

"The spray would have to be a large area so to be sure of contact with the skin, but once administered, the drug would take affect within a few seconds."

"Thanks, Perry. So let's discover who sprayed Victoria and probably killed Mary Waite." Marc unsealed the first parcel and removed a bottle labeled midazolam. The second parcel contained a bottle labeled dimethyl sulfoxide. He then reached in and removed two perfume sprayers, one labeled 'Wonderstruck', the other a paisley bottle without a label.

"I believe our suspect thought she was not going to get caught. Otherwise, she would have removed these from her residence."

Monica asked, "How were these items obtained?"

"A properly signed search warrant was executed by Tom and me this morning. It was restricted to these items which were gathered and sealed at the scene."

"Was the resident present when these items were discovered?" Monica asked.

"I do believe you are wondering about the entry to the apartment. The superintendent admitted us as a courtesy."

"This search may be problematic to getting a conviction."

"Yes, except for the theft of the midazolam from a Bellingham hospital about two months ago. Tom, go get our doctor." Tom opened the door and signaled for the lady who waited in the corridor. Dr. Giselle Selandian entered and a gasp escaped from Monica's mouth.

"People, I would like you to meet Monica's older sister, Giselle, or Ginny, Selandian. She is a neurologist in Bellingham, Washington and is missing one bottle of midazolam."

Ginny moved toward her sister. "Why, Mon, why? You have everything going for you."

"Shut up. They have nothing to go on."

"Actually, we have everything we need. You visited your sister at the time of the missing drug. You borrowed her hospital clothing and badge, not realizing they had reissued scrubs and badges. We have a picture of you in the pharmacy. The missing bottle is this one." Marc picked it up with a gloved hand. "It has your fingerprints on it, and is marked as belonging to St. Joseph's.

"I do believe this sprayer is yours, and I found but did not remove an instillation kit for interstitial cystitis medicine, which included Solu-cortef, DMSO, and sodium bicarbonate in solution. I met with several medical personnel who confirmed this is a medical process to help with the treatment of I.C. I can't think of any reason for you to have these items unless you have I.C."

Selandian spoke. "She complained to me four years ago about pain in her bladder. I sent her to friend of mine who specializes in renal medicine. She diagnosed Monica with I.C. and started her on instillations of the medicine. It's usually done in a doctor's office by staff, but to save some money for Monica, she learned how to instill her own bladder."

Monica stood up. "You have no idea the humiliation I suffered because of that bastard. He made love to me and told me I was the one he wanted forever. I fell in love with him and then I caught him fucking a freshman in his apartment. She wasn't even as pretty as me. He just lied to me to get me into bed. I did things with him I never had done before. I broke off our relationship and went on with my life."

Marc said, "But he met Mary Johnson and all the nasty things he did to all those other girls stopped. That must have really fried you."

"I'm not saying another word. I'm entitled to an attorney."

"Don't look at me." Woodbury declared, "I can't take on another person in this matter, especially you, Miss Atherton."

Duncan responded, "I can advise you until you get an attorney, and I advise you to stop talking."

Monica walked away from the others at the table and stared out the window. Her sister approached but was rebuffed. Monica turned around. "Funny thing is I would have been the perfect wife for you, Roger. I have a law degree and my first case to try. Too bad it was you." She faced the window again but kept speaking. "When I finally tracked you down, I wanted so much to contact you and see if I could win you back. But that little bitch you married bore you two kids. I knew you wouldn't leave her. So I had to devise another plan."

"Monica, you need to stop talking." Duncan had walked to her and placed a hand on her shoulder. "This can be used against you in court."

"Why yes, Mr. Jefferson, you seem to have neglected your duty of reading my Miranda Rights to me. I can get all of this thrown out of court and nothing will remain to convict me."

"Alright, Miss Atherton you have the right to remain silent ..."

"Oh, shut up. I understand my rights." Monica approached Victoria, who cringed. "You just happened to be fucking my boyfriend and forgot to tell your sister. I had a laugh when I discovered that. I followed you for three months, watching you go into those houses Roger bought for your little trysts. I was present when you bought the gun. I was behind you every Sunday you went to Roger's place. All I had to do was figure out the schedule. But what surprises, when I witnessed you fix tea for your sister, and then you just shot her."

"I did no such thing."

"How do you know? You've admitted you don't remember anything."

Marc spoke, "Miss Atherton, you are under arrest for criminal trespass and assault. I think we can get those charges to stick long enough to provide you time to arrange for defense of a murder charge."

"Marc," Duncan said, "We need to talk as soon as everyone leaves." He nodded his assent. "Monica, I cannot tell you anything you don't already know about the trouble you have brought to you. I can say that you will need a good defense attorney. I am pursuing criminal charges for invading the Waite home and for apparently stalking Victoria Johnson. You have violated almost every standard of ethical attorney behavior. I will be contacting the bar association and recommending your disbarment."

"Go ahead. I don't need this job. I only did it to get a chance at Roger."

Roger said, "You really screwed up this time. Threatening me in college and then here at the sheriff's office, I can be a witness against you."

"Oh, yes," Marc said, "About that conversation with Roger at the stationhouse, Tom and I witnessed it and find it interesting you wanted to coerce a confession out of him."

"I just wanted to scare him."

Dr. Selandian said, "Monica, just tell them what you told me when you came to my house."

Monica turned to face her sister. "I must say, I really don't know what you are talking about. We had a nice visit and chatted about the weather and our parents."

Ginny responded. "She told me she found Roger and she was going to destroy his marriage. She still wanted to be with him, even after what happened. She's obsessed with him."

"When did you discover she had taken your old badge and scrubs?" Marc asked.

"When you came to me at the hospital and related your story, I knew she had strayed too far from reality," she said. "My sister is very smart, and when she told me about meeting Roger in college, I thought she had a person who matched her ability and personality. When they broke up she said she'd get revenge. I didn't think she would carry a grudge this long."

"You didn't report the threats to anyone. Why?"

"She's my sister. I couldn't just turn her in. She's smart enough to know what can happen."

"Monica," Marc asked, "did Roger know of your obsession for him. Did he act against you in school because he feared what you might do to him?"

"I don't have to answer your questions."

"No, you don't. I figured you wanted us to understand how rotten Roger is. I still see him as the victim here. You haven't convinced me with your tale of woe is me. Roger is the one suffering a loss here."

Duncan sat back as Marc continued. "Mary was an innocent person. She happened to fall for the wrong guy and got in your way. I am sorry you had to endure such a strain on your heart. Ridding Roger of her as soon as possible could only be good for you. When you spoke with Victoria, did you convince her to shoot her sister or was she willing all by herself when you suggested it?"

Victoria whimpered when Monica said, "The little bitch refused to do it. They were getting Mary help. That wasn't going to be an option. So I asked her for the gun. She gave it to me when I advised her it was dangerous to have it in the house with a crazy person."

"Did you wipe off the gun so as to hide the fact you were in the house?" Marc asked.

"You didn't find any prints on it, did you?"

"Actually, we found one print which has enough markers to identify you. It's not perfect but can be used," he answered.

"Duncan, can I go now?" Monica asked. "I promise to stay in town until this clears up. I know I should suffer some penalty for my actions in this office. I'm willing to do that. I'll then leave and practice elsewhere, when my suspension is complete. I admit I entered Roger's house after he left for church. I admit to spraying Victoria with the cocktail. I admit I watched her shoot her sister without any provocation by me to do so. I stipulate to following Victoria Johnson, although not to stalking her."

"If you had the gun in your hand, when did you return it to Victoria so she could shoot Mary?" Marc asked. "Were you both in the bedroom? Did Mary get to see you before she died?"

Monica sat stoic to Marc's questions. He persisted. "What look did she have on her face as the gun pointed at her? And I guess the big question which comes to my mind, is, why didn't you stop Victoria from shooting her sister? You admit to being there. You admit you took the gun from her and yet you say she pulled the trigger and you witnessed it. I don't understand how Victoria got the gun back to shoot her sister, whom she professes to have loved." He put his hands on the arms of the chair in which Monica sat and asked, "How come you didn't stop her?"

"She walked out of the room. Because the little whore wouldn't do it, I had to finish the job she was supposed to do."

Marc stood tall and looked at Duncan. Tom retrieved the deputies who cuffed Monica and led her to the detention cell in the sheriff's office across the parking lot.

CHAPTER 44

"Thanks, Marc," Duncan said. "I never would have guessed she did it."

"What happens to us?" Roger asked. Dr. Selandian had been taken to another room for a statement leaving Tom, Marc, Victoria, Roger, and Jeff Woodbury as the remaining witnesses to the confession. "Can Victoria be exonerated of any involvement?"

"Jeff, what do you think?" Duncan asked.

"I can see Victoria being freed from any charges. She certainly didn't do anything wrong."

"Except for purchasing a gun under an assumed identity."

"Yes, well, we can work something out about that, which shouldn't involve jail, can't we." Woodbury asked. Duncan smiled and nodded his head.

"As for you, Roger, you face more serious charges of tampering with evidence, criminal intent to defraud an investigation, and hampering police in that investigation. Each of these can carry jail time."

"Yes, sir, I understand," he answered.

Woodbury spoke, "Let me speak with Roger and see if I can get him to agree to probation of some sort."

Duncan said, "I think we can work out something, but it may involve a little time spent in custody." Woodbury, Roger and Victoria, left the office.

"Do you really want to punish him for what he did?" Marc asked Duncan.

"Probably not, but he needs to know the firestorm created because of his actions in college. It doesn't surprise me anymore to find out people don't get it. What we do early in life has a way of coming back to haunt us."

"What about Victoria?"

"I'm guessing the DA will go for a probationary period for her. She hasn't done anything truly criminal. It's sad though, to think someone so beautiful and young can experience so much in so short a period of time. She better learn a lot about living a decent life."

Tom said, "I wonder if she and Roger will stay together. They seem to care about each other, and I sensed she really did care about her sister."

"I don't know," Duncan said. "Maybe they can make something work, but those children are going to need a lot of therapy to get through what happened. I know they're young and can grow up with Roger and Victoria as loving parents. But how can those two explain the death of their mother without lots of confusing issues to muddle through? This has been a most inopportune event."

Marc and Tom bid adieu to Duncan and headed out to solve other crimes occurring in Wendlesburg. Marc finished with the necessary paperwork and called it a day. He had motives of his own at home and wanted to see his wife and children. They deserved more than he gave. An explanation about Uncle Jerry would clear his mind of troublesome issues which Joan might accept and deal with better than anticipated before now. He knew she was right about police work being more important than the family. A change in his life was required to reverse her thinking. Could he? Only time would tell. He drove to the elder care facility to see her and invite her to dine with him without the children. He wanted to describe his thinking to her and in days and weeks to come exhibit changes to his way of life as an officer of the law.

CHAPTER 45

Joan smiled as Marc handed her a glass of wine. They sat in a favorite restaurant away from the noise and crowd. The children agreed to have a pizza delivered at home.

"I realize you needed to finish this investigation and I hope we do not need to endure another such case for a long time." She raised her glass for a toast. "To the most ingenious detective I know." Marc tapped her glass, smiling, and truly relaxing for the first time in many weeks.

"To us, and to no more crazy people coming between us," he said. They each sipped from their glasses. Joan placed hers on the table.

"When did you first suspect the Assistant D.A.?" Joan asked.

"As I entered the bedroom something seemed out of place. I reserved judgment until I spoke with the husband, but his story sounded contrived. With the tale unfolding, I realized another person must have been present before he returned home. He was covering for someone. When his relationship with the younger sister came to light, she became my prime suspect. Roger's confession was a cover-up for the sister murdering his wife. The amnesia act was so shallow, her buying the gun, and the professed love for her sister, prompted further study to find concrete evidence to convict her." Marc finished his wine and set it down with a push toward Joan. She poured another drink as he continued.

"The challenge for a conviction lay in the reasonable doubt. If Victoria was guilty of pulling the trigger, no direct connection seemed evident. Unresolved loose ends such as the second bullet in the wall, the garlic odor on the body as well as other places in the house, and the timelines for Roger and Victoria, left questions about her guilt. No amount of prodding could get Roger to recant and Victoria stuck to her amnesia story. I knew he was covering for her and she never denied shooting Mary. At the same time she didn't confess."

Then Roger and Monica's history surfaced, so I quietly instigated an investigation to see how she fit into the events of that fateful Sunday."

"What motive did she have for wanting Mary dead? That affair ended in college."

"Not for her. She felt humiliated and dishonored because of Mary. Her hatred for them slowly festered and a plot materialized, and what better way to get even with Roger than to kill Mary and have him convicted for her murder?"

He drank the rest of his wine and continued. "The break came when I discovered Monica's sister, a neurologist in Bellingham, and she revealed the use of DMSO because of IC. Creating the short term amnesia with midazolam and DMSO finally made sense. If Monica hadn't taken that bottle from her sister, I probably would not have been able to get her to confess. Then I had to prove Roger knew nothing of the events, but I still wasn't sure who pulled the trigger. Victoria's unwitting complicity didn't free her of any obligation. When I confronted Monica with the evidence, her vitriolic hatred spewed out in a confession."

"Victoria was a problem wasn't she?"

Marc called the waitress over to the table. "May we have our check please?" She retreated to run the bill.

"Victoria caused Monica to revise her plan, but I doubt she was much of a problem. I think it was easier to get Roger to think she did it and get him to confess."

Joan replied, "Congratulations are in order. Patterson is pleased, isn't he?"

"Yes, as are Roger and Victoria, now no longer bearing the guilt of killing Mary." The waitress returned. Marc placed a credit card in the folder, which she picked up and disappeared again.

Joan gazed at her husband. "What's going to happen to them?"

"Duncan doesn't see much purpose in pursuing convictions in court. Roger has pled guilty to tampering with a crime scene. Victoria is free of any charges. Those two are going to have to figure out their own futures. As for us, I guess I have motive to figure out what we want."

"So you can rest now?"

"I guess."

"What does that mean?" Joan looked puzzled.

"Nothing, really, but I want you to understand something about me which I haven't told you before. As a matter of fact, I haven't told many people."

The waitress reappeared with folder in hand. "Well?"

"I'll tell you in the car on the way home." He signed the restaurant copy leaving a generous tip. They departed for home and the explanation of his disdain for suicide because of Uncle Jerry's death, which created his motive to convict perpetrators for murder. Joan looped her arm in his and leaned her head on his shoulder.

Marc just knew Joan should understand this disdain for suicide. He figured Uncle Jerry would approve another examination into his untimely death. Would Joan?

ACKNOWLEDGEMENTS

This labor of love has many helpers whom I wish to acknowledge. When I retired I had already begun writing Motive. I knew nothing of the craft of writing a marketable manuscript. I spent two years creating my book and assailing my wife, Sandy, with the next great piece of writing. She feigned sympathy and interest. Her voracious affinity to read fueled my desire for her constructive critique. And she didn't disappoint.

I guess the earliest people to read and hear about it were the agents I spoke to at Pacific Northwest Writers' conference at the Hilton in SeaTac, Washington in 2009. I had joined PNWA early in June and signed up when I found out about the conference. One suggested I lose the beginning and start with the back story which was where the action began. Another explained how the action needed ramping up. I realized then how important the conference was, for me to listen to the writers, agents and editors who were telling their stories and anecdotes. I had to learn the craft of writing for the marketplace.

Before attending PNWA's conference I had purchased and read Donald Maas's book The Fire in Fiction and attended his one day seminar at the Hilton in Bellevue, Washington. We used the book as a teaching guide. There's nothing like having one of the premier agents in the writing business chop apart the hard work of many months into so many little pieces. However, I recognized the improvement in my writing and decided I needed to continue attending workshops and conferences.

While attending the PNWA conference, I met many fine people in the beginning stages of a career in writing. Other people had completed manuscripts to pitch and still others were published writers. I sat and listened to several writers who espoused their writing careers and the accomplishments of years of hard work.

I discovered the International Thriller Writers had a conference in New York City. I explored the agenda of Craft Fest, Agent Fest, and Thriller Fest, along with the parties, dinners, and other events and knew I wanted to be there. I presented the idea to my wife, Sandy, who accepted, and I signed up to attend. We decided to make a family vacation happen, so my daughter, son-in-law, grandson, and son became part of the trip. We flew to Newark and rode a stretch limo to the Grand Hyatt Hotel. We enjoyed a couple of days exploring before the conference. When the conference started my family continued seeing New York while I met some of the best thriller writers in the game. Steve Berry, David Morrell, Jon Land, Lisa Gardner, Robert Dugoni and others taught classes on the craft of writing. Jon Land and Kathleen Antrim trained us how to develop the perfect pitch for Agent Fest, a time to meet agents and pitch our manuscripts. I uncovered several agents who were interested in my sending material.

As my interest in creating a manuscript worthy of publishing increased, I attended the Writer's Digest Intensive weekend in Cincinnati in October of 2009. I went to the Writers on the Sound weekend held each year in Edmonds, Washington in 2011. Each experience increased my ability to craft better writing. I finally arrived at the point of completing a manuscript. I asked several people, Anne Lindsey, Kathy and Larry Little, Susan and John

Wall, Maggie Scott, and Sandra Stockwell, to read and critique my book. Their valuable input helped me understand a reader's need when reading a book.

Jason Black was engaged to edit and critique <u>Motive</u> for character development, story line, point of view, and any other writing improvements deemed necessary. His masterful application of editing skills and advisory comments changed my book again for the better.

David Smith, a pharmacist friend of mine, provided the operant action which Monica used to disable Victoria. I asked him how a person could have a memory loss without being completely sedated to unconsciousness. He e-mailed me the midazolam, DMSO cocktail. Now the likelihood of this form of manipulation being used is remote as this is a work of fiction, but it provided the intrigue which brought me to a story twist that surprised even me.

D. P. Lyle, M.D., provided forensic background through his book, <u>Forensics, A guide for Writers</u>. This book helped to understand the process by which a medical examiner can unravel the intricate evidence gathering needed to solve a crime.

And so I have arrived at a book which I hope you enjoy and are willing to pass on to others. It may not be a great literary marvel, and probably will not challenge any other mysteries written by so many talented crafters of storytelling. But I have enjoyed writing it and look forward to unveiling the many characters rummaging around in my head looking for a way to escape to the pages of another book. My second book, tentatively titled <u>Motivations</u>, about the beginnings of these tragic families' lives will be forthcoming in the next few months.

Finally, I must thank Darcy McKnight, who patiently and diligently invested time and energy into a final reading, uncovering what I hope were the last of the mistakes needing correction to make this a proper story which I hope you have enjoyed.

For all the help from the many who have not been named and whose advice has been so carefully followed and who do not know the extent to which they contributed to the education of this newbie in the world of story crafting, I thank you.

Any errors of writing or crafting, misuse of legalese, court procedure, or equipment mentioned in this story are solely the responsibility of the author.

This is a work of fiction and no one who appears in this story is a real person living or dead. But ideas stem from reality and if anyone thinks they recognize themselves in my book, please be thankful you do not in reality act the way these characters have acted.

Made in the USA
San Bernardino, CA
29 July 2014